THE STORY OF GRENVILLE KING

THE TOUR SERIES - BOOK 3

JEAN GRAINGER

www.jeangrainger.com

Created with Vellum

CHAPTER 1

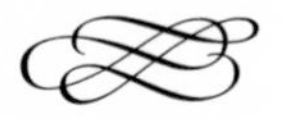

Conor O'Shea locked eyes with his lunch companion. The glossy brochure for the almost derelict property lay on the table between them.

'Well?' Corlene smiled slowly.

Conor sighed. Corlene's suggestion had taken him by surprise, but the more he thought about it, he had to admit it sounded tempting.

'I don't know, Corlene. I never expected Bert to leave me anything – I was stunned when I got the letter. Half a million euros! To be honest, my instinct was to give it back, but as you say, he was a very wealthy man and he spread his wealth around.' Conor shook his head.

'Yeah, well, I knew he was going to do it – we discussed it. When we came on that tour with you all those years ago, he spotted something in you, Conor. It all seems so long ago now, but he really felt you brought such joy and happiness to people on the tours, going far and above what you needed to, and he wanted to reward you.'

Conor smiled at the memory of how Corlene thought of Bert as her next victim at the time. Bert was a very wealthy man who liked to do good things for people with his money. He'd spotted something vulnerable in Corlene and her teenage son and wanted to help them.

Corlene had lived in Ireland since that tour and seemingly felt at home.

She went on. 'Honestly, Conor, don't overthink it. He wanted to give you something. He left me considerably more. Just accept it in the spirit it was given. So back to my idea – what do you think?'

Conor picked up the brochure again. 'I know this place – Ana and I walk there sometimes. It's in an amazing location overlooking the ocean, and it's in better shape than many of the other castles that are dotted around the place. But to buy it… I don't know. The amount of work and money it would take…'

'But we have the money, Conor.' Corlene was insistent. 'Bert made sure we had it before he passed away. I'm suggesting a partnership. I put up a million, you put your half in, and we can finance the rest. Bert had some friends, investors, bankers, who would be happy to talk to us – he told me that only a month ago. We'll be able to buy it and renovate it to a five-star standard.

'Castle Dysert could be the next big luxury resort, the most sought-after wedding venue in Ireland, the place to have your annual golf holiday when you want to impress your corporate clients. And of course there's the fact that I could use it for my self-improvement courses. My business is thriving, so we have instant clientele right there. Who knew so many women needed help getting their men to behave themselves? To be honest, most of the guys they're so desperate to have aren't worth it, but that's not my job – I keep quiet about that end of things. With Bert's investment and help along the way, it has turned into a great business and I make a lot of money.

'At the moment, I host my workshops, training sessions and all of that in a hotel in Dublin, but imagine if we had our own place? We'd have other guests too, obviously, but it would be perfect! And believe me, there is no end to the clients. I am working around the clock, taking on staff, training them to do what I do, and the demand seems to be endless.'

Conor smiled at her. 'If you're determined to do it, Corlene, I'm sure you will, but I don't know about getting involved. I'm a tour bus driver – what can I bring to the table apart from investment? Sure,

I've lived in hotels for years, but that doesn't mean I know anything about running one.'

Corlene sat forward, resting her elbows on the table, her painted fingernails and perfect make-up not far from his face. She reminded Conor of a cat watching a canary. 'Well, Mr O'Shea, that is where you're dead wrong.' Corlene had never lost her Alabama drawl. 'You're going to be the public face of Castle Dysert. You know everybody in Irish tourism, you have all the right connections, and you can manage the most difficult of people – you've been doing it with grace and good humour for years. But more than that – and I know you're going to be all embarrassed – you're the sexiest Irishman I know. Those eyes, that silver hair, that hunky body… Honey, you're like catnip to those American ladies. We make you the face of Castle Dysert, and every red-blooded woman in the States will be booking flights to get here.'

Conor laughed. 'Would you go away out of that, you lunatic. I'm the wrong side of fifty years old. I know exactly what you're doing, trying to sweet-talk me, and it won't work. I'm one of the few men on earth impervious to the charms of Corlene Holbrooke.'

'Be that as it may, but I do want you.' She paused and grinned wickedly. 'For the hotel, of course. But think about it. You have the skills and would do such a great job. And think of the security it would bring to you and Ana and the boys. It would mean you'd be home more, and you'd have something to leave to them. Do you really want to be dragging suitcases around all your life, living in hotels, missing out on so much of the boys' childhood? This is a great opportunity, and I want you to take it. And if Bert were here, he'd want you to take it too.'

Conor took a sip of his coffee. 'I don't know, Corlene. I'll have to think about it, talk it over with Ana. You're some operator, though, I'll give you that much.'

'Well, OK,' Corlene said seriously, 'but we need to move fast if we're doing this. A property like that won't stay on the market for long.'

She was probably on to something; the west coast of Clare was stunningly beautiful and badly needed a resort of that standard. Conor knew from years in the tour business that the demand was there. The Irish Tourist Board had recently begun to market the Wild Atlantic Way, a coastal route that went all the way along the Atlantic seaboard, and it had really taken off. It was kind of funny really; it had always been there, but now that they'd named it, it had become a holiday destination. It was great, though, and all the pubs, cafes, shops and accommodation vendors along the route had seen a huge upturn in profits. Castle Dysert was right on it and would benefit in a similar way if it were up and running.

Corlene changed the subject. 'So how are Ana and the boys? Dylan showed me some pictures on his phone. They're growing up so fast – it seems like two minutes ago they were born.'

'I know. They'll be seven this summer, and they love to see Dylan and Laoise. Your son is quite the babysitter, Corlene, and believe me, they need plenty of minding. They're great craic, but you'd need to be in the whole of your health for them, as they're always dreaming up some new kind of mischief. Ana says her mental health is improving by the month now that they are someone else's problem for five hours a day. She's really getting stuck in with the women's refuge thing. I don't know if I told you, but I had a woman on a tour a few years ago who was married to this desperate oaf altogether. It turns out he trafficked her into the States from someplace in Siberia. Valentina, her name was, and Ana helped her escape from him. He was arrested and charged and everything. Good enough for him too, as he hit me a clatter one day. But anyway, Ana got involved with the organisation that supported Valentina through the whole thing, and because she speaks Russian and Ukrainian, she's a great asset to them.'

When he'd met her on a tour of Ireland, he was the driver and guide. She had been determined to find a new husband and, more importantly, a meal ticket. Conor was still single in those days, and she often said she was amazed nobody had snapped him up. But she had been so desperate for a cash injection in those days that a bus driver wasn't going to fit the bill.

She never found that elusive millionaire, but she'd made some great friends, and her son, Dylan, had fallen in love, not just with Laoise, an incorrigible Irish wild child, but with the music of Ireland. He went from being a surly goth, all make-up and growls, to a charming, well-dressed, slightly shy young man. He and Laoise had a very successful band, and they toured all over playing traditional Irish music.

Conor picked up the brochure again and leafed through it. 'I've often wondered what it's like inside now. It's too overgrown to get at it, but some of the plants on the grounds are really unusual. I've seen photos of it back during the First World War. They used to have balls there for the British soldiers who were stationed here in Ennis. The family – I forget their names now – were well in with them, being English and Protestant themselves. It was absolutely magnificent back then – stables, walled gardens, orchards, the whole lot. It was burned in the twenties by the IRA in an effort to drive the family out. That happened often, as those wealthy landowners were seen as symbols of British imperialism. The family went out to Australia then, I think, and that's where they made their money, in opal mining. But one of them was a botanist, and she brought back all kinds of exotic plants and things from the tropics. Because the Gulf Stream hits the west coast of Ireland, it makes the soil temperature higher than it would normally be in a country with our climate, so those plants can grow here.'

The brochure showed an impossibly romantic image of a castle perched on a clifftop. Its cut limestone and red sandstone façade was obscured by a tangle of weeds and climbing plants, but he could see that beneath the vegetation, it was an ornate structure. The gardens swept down to the rocky shore below. Mother Nature was threatening to choke the place with briars.

'I should have guessed you'd know all about it. How come nobody fixed it up?' Corlene was fascinated.

'Well, I'm not totally sure. There were always rumours, you know? I do know that after the castle was burned, the family left Ireland. Then one of the sons of the original family came back with his wife – she was the botanist – sometime in the fifties, I think, and did it up.

The daughters of that family were the last people to live there, and they stayed there for most of their lives. They were reclusive, neither married, and when one of them died last year – cancer, I believe – the other one committed suicide. The poor woman threw herself from the roof.'

'Wow, not just a gorgeous building but one with a dramatic past. I like it. Good for business.' Corlene grinned.

Conor knew better than to reprimand her. She was incorrigible. 'So apart from trying to recruit me into acts of insanity, how's life going for you?' he asked, changing the subject as he needed time to mull things over. 'We haven't seen you since the launch of Dylan and Laoise's new album, so that must have been last autumn?'

'I know. I've been so busy. The website is getting so much traffic, I honestly can't keep up. When I did that makeover job on Cynthia, who could have guessed what it would lead to? She and Patrick send their love, by the way. They are so funny, such a mismatch, but it works so well. Your tours really do have something magic, you know, Conor. All over the world there are happy people, all because they sat on your bus for a week. There was a TV show in the States, years ago, called *The Love Boat*, and Bert and I used to joke that your tours were a bit like that, only not so corny. I mean, look at me. I was a mess, a total disaster, but I met you and Bert, and, well, I could never have imagined how great things would turn out.'

Conor listened as she updated him on all the strides forward her business had taken. He'd thought it was a daft idea when he heard it first, but Corlene had turned her business into something huge. He tried to reconcile the polished, prosperous, good-looking woman who sat in front of him now with the person he met all those years ago. She'd arrived on his tour without a penny, dressed far too young for her age in clothes too tight, drowned in cheap perfume and caked in make-up. She shamelessly flirted with anything in trousers. When she found herself drawing blanks romantically, and with funds at an all-time low, she even resorted to placing a personal ad in the paper in Killarney. Conor had thought he would choke from laughing when she recounted that tale at his and Ana's wedding. The whole story, from the tight shapewear digging into her to the potential beau's mother being some kind of old crone in a pub, had the entire gathering in stitches. Even Dylan laughed, and his mother's antics up to then had caused him nothing but shame. It was great to see Dylan and Corlene so relaxed around each other now. There was a time when everything she did embarrassed her son.

Conor knew that Ana wasn't that keen on Corlene. She loved Dylan and Laoise, but Corlene flirted with Conor all the time, touching him unnecessarily and constantly making suggestive remarks. It didn't bother him – she was only messing and she went on that way with all men – but he knew it grated on Ana.

On the other hand, she was a great businesswoman. If he went into business with her, it would have to be with his eyes wide open. She could size people up in seconds and knew instinctively how to get what she wanted. But he also knew that beneath her polished image there lay a heart of gold and that she'd seen more than her fair share of rough times. She was a very complicated person.

He glanced through the brochure once more. 'And you want us to buy it, just like that?' he asked.

'Yes. We buy it together. I do the business end, and you're the front man. Together, we turn Castle Dysert into a serious five-star, really high-end hotel – well, more of a resort actually. A spa, leisure centre, the usual, but more than that. I've thought this through. We could offer tailored holidays. People searching for their Irish ancestors can come, and we'll get the right people to help them find them. People who want to learn about Irish literature can take classes, go to readings, that sort of thing. We could do a lot with Irish music – workshops, classes, sessions. There's a market for it – I know there is – and we're going to tap into it. I can do all the business stuff, the schmoozing, dealing with banks, builders, all of that, but you have to be the man people think of when they think of Castle Dysert. You are the quintessential Irishman, with the accent that makes women want to drag you into bed, the crinkly-eyed smile, the knowledge of the country… You are the whole package, Conor. Men like you and women love you, and it won't work without you.'

Corlene paused and gazed at Conor intently. Her hazel eyes with flecks of amber were made up perfectly to accentuate her best feature. She looked much younger than she had before, and when he'd remarked on it last year at Laoise and Dylan's launch, she simply whispered, 'Surgery,' in his ear and gave him a pat on the bum that Ana had noticed.

Conor wished Corlene would rein it in. His wife trusted him, and he never gave her reason not to, but while he knew there was no harm in Corlene really, Ana didn't see it like that.

'Conor, we need someone with your skills. Not the day-to-day running – that's someone else's job. We don't want to waste your considerable talents on housekeeping and balancing the books – we'll get a manager for that. No, your role is much more important and only you can do it. You can call it what you like, but ultimately everyone there would be answerable to you. Our success in this venture – and believe me, it will be a huge success – is totally dependent on you being part of it. Normally when you recruit someone, the idea is to make them feel like they would be lucky to get the job, but not in this case. I need you, Conor. What I'm proposing is that once the repayments and so on are made, we split the profits fifty-fifty. I know your investment is half of mine, but you'll be doing most of the work, so I think it's fair. We'll get it all drawn up legally, and it will be very clear-cut. You get to do what you do so well every day, only this way you earn more money. And more importantly, you get to go home to Ana, Artie and Joe every night.'

Conor didn't answer. This was so much to take in.

'Take some time to think,' she instructed as she gathered her things into a voluminous Versace handbag. 'But not too long. Talk to Ana, and I'll call you tomorrow. I've got to go.' She placed several notes on the table to cover the lunch bill. 'Dylan is leaving for Sweden and Denmark this evening with Laoise. They have some gigs lined up there, and I want to see him before he goes.'

He stood and she embraced him, kissing him on the cheek and giving him a squeeze, and then she was gone.

CHAPTER 2

Conor pulled into his driveway and sat in the car for a few minutes. He and Ana had loved the home and garden the moment they saw it – a big old two-storey house, built of rough stone and covered in Virginia creeper.

The house had needed total modernisation, but now that it was done, it was lovely. He remembered the small terraced house of his childhood, with no garden and just a small yard, and thought how it was often cold and empty.

He sat for a few minutes, watching the boys playing football in the garden, Joe scoring a goal and doing a victory run that involved pulling his shirt over his head and yelling. Artie then took advantage of his twin's temporary blindness and tackled him to the ground. Conor smiled. They were like a pair of tiger cubs, constantly jostling and wrestling, but they were so devoted to each other that no fight lasted more than a minute.

Everyone said they looked like him. He had one or two pictures of himself as a kid, and he supposed they were right, though he was sure he had never been as good-looking as his boys were, with their white-blond hair, olive skin and Ana's green eyes. They were universally adored wherever they went.

His childhood was starkly different to theirs, however. Reared by his mother when his father left, he and his brother never knew the carefree happiness his twins did. His mam worked so hard and tried her very best, but the shame of being a deserted wife and the constant financial pressure killed her in the end. Conor had left school at sixteen and worked hard as an apprentice mechanic for a man called Joe Kelly, who had become the closest thing to a father Conor had ever known.

He smiled as he reminisced and watched little Joe, named after his old boss, who was now hanging upside down from the goalpost while Artie tried to kick the ball into his brother's arms.

He heard Ana calling the boys for their dinner, her accent as undiluted now as it was the day she arrived from Ukraine. She was many years his junior, and at first, he had been reluctant about the relationship. Now, the idea that he might not have grabbed her with both hands and never let go filled him with horror. She was the best thing to ever happen to him, and he adored her. He was looking forward to telling her about Corlene's proposal and wondered if she'd be in favour of it if it meant he could be at home more.

He loved driving tours, and he was good at it – Corlene was right about that – but he hated being away. When the lads were smaller, before they started school, Ana used to bring them to various hotels to meet him in the evenings, but it was more difficult now. He worked for one of the best tour operators in the country and was their most senior staff member. He had almost total control of itineraries and hotel choices, as they trusted him and paid him well. It was a lot to walk away from. He sighed. Once the boys were in bed, he'd hammer it out with Ana; in the end, he'd do whatever she wanted.

He got out of the car, crept up behind Artie just as he was about to score and lifted him bodily off the ground. Within seconds, all three of them were on the grass, rolling and playing. Conor scrambled to his feet, took the ball and scored, dodging his sons' efforts at tackling. He pulled his shirt over his head and did the victory run, much to their delight. Ana arrived then and he ran to her, picked her up and kissed her as he swung her around.

'Urgh, Dad, yuck! Stop kissing Mammy – it's so gross!' Artie tried to get between them.

Joe just giggled and jumped on his father's back.

'OK! You is all like wild animals. And you' – Ana pointed at the middle of Conor's chest – 'is making them worse.' Her words were softened by the huge grin on her beautiful face. 'Come inside, wash your hands and eat your dinner. You don't even do your homework yet. And Joe, Miss Carney say to me your handwriting is very bad, so please let me or Dad see it before you put it away, OK?'

'OK.' Joe grinned as he caught his father's eye. While Artie was studious, Joe didn't give a hoot about school.

Ana gave Conor the look, the one that said, 'Back me here,' and Conor instantly responded. He bent down to be at eye level with the boys and put his arms around them. 'That trip to Tayto Park we promised is not going to happen unless there is a big improvement in the writing. Do you hear me, Joe? Mammy is going to check with Miss Carney and so am I, and she needs to be telling us that there are no more scribbles and words she can't read. You're well able to write neatly. Remember the lovely writing you did on my birthday card? That was such brilliant writing, I thought Mammy had done it for you. But you're in such a rush to finish the homework, sometimes you can be very sloppy. And also, Artie, I asked you to clear all the old toys out of the garage two weeks ago and put them into three piles – ones you want to keep, things to go to the charity shop and, if they're totally banjaxed, ones that need to go to the recycling centre. Both of you need to get cracking seriously now if you want us to take you there. Clear?'

They nodded. They loved their dad unquestioningly, and when he gave instructions, they were followed. He was never cross with them, but they hated it if they felt they had let him down.

'Now, let's get inside and do what Mammy says, no messing. I want to see you at the table, hands washed, in five minutes, OK?' He tousled their hair and they scampered into the house.

'Thanks.' Ana smiled, slipping her arm around his waist. 'Sometimes they don't take notice of me. And thanks for saying something to Artie too. It's hard for poor Joe, Artie always getting the best in the class and he doesn't.'

'Ah, they do listen to you, but they see you all day. It's 'cause I'm away so much. Familiarity breeds contempt and all that.'

'What?' She looked at him, confused by the saying.

He grinned. 'It just means that people you see all the time have less impact than someone who isn't there as much.'

'This English, totally ridiculous language. In Ukraine, we just say that, the explanation, not the mad old saying from so many thousands of years ago…'

'I know, I know.' He chuckled, put his arm around her shoulder and kissed the top of her head. They walked in to join the boys for dinner.

After dinner, Ana FaceTimed her parents in Kiev while Conor cleared the dishes. Despite valiant efforts on Conor's part, the Ukrainian language had eluded him, so he had no idea what she was saying. Ana tried teaching him Russian as well, as both languages were similar, but the Cyrillic script didn't help, so eventually she gave up. His parents-in-law were wonderful people and loved Conor, despite never having had a conversation with him without Ana to translate. It was hard for her, he knew, and she wished he could pick it up, but he was never great for the books, even back at school. Practical things were no bother to him; things that he could see the benefit of, he learned very easily. But he remembered years of sitting in school with teachers going on about glacial rejuvenation or conjugating irregular French verbs, and he just couldn't see the point of it. His mind would wander until the roar of the master or a clatter across the head brought him back to the present. He lost count of the number of times he was beaten at school. The brothers had told his mam he was just plain thick, and for a long time he'd believed it. But now he knew that wasn't the case. He just needed there to be a reason to learn something. He felt ashamed – Ukrainian was his wife's language and that should be enough of a reason to learn the blasted thing. But she spoke English and the boys were completely bilingual, so he just couldn't summon the enthusiasm.

Ana had spoken in her mother tongue to the twins since their birth. They even went to a little Ukrainian school in Ennis every Saturday morning to learn about the culture, and while Artie enjoyed it, Joe absolutely hated it.

While she spoke, Conor tidied the kitchen, made the boys' lunches for school the next day and gathered their clothes for the laundry. Ana was still speaking to her parents, so he hurried the boys upstairs to bed amid much protesting. He wanted time with Ana alone to talk to her about Corlene's proposal.

Eventually, after he'd ensured their teeth were brushed, read them stories and issued dire warnings of the trip to Tayto Park being cancelled if there were any shenanigans out of them, he came downstairs. Ana was sitting at the table lost in thought, the call finally over.

'What's up?' he asked, leading her to the sofa.

She sighed. 'It's Papa. The place where he is working always is going to close. Some big Russian company buy it and now they move it all to Russia, so everyone is unemployed. You know how the town is – everyone work there, so when is gone, he won't get other job. Also, their apartment is with the job, so no job means no home. They don't know what to do. They can't go in Russia, and anyway, Papa hates Russia after everything they do in Ukraine and to its people…'

Conor thought for a moment. Ana was the youngest in the family. She had an older brother who lived in Moscow and a sister who was married to an awful lout altogether by Ana's reckoning. Conor had never met the brother, Sergei, and had only met her sister, Dorota, once.

'Well, a conversation I had today might help.' He told her quickly of the plan Corlene had put to him that afternoon.

Ana looked astounded. 'And we could do this, buy this old place?'

'Well, technically I suppose we could,' Conor confirmed. 'To be honest, I dismissed it at first, but then I found that the idea of being at home with you and the lads and running my own business does appeal to me. Maybe it's a crazy idea. We'd be in debt up to our eyes, and I don't know if I could even do it. What do you think?'

Ana thought for a moment. 'And just you working there, not Corlene?' she asked.

'Well, she'd be the major investor, so I'd be in touch with her, but she wouldn't be there day-to-day, no.'

'And you would not have to do more tours and stay away from us?' She seemed to be warming to the idea.

'Yeah, I'd resign and take over the castle full time. The renovation first, then run it. Sounds easy if you say it quickly.' He smiled. Then something struck him. 'And I just thought of something. Maybe your parents could come here. There'll be loads of work in the hotel, and your dad is very good with his hands – he can do anything. I'd definitely take him on, your mam too if she wants a job. You said yourself they like it here, and they don't have much to do with Sergei or Dorota anyway. They could stay with us for a bit, and then if they're happy here, we could get them a little house somewhere near us.'

He knew by Ana's face that she was torn. She wanted to care for her parents and he knew she hated him being away on tour, but she was nervous.

'OK, so if we do that, and my parents come here, that is good. But, Conor, why is Corlene ask you? I know you are so good at the tours and everything, but look – I am sorry if it sound bad, but always we are honest – I don't like the way she is with you, all touching you and saying how nice you are and everything. The last time I meet her, she looks so perfect, hair and make-up, and me just boring old housewife in jeans and a T-shirt… And don't say I imagine it, because I do not. Even Valentina say it. She say, "Don't let Corlene near Conor."'

Conor pulled his wife gently into his arms. 'Listen to me now. That's just the way she goes on – she's like that with all men. I don't take a tack of notice of her, and neither should you. Valentina can think what she likes, and Corlene can as well. You're the only one who matters to me – forever. You're my wife and I'm your husband. We are true and faithful to each other, and Corlene could stand on her head in the nude in front of me and it would not change that one iota.'

Ana giggled at the image, and Conor was relieved. 'Anyway, if we do it, she'd be around a bit at the start as we set it up, but once it's running, she'll be in Dublin. She lives there, her business is there, and she won't be down here much at all, I'd imagine. But either way, you need never worry, Ana. I swear I would never look at another woman. You're all I want or need. You know you can trust me, don't you?' His sapphire-blue eyes searched hers and she nodded. 'But this might be a good opportunity, and now it would help your parents as well. What do you think?'

'It is not you I do not trust, but I suppose it is a good solution, and if it means you will be home every night, then it is worth it. But what about you? Papa and Mama can't speak English. The boys would be talking to them in Ukrainian, and you won't understand. Conor, will it not be a big strain for you if it is possible?'

He rested his arms gently on her shoulders. 'Ana, they're your parents. You're my wife. That makes us family, and we'll figure it out. The boys are mad about them, and your mam would be a great help to us looking after them. You saw how they were when they visited last year. You were only saying the other day how you can't give as much time as you want to the refuge because of the boys, so maybe now you could do a bit more if your mam is here to help out. And I'd be around too, not like before.'

'Well, that is true, especially now. Most people are look forward to summer, but I do not. It means you will be gone. I know it is the job you have and everything, but we hate it when you're away.'

To his dismay, he saw her green eyes fill with tears, which she wiped angrily away. 'I'm sorry, Conor. I should not to make you feeling bad. You take so much care of me and the boys, but... Ignore me... I don't know what's wrong with me these days. I feel sometimes like I am disappearing. I am just the mother, cooking, cleaning, washing clothes, driving to school, to football and hurling... I look bad. I don't know, Conor... I'm sorry.'

He loved her so much, it upset him to see her like this. 'It's been hard on you, I know, in a foreign country with only the boys for company when I'm away. But this could change all of that. You could do whatever you want – go back to college, get a job, volunteer more at the refuge, whatever you want. And as for not looking good, well, that's just wrong. You're gorgeous. Sometimes I watch you when I come home late and you're asleep, and I can't believe how someone like me got to marry someone as beautiful in every way as you, my darling girl.'

They sat peacefully together for a long time, each lost in their own thoughts.

Eventually, Ana broke the silence. 'Let's do it. But if Corlene starts all the flirting again, you will stop her, OK?'

'I'll try. You know I have said it to her loads of times, but she just ignores it. She's relentless. Honestly, the best way to deal with it is to ignore it. You've nothing to worry about with me on that score, Ana, ever. You know that, don't you?'

She nodded and smiled. 'I trust you, Conor, but maybe not so much Corlene. She looks always like she wants to eat you, like a lion.'

There was no point in denying it, but he wanted to reassure her. 'Well, she can look all she likes, but she won't get anywhere with me. She knows that too – that's why she does it. The funny thing about Corlene, for all her flirting and now this business she has, she has never once in all the years I've known her had a man of her own. And even before they came here the first time, Dylan said the same thing. She got married loads of times, sure, but never to anyone she had even the slightest feelings for. The only person she loves is Dylan, and even that's a relatively recent phenomenon. I don't mean she didn't always love him, but she didn't do a great job of showing it in the past.'

'What about Dylan's father? Does she ever talk about him?'

'Nope, not a word. Even Dylan doesn't know. She told him years ago that it could have been any number of people, that she couldn't be sure. Poor lad. He told me once he used to imagine what his dad was like, tried to make up stories about how he was looking for Dylan but couldn't find him because Corlene moved them around so much.'

'Poor Dylan.' Ana sighed. 'He had such a hard life before here, before meeting you. But now it is so much better. He is so happy with Laoise, and even they are happy to live with her parents. Most young people would want a place of their own, but I think Siobhan and Diarmuid are like his family too. At the start, when I see him looking at

Laoise, I getting scared for him. He so much loves her. But then she is not so crazy as she looks and acts. She is more sensible, really, and they are good, solid, I think. Anyway, tell me more about this plan to be the king of the castle…' She grinned, and Conor was relieved to see her back to her old spirits.

'Well, Corlene and I are going to buy it. We'll need to borrow from a bank, but Corlene arranged all of that with Bert before he died. So I'm just investing my share, and I'd be what she calls the face of the resort. She has big plans, a place not like anywhere else in Ireland, and I know if she sets her mind to it, she'll make it happen.'

Ana thought before she spoke. 'And could you be happy, staying in one place after so many years always going, going, everywhere in Ireland? Always since I know you, you do this, and it is, I think, part of what you are. Of course, me and Artie and Joe want you to be here with us, but also you must be happy for yourself. If you are lonely for your job, for all the friends you have in the hotels and other drivers and guides… It must be right for you as well as for us.'

Conor sighed. He wondered how he got this woman in his life. He looked down into her face. She was tiny in comparison to him. Her blonde hair had been cut in a cute pixie cut ever since he'd met her, and her ears were pierced several times. She had high cheekbones and skin that took the sun well. Though Artie and Joe were very alike, they weren't identical, with Artie looking much more Slavic and with an open expression, like Ana.

'Ana, I want us to be together as much as we can. I also want financial security for my family. I'm not getting any younger, and to be honest, I'd happily say goodbye to the long days, the early starts, and the lifting of heavy suitcases every day on the tours. So if you're OK with it, I'll call Corlene tomorrow and tell her I'll do it.'

'Are you sure? You won't be so sad?'

'No, of course I won't. I love the job, but I hate being away – you know I do. It suited me for years, the life I had before I met you, but not now. As for my friends, drivers and all of that, I'll miss the craic, I'm sure. But I like those people – I *love* you, Joe and Artie. You are my people, the people I want to be with, so if I can make enough money and get to come home to you every night, then that is exactly what I want.'

'And what about Mama and Papa? Will we ask them if they want to come? Maybe we can talk to the embassy and ask if they can do the papers...'

'Sure we can. I know a fella who works in the Department of Foreign Affairs, and I'll ask him what the story is. Don't say anything to them yet. Let's see if it's a runner, and if it is, then we can put it to them, OK?'

'OK.' She cuddled up to him and yawned.

'Are you exhausted?' he asked. 'Maybe you should get an early night?'

'That is a really good idea. But, Conor?'

'Yeah?' he replied as he searched between the cushions of the couch for the TV remote.

'I'm not tired.' She ran her hand over his chest, leaving him in no doubt of her intentions.

'You'll be the death of me, Mrs O'Shea.' He grinned as he followed her up to their bedroom.

CHAPTER 3

A month later, Conor stood in the arrivals hall at Shannon Airport, chatting with Mad Mike Murphy, a tour driver for many years who had a cavalier attitude to personal hygiene and a very overinflated opinion of his own sex appeal. He was notorious among the female guides as a lecherous old goat, and they dreaded being paired up with him. The only woman who could manage him was his acerbic wife, Mags, who had a face like a bag of hatchets and of whom he was absolutely terrified.

'So anyway, as I was saying, Conor...' Mike rambled on while Conor checked the electronic board for the arrival time of the flight from Boston. He was meeting Corlene, who had been in the States arranging the loan for the hotel with Bert's bankers.

'This wan, Swedish or Swiss or something, jays, she was mad for me altogether, and she was a fine-looking bird, y'know what I mean?' Mike nudged Conor forcefully in the ribs, followed by a gesture that suggested the ample proportions of this woman.

'What? Oh, yeah, right...' Conor was distracted. He hadn't told Corlene he'd collect her, but she'd texted from the airport to say the whole thing was going ahead, so he decided to be there to pick her up.

If Corlene didn't see him in the waiting throngs at arrivals, she might miss him and go straight to get a taxi.

'Are you even listening to me?' Mike was indignant.

'I am, yeah… A Swedish woman…' Conor scanned the groups emerging from the baggage hall.

'Well, she wanted more than I was willing to give. I mean a roll in the hay is all fine and well, but she reckoned she could come over here and set up shop with me. But sure you know Mags'd eat her alive if she ever got wind – a very jealous woman my missus – so I had to let the poor girl down gently. She's gone modelling bikinis now in the Seychelles, trying to get over it, but 'tis hard to see that pain, y'know…'

Conor had worked with Mike for over twenty-five years. They drove for the same company and often swapped coaches or did each other favours, so despite many years of listening to Mike's nonsense, Conor never said a word about his alleged romantic encounters. Now that he was leaving the tour business, he had no more need of Mike, and an uncharacteristic urge to not be diplomatic rose up within him. 'Mike, I'm actually waiting for someone, a friend actually, so I'll have to leave you…'

'Oh, you're too high and mighty for us these days, are ya? Sure, we hardly saw a hair or hide of you last summer. Ah, 'tis the little woman has you well and truly whipped, I'd say, making you drive all the way home instead of landing yourself in the lap of five-star luxury in the hotel. And even on the nights you did stay, sure you were in the bloody gym or above in bed. She's after catching you good and proper, another good man down. But you're not the first, I suppose, and you won't be the last. The Irish wans are bad enough, but sure them Eastern Europeans are the devil, fierce strict, if you know what I mean…' Mike's remaining teeth were bared in what he thought was a suggestive grin and he winked theatrically, but the whole image only served to make him look like a total halfwit. The ridiculous comb-over of suspiciously dark hair that scraped across his shiny pate contributed to the village idiot look. The idea that any woman on earth with eyes or ears would go within a donkey's roar of Mad Mike was laughable, yet he persisted with this nonsense. Conor had had enough.

'Mike, listen to me because we won't be talking again after this. My wife is not strict – she is lovely. Would I rather spend my evenings with her or you? Well, I'm afraid there's no contest. I go home when I am anyway close, not because I am whipped or under her thumb or anything else. I go home because after a day's work, I want to see my kids and relax in my own house and sleep in my own bed with my own lovely wife. The very last thing on earth I want to do is listen to your bizarre fantasies about sexual conquests that happened nowhere but your own sordid imagination.'

Mike's face turned a variety of colours as he struggled to formulate a riposte. Just as he was about to open his mouth to speak, Conor spotted Corlene and waved, relieved to have found her. She looked amazing, and he wouldn't have been surprised if she had used the trip back to the States for another bit of 'cosmetic help' as she called it. She was managing to hold back the tide of time, but the suspiciously while teeth and fake boobs did nothing for Conor.

They had a busy few days ahead, meeting the various people needed to get the project underway, so she was staying in the Old Ground Hotel in Ennis, a lovely hotel that oozed tradition and old-world charm.

'Conor! It's so great to see you! I didn't know you were coming – what a treat.' Corlene's Alabama drawl made Conor smile every time.

He put his hand out to shake hers but found himself drawn into a hug. She rubbed his back.

As they were about to leave, Mike, clearly recovered, scampered after them, determined to have the last word. 'You're a right pain in the arse, Conor O'Shea. You always were and always will be. Everyone knows you got that young Russian wan out of a catalogue or off the internet. And here you are now picking up another wan, and you being all so high and mighty to the rest of us.'

Conor and Corlene turned. Corlene was bewildered, but Conor burst out laughing and then walked away, leaving Mike fuming in the arrivals hall.

As Conor pulled out of the airport car park, he recounted the exchange with Mike.

Corlene chuckled. 'Well, I reckon you've gone and burned your bridges with that guy, handsome, so I guess you'll have to stick with me.' She placed her hand on his knee and squeezed gently.

Several tourists were stalling and jerking their newly rented cars out onto the narrow Irish roads, unused to stick shifts and roundabouts. The roads around Irish airports were hazardous to everyone as the visitors did their best to get used to what must seem impossibly difficult driving conditions. Conor gave way to a pair of elderly ladies who were having a particularly bad experience, and once they were on the road again, he spoke. 'Well, like I told you, Ana's happy. She'd love me to be around more to help with the boys. And as you say, I'm in Mad Mike's bad books now, so I've no choice.' He chuckled.

'I'm glad she talked you into it. I must admit now to being less confident than I seemed that day we had lunch. I thought you were kind of a fixture of Irish tourism in the bus tour world and I'd never lure you away.'

'Well, there wasn't much convincing needed, to be honest. It suits us to do this now, for a variety of reasons. I had no idea what to do with the money Bert left me. I'd probably just have invested it in something, but I like the sound of this and it's a great opportunity.'

'Well, the money will work out fine. The finance guys in Houston were full of enthusiasm, well primed by Bert, the old sweetheart. I talked you up, explained why we need you, and I think you'll be happy with the arrangement. Obviously, have your own accountant look over the figures, but these are good guys, worked with Bert for years, so there's no funny business. The company will provide you with a company car, travel allowance, healthcare, all that stuff. You talk to your accountant and let me know what you want, and I'll see to it that it gets done. The way I see this playing out is that you do all the publicity, the media, TV interviews, Facebook ad campaigns and all of that. We should set up a familiarisation trip for travel magazine people, tour operators and that sort of thing as well.'

'Sure. I have plenty of connections both here and in the States, so that won't be a problem. I'm not a big social media person, though – I don't go on it at all really.'

'Oh, don't worry about that end. I have a company of young hipster types in Dublin who take care of all of that. You just show up, we'll shoot the ad, and we'll leave the tech to these kids. But I'll tell you what, Conor, you are going to be clickbait, and when those ads start runnin' in the US, we'll be booked out.'

Conor laughed. 'I've been called a lot of things, but clickbait isn't one of them. Whatever gets bodies in the beds is fine by me.'

'Anything?' Corlene glanced at him out the side of her heavily made-up eye. 'I'm thinking you come running out of the crashing surf, wearing only a small swimsuit…'

Conor considered talking seriously to her about the suggestive remarks and all of that, but it felt ridiculous. It really didn't bother him and, so long as she toned it down in front of Ana, wasn't worth making a big deal over.

'Go way out of that, you hussy. Anything with my clothes on, right?'

'Spoilsport.' She grinned wickedly.

They chatted happily about the renovations, and soon they arrived to the hotel car park. The sun was streaming through the window as Conor reversed into a space.

'I'm so excited,' Corlene announced. 'This is going to be such an adventure.'

Conor decided to voice his insecurities. 'Corlene, I know how you envisage this working out, but you do know I've never done anything like this before, right?'

'Look, Conor, you'll bring out the best in the staff, the clients, the operators, and that's what we need. You make people feel special, like their issues are important and that you can help them, whether it's finding their great-grandma's grave or the perfect night's entertainment, or just helping people over a hard time. People come on vacation for so many reasons, not always just to relax and enjoy themselves, and you know that better than anyone. That guy Declan, who used to be a priest – remember I met him at Dylan and Laoise's party – he told me about how you helped him and his wife when she was expecting and they were on the run. Conor, nobody else could handle that, could solve their issues like you. We just need you to keep doing that, except not on a bus tour but in our resort. Simple as that. You are the face of Castle Dysert. When people think of the hotel, immediately they'll think of you. You meet the guests, you get to know them, and if they need help with anything, you work your magic. Same with the staff. You manage the people. Not the day-to-day – just keep everyone happy and doing their jobs. Simple. Of course, before we get to that, we're gonna need you at the site, overseeing things, making sure we're not being taken for a ride. Bert always said some of the most hard-working guys he met in sixty years in building were Irish, but some of the biggest crooks were Irish too.

'Now, I gotta get me some coffee and some of that great Irish bread. I almost never eat carbs, but I just can't resist that stuff. What do they put in there, cocaine?'

They chatted amiably as they walked towards the hotel.

'Hey, guess who I met for lunch on the layover in Boston?' Corlene said.

'Not Ellen?' Conor was glad to hear Corlene had stayed in touch with Bert's old friend. 'How's she doing?' He smiled at the memory of Ellen O'Donovan, who had come on the same trip as Bert and Corlene. She'd discovered an incredible family story, and she finally slept in the bed that she was born in.

She'd written to him at Christmas and sent lovely gifts for Joe and Artie. She was always offering to put them up if they ever came to Boston. He and Ana had talked about making the trip; they really should now that the boys were older.

'Oh, you know Ellen, quiet and determined and still as sprightly as ever. She couldn't make the trip to Texas for the memorial service as she's getting a bit too frail for that kind of travel on her own any more. She misses him, just like I do, but she told me he'd made the trip to Boston to see her only a few weeks before he died. He stayed with her for a few days, and they said their goodbyes then. It's tough at their age – so many goodbyes.'

'I must send her a card. We might try to get over to visit. Ana has never been to America, and the boys would love it. I suppose I could never travel during the summer, and now that the lads are at school, we are kind of restricted, but we should try.'

The ivy covered old hotel seemed to glow in the morning sunlight. It was the epicentre of the the hustle and bustle of the busy market town and Conor greeted several people he knew as he entered the beautiful old lobby.

He and Corlene had a busy schedule of meetings for the week ahead – builders, architects, planners, interior designers. No expense was being spared, and the old castle was going to be unrecognisable.

A young waiter showed them to a seat in the sunny dining room overlooking the hotel gardens.

'Eat up! It's going to be a long day.' Corlene smiled as she buttered soda bread, while Conor tucked into a full Irish breakfast despite his intention to only have toast. The smell of bacon and sausages and freshly baked soda bread was too much for him.

'I know. I've a bit of juggling to do as well because I've a few tours booked in since last year that I'm trying to either offload or manage myself if all else fails. I've a tour going out tomorrow, but I'm only behind the scenes. I've a young lad driving for me. I'm hoping he'll take over for me so when I give my notice, I'll be able to present them with a good replacement.' Conor ate his breakfast hungrily; he'd been up at six to take Joe swimming. Joe was hoping to make the county swimming team and was training every chance he got.

'I hope he works out, as we need your full attention. So how about we finish up here and head on out to our castle? The auctioneer, as you call him – though what's wrong with real estate agent, I'll never know – won't be out there until tomorrow morning with the keys, and the building guys aren't scheduled to start until later in the week, but I'd like to see it for myself before all of that, y'know?'

'Of course. No problem.' Conor smiled. This was exactly how Corlene had amassed her fortune, by always being one step ahead. Corlene was as sharp as a razor.

They finished breakfast and walked out of the lobby.

'Aren't you changing?' he asked. Corlene was in a tight cream skirt, a baby-pink leather jacket over a low-cut top and impossibly high heels.

'No. Why?' She grinned.

'Because this place is totally overgrown, probably mucky outside, and could well have rotten floorboards and God knows what else inside. So maybe that isn't the most practical outfit?'

'Conor,' she drawled, her hand on his lower back, 'how long have you known me? I don't *own* any practical clothes, nor do I intend to buy any.'

He shrugged. 'Suit yourself, but don't go getting all damsel in distress on me, right? I'm not lifting you.'

CHAPTER 4

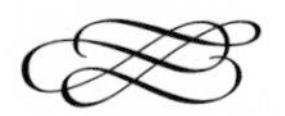

Conor and Corlene left Ennis and drove out to the coast and along the narrow strip of road that approached the castle entrance. Conor thought about how nice it would be to work twenty minutes' drive from home. He could collect the boys if Ana was stuck or pop home for lunch if the humour took him. After years away on the road, and in recent years feeling guilty about leaving all the parenting to Ana during the summer season, this new opportunity was ideal. He glanced at Corlene, who was checking email on her phone. She had reluctantly put on the pair of Ana's wellington boots that Conor had put in the boot that morning. He, unlike Corlene, had come prepared, in old jeans and hiking boots. He had pulled off his fleece and given it to her, and had instead put on his well-worn dark-green waxed jacket that was on the back seat. She looked hilarious in a skirt and green rubber boots, with a long grey fleece over the whole ensemble.

He pulled the car as tight to the wall as he could to facilitate passing traffic as they approached the entrance. The avenue up to Castle Dysert was barred by a pair of very ornate but rusty gates held together by an even more ancient-looking padlock, so Conor stopped the car and they got out. Between the pillar to the right of the gates and the hedge, there was a gap wide enough for them to slip through. The weather had been wet, and the mile-long driveway was muddy and dark, as the canopy of huge oak and beech trees almost obliterated any light. There was a distinct chill in the air, and Corlene shivered. The winding path was anything but inviting. Together, they trudged up the avenue.

'It will take some work, Corlene. At the moment it looks like a place you'd film a horror movie,' Conor joked as they avoided the worst of the puddles in the rutted path.

'I'm sure glad of these gumboots.' Corlene grinned as her foot sank into a deep pile of wet mud.

She opened her mouth to say something else, but Conor put his hand on her arm to quiet her. Silently, he pointed through the trees into the undergrowth ahead to the left. There was a wall, probably the wall of the old orchard, and beside it stood a stag, a huge muscular animal, his antlers rising majestically from his head.

They stood there for a few moments, just observing each other, and then the stag turned and stalked off into the woods.

'Are they wild round about these parts?' Corlene asked quietly, though the stag was gone.

'Not usually, but this is such a big estate, and the gentry long ago would have stocked it for hunting. I suppose nobody's hunted here for years, so the herd of Irish red deer just prospered. You would hear of deer roaming around occasionally. The sisters who lived here hardly ever ventured outside, I believe, so the deer would have bred and lived without fear of hunters. People tended to stay away, so much sad history or something. Well, that and the fact that everyone thinks the place is haunted,' Conor added with a wink.

'What? Are you kidding me? This place is supposed to be haunted?' Corlene chuckled. 'Great! Us Americans love that kind of thing. Come and stay in our haunted castle! See, you're earning your money already.'

They tramped up the avenue to the castle, the land on either side of the path a tight tangle of briars and thorns, and they were relieved to emerge into the bright spring sunshine once more. To the left was a stone wall, behind which Conor pointed out extensive stables. To the right there was another winding path that, according to the plans, led to the ornamental gardens, a pond and the vegetable and rose gardens. Behind the castle itself was the orchard, which overlooked the bay. At least that's what the grove once was; now the whole place looked like a jungle.

The castle was made from white limestone and red sandstone, and the front door was easily six feet wide, with marble columns and stained-glass panels on either side, making it an imposing entrance. The sun glittered off the remaining glass. Many of the Georgian panes were missing, and some had been crudely boarded up. Conor counted twelve enormous windows across each of the four floors.

The front door was locked, so they walked around the back to see if there was a possibility of gaining entry some other way. They could have waited, but they were both excited to get inside before the place was crawling with experts. There was a rotten window at the back, and the pair exchanged a glance.

'I could probably push it through if you want?' Conor examined the splintered wood.

'Sure, let's try. We own it now anyway, and the whole thing will need to be replaced eventually. Just be careful.'

Corlene stood back as Conor found an old stone to stand on so he could reach the window better. He then shoved his shoulder against the frame, and as he suspected it would, the window gave way and the entire frame disintegrated onto the floor inside.

'I'll climb in and see if I can open the back door from the inside. You wait here.' Conor heaved himself up through the open space and jumped down inside onto the tiled floor of the old kitchen, narrowly missing an enormous stone sink hanging precariously off the wall. Ominous scurrying told him he had disturbed the residents, and he shuddered. He was OK with mice, but rats gave him the creeps.

The kitchen was huge, and as he scanned the room in the gloomy light allowed in by the filthy windows, he spotted a large cooking stove, pots and pans of all sizes hanging over it, and an enormous rectangular table, attached to which were several ancient-looking kitchen tools. Cobwebs hung in festoons from the corners, and some even stretched the full width of the room, so much so that he had to use his arms to cut through them to get into the hallway where the big back door was.

'You OK in there, Conor?' Corlene called from outside.

'Yeah,' he shouted back, causing even more scurrying. 'I'm going to try to get the door open. If you can give it a shove when I say, we might get it open.'

'I could just try to climb in the window,' Corlene suggested.

'Yeah, right. I can just see that all right. No, this will work,' he called as he eased a rusty bolt back. The timber door had swelled and was wedged tight to the frame. There was nothing for him to pull, but at least he had the bolt off. Corlene pushed, but to no avail.

'Hang on, I'm coming back out. Just stay put.' Conor went back into the kitchen and climbed back out the window, this time by standing on the sink. When he appeared beside Corlene, his jeans were filthy and his shirt was beyond saving. He ran his hands through his silver hair to remove cobwebs.

'You're even more gorgeous filthy.' Corlene chuckled. 'Lucky Ana.'

Conor ignored her comment and examined the door. 'Stand back.'

He moved a few yards away from the door and then ran at it, shouldering it powerfully. The door moved slightly out of its frame, so Conor repeated the exercise. This time the door burst open and the wood scraped across the filthy tiled floor. They were in.

The smell of must and decay was strong, and it combined with the unmistakable scent of mouse droppings. They ventured through the old kitchen and along a passageway into the main reception area of the castle. There was a warren of corridors and hallways going in several directions, but they followed the main hall to a huge entrance room, in which rose a magnificent staircase.

He tried to get one of the many shutters to open to let some light in, but the locks were too high up for him to reach. The cantilevered staircase rose and split to form two semicircular balconies, which overlooked the gardens outside on one side and the entranceway below on the other. The stairs were carpeted, but the carpeting had fallen foul of moths and almost disintegrated in a puff of dust when they stepped on it.

'I think it's sound enough,' Conor reassured Corlene as he tested the wood of the stairs with his weight.

'It's like that house where they shot *Gone with the Wind*, isn't it? Or at least it could be...' Corlene was enthralled. Conor could see the gleam of enthusiasm for the project in her eyes.

'Will we go up?' Conor glanced up the stairs.

'Sure.'

As they climbed, they held the beautifully carved banister just in case the stairs gave way. Suddenly, they both stopped and strained to hear.

'What's that?' Conor whispered. The sound was faint but distinct.

'Is that a train?' Corlene whispered back.

'There are no trains around here, no tracks or anything, but it sounds like a toy train set, like an old-fashioned one.' Conor was perplexed. The noise stopped just as suddenly as it started, and slightly rattled, they continued.

Upstairs, room after room revealed old furniture, even some artwork, though the lighter rectangular shapes on the walls gave truth to the rumours that the sisters had died penniless. They had lived there, but in miserably poor conditions, having nothing but the bare minimum to do with the town nearby. Nobody really knew them. Corlene and Conor wandered from room to room, taking it all in.

They left the way they came in and made their way back to Ennis. Corlene wanted to stop at the nearest hotel to the castle to check out the competition, so they sat in the bar having coffee.

'It's a totally different market,' Conor explained. 'This is a family hotel, mid to low budget with self-catering houses attached. We won't be putting in on them nor them on us.'

They chatted about all they had seen in the castle, trying to visualise how it was going to look. Corlene had already engaged an interior designer, who was coming next week.

By the weekend, the place would be crawling with workmen. Corlene was not a woman to be slowed down by regulations. The planning was in order, and she had the full go-ahead to get started on the job. She'd been busy since they last spoke.

'That was fast,' Conor remarked when she told him how all the paperwork was sorted out so easily. 'The county council isn't known for the speed at which they deal with planning applications. How come it went through so quickly?'

Corlene grinned. 'Well, let's just say there is more than one way to make an application, and when it's made over dinner at a nice hotel and the planner's wife is visiting her mother in England, things can get done remarkably quickly.'

'I don't want to know!' Conor laughed. 'If I don't know, then I can't be implicated. Though there will be a lot of head-scratching as to how you got it through so quickly when people who just want to build a small extension onto their house are made to jump through all kinds of hoops. So I'd keep that to myself if I were you.'

'You don't think I got where I am by shooting my mouth off now, do you?' Corlene replied with a wry smile. 'Say, what do you think about that sound we heard? Weird, eh? What's the story with that place anyway? I know two old ladies lived there alone for years, but what about before that? And why do people think it's haunted? This could be a great angle – ghost-themed holidays! Hey, we could even get that *Most Haunted* TV show to come.'

'Look, that's only old gossip. Every old building in Ireland is haunted according to someone. I wouldn't take a tack of notice of that. On the history of the place, though, I've only heard bits and pieces, but I know a man who would know. Do you want to meet him? He's a carpenter and an electrician by trade, but he spends most of his time now as a local historian and folklorist. In fact, he works for the Folklore department of the library, gathering up all the old stories and that around the county. He's a fascinating man – he's a train expert, a botanist, a musician. Martin O'Donoghue is his name. What he doesn't know about local history isn't worth knowing. He's a bit of a character.'

'He sounds like just the guy for us. Can we meet him tonight?'

Conor marvelled at her energy. 'I'll see if he's around and let you know later.'

'Sounds good, Conor. I'm looking forward to hearing what he has to say. That train sound – it was coming from inside the house, wasn't it?' She was not letting it go.

'It sure sounded like it was, but who knows?'

CHAPTER 5

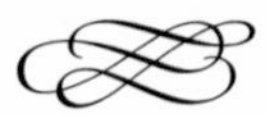

'Come with me. We are going out to Martin's place after dinner to have him tell us the story of Castle Dysert. We'll get a sitter, and you can have a glass of wine. I'll drive. Come on, you'll enjoy him – he's great craic.'

Conor and Ana were preparing dinner together as the boys played in the other room. He thought she looked tired and needed a break. She was still worried about her parents. Conor had made enquiries with the Department of Foreign Affairs but had not had a reply yet, and he didn't want to get their hopes up.

He hoped the prospect of the hotel would give her a new lease on life. He'd read a bit about depression and how, for women in Ana's position, life could be hard. He spent all day out and about, meeting people and getting things done, and he thought it must be difficult being at home all day, just the repetitious monotony of housework and childcare, no matter how much she adored the lads. He loved that she was at home full time, but he also knew she needed intellectual stimulation beyond making rockets out of cereal boxes and cooking dinners.

In the past, she'd talked about having her teaching qualifications from Ukraine translated, but she was disappointed to realise getting a teaching job would be almost impossible because she had never learned Irish. The national language was a compulsory subject in all Irish primary schools, and teachers had to be able to speak and teach it as a prerequisite to employment.

When he met her, she was working as a waitress at a hotel he stayed in frequently. Waitressing in Ireland paid more than teaching in Kiev.

'Thank you, but I won't tonight. I am so tired. Joe won't do his homework, and he get into big fight with the teacher again. And Artie tells me that always Joe is in trouble. And Mama was on the phone, say they get notice to leave the apartment next month, and I can't say anything. They ask Dorota if they can stay with her, but she say she don't have space. *Tato* won't ask Sergei, so...' Ana looked like she had the weight of the world on her shoulders.

'Look, I'll ring Tony at the department again tomorrow, but either way, let's just book them a flight. They have passports, and they came in with no bother before, so tell them just to say they are visiting their daughter and her family for a holiday. We'll work out the details of them staying once we have them here. Go online and book the flights now. I'll finish this.'

Ana's eyes filled with tears. 'But how? You can't pay for all of it. It's not –'

'Not me – we. Everything we earn is ours.'

'But you do all the working, and I –'

'Ah, Ana, stop that this minute. We've had this conversation before. I go out to work so that you can stay here and look after our lads and give them the amazing childhood they have. When I was a kid – you know, I've told you – it was hard. My mam was never home, working all hours to make ends meet, and my old man was gone, so there was nobody there for me or Gerry. I managed, but it was crap and a lonely way to be a child. Joe and Artie have you all the time and me a lot of the time, they can have their friends over to play, they have dinners made for them, you help them with school projects and bake them cakes on their birthdays. You're on the parents' association for the school, and you make those kids' lives so magical and fantastic. I lived in hotels, and you made us a home. This is the first proper home I've ever had, Ana, and you're the reason we – me and the boys – are so happy. So never, ever let me hear you say you don't pull your weight in this family, because you *are* this family. Now, I don't care what it costs – we have the money anyway – just book them a flight into Shannon and tell them to bring as much stuff as they can, OK?'

'Well, it will be expensive last minute, and he won't let us pay, let us give them a home. My *tato*, you know he is proud man –'

'Ring him.'

'What?" Ana was confused.

'FaceTime him now, on his mobile, and translate for me exactly what I say. Promise you'll do it exactly now, otherwise I'll ring Valentina and ask her.'

'But he –'

'Ana, please, just do it, will you? I want to talk to him, man to man. You aren't involved except as a translator, OK?' Conor sighed.

'OK.' She took out her phone and called her father. He answered and she had a short conversation with him. Artur was a big man, as tall as Conor, but he was quiet, a gentle giant.

'So what you want to say?' Ana asked.

'Did you explain that you are translating for me?'

'Yes, I did. He's happy to talk to you.'

Conor turned the phone so he could see his father-in-law and so that Ana could be heard translating. 'Hi, Artur, I'll keep this quick. Ana tells me that your job is gone and you and Danika are being evicted.'

Ana translated. Her father nodded and was about to speak.

Conor held his hand up, begging for silence. 'I have a suggestion. How about we bring you both over here to Ireland and you both stay here with us. I have bought into a hotel, and I will need a maintenance man to do all the jobs – a bit of security, a bit of woodwork, metal-work, that kind of thing. You can turn your hand to anything – I've seen the work you've done on your own place there – so I want to give you a job. Once you are here, we'll apply for residency here for both of you. We'll get you a little house near us so Danika can help Ana with the boys, and you can work with me. How does that sound?'

Ana looked at her husband, and her eyes gleamed with love and gratitude. She spoke in rapid Ukrainian, and Conor saw his mother-in-law, Danika, appear behind her husband, tears in her eyes, as Ana explained the plan. Once she'd finished, Artur remained silent for a few seconds. He was a proud man who had worked all his life. He hated being so dependent, and Conor could see it.

Eventually, he spoke, his voice quiet.

Ana translated for Conor. 'He says how can he work here when he can't speak English?'

Conor thought. The last thing Artur needed was to be made to feel like a charity case. 'He'll have to learn, simple as that. He's a smart man. Joe and Artie and you can teach him, and he'll soon have enough to get by.'

Conor couldn't care less if Artur never learned a word, or if he never did a day's work again in his life, but Conor knew that for Artur, it was vital to think he would repay the debt. If he had to learn English into the bargain, then it would seem even less like charity.

Once again, Ana spoke rapidly, and Conor managed to catch a word or two but nothing more.

Artur smiled and said something.

'He's asking Mama to get the dictionary,' Ana whispered.

Within moments, Danika handed her husband a huge book. They didn't use the internet if they could help it because it was expensive. They used their full data allowance every month talking to Ana and the boys on FaceTime. Artur rifled through the pages, finally stopping and running his finger down a column of words. 'Thank you, Conor,' he said in heavily accented English.

Ana and her mother burst into simultaneous tears, and they both started talking in rapid Ukrainian at once. Conor just nodded and smiled at them both as they signed off. Once they were done, he drew Ana into his arms, and she cried tears of silent relief.

'Thank you, Conor, so much. You are so much kind, so... Remember the day you gived me your phone to call because Mama was sick when I working in the Dunshane Hotel? I think that was the day I fall in love with you.'

'I remember it well, and Carlos Manner looking like a bulldog chewing a wasp. There's one hotel manager we won't be offering a job to anyway. He's still there, you know, looking po-faced. I don't know why they keep him.'

Conor got on with most people, but Manner was a right plonker. He'd made Ana's life hell when she worked there, and he really resented it when she and Conor got together.

'Oh, he was so horrible. Remember how he maked me clean the windows in the dark and the rain and how always he maked new girls cry? They keep him because all the poor staff are afraid of him. The owners don't want the people to think they are mean employers, so they put someone like Carlos in charge and he do all of this bad work... What you call, not bad work...'

'He does their dirty work. You're probably right. Behind every nice boss, there's someone doing all the nasty jobs. Carlos always looked like he was enjoying it, though.'

The conversation was interrupted by the arrival of a very put-out-looking Artie with a mutinous Joe behind him.

'Dad! Joe didn't finish his maths 'cause he says he's going out to play football, and now Miss Carney is going to keep him in at lunchtime –'

'Shut up, you, ya little rat!' Joe punched his brother.

'OK, OK, OK! Settle down and stop calling each other names. Joe, I thought you had finished all of your homework?' Conor looked down at the belligerent expression on his little son's face, and his heart melted. He addressed his other son, equally adorable. 'Artie, have you finished?'

'Yes, ages ago when Mammy said we had to do it, but Joe was playing with the Lego 'cause Mammy was on the phone to *Babusya*. If Joe gets to go out to play...' The unfairness of it all was too much for the more studious of the two.

'Right, I'll tell you what. Joe, you bring yours in here to me, and

Artie, will you go up and sort out a story for later on? It's your turn to pick.'

Conor caught Ana's eye as Joe sighed and went to get his school bag. Joe really struggled with all subjects, but he found maths especially boring and mystifying, and the gap between Artie's ability and Joe's was becoming more and more obvious. Conor hadn't really thought much of it until Ana started worrying.

Ana had said she was beginning to think Joe might have special needs, but Conor dismissed the idea. He could see himself in his son so clearly; if Joe was interested in something, he'd excel, but he just didn't see the point of school.

The next twenty minutes were spent trying to get through subtraction, and eventually they managed together to get the homework finished, though Conor noticed he had to tell Joe the answer almost every time. Joe just didn't get it.

Joe was putting his book away when he looked up at Conor. 'Dad, am I thick?'

Ana was in the other room with Artie.

Conor drew his son onto his lap, even though he was getting a bit too big for it now. Joe put his arm around his dad's shoulders.

'You are absolutely not thick. Why would you think that?' Conor's heart was breaking for his boy.

'Well, 'cause usually brothers or friends aren't allowed to sit together in school – Miss Carney moves people around. But Josh Harrington said I was only allowed to sit beside Artie 'cause he's the smart one and I'm the thick one and there is a smart fella and a thick fella at each table.' Despite his best efforts to keep them at bay, tears were forming in Joe's eyes.

'And who does Josh Harrington sit beside?' Conor asked calmly, while inside he was thinking how much he'd love to wring the little monster's neck.

'Tom Callahan.'

'And is he smart or thick?' Conor hated using those words, but that was how Joe saw the world.

'Really smart, like he won a prize for a story he wrote and everything, and his mam is a teacher and his dad is a doctor or something.'

'And so if every smart fella has a thick fella beside him based on Josh Harrington's theory, then what does that make Josh?' Conor asked, smiling.

'Er...thick?' Joe responded, the realisation dawning on him.

'And do we trust the opinions of thickos like Josh Harrington? We do not! So if he starts that again, you tell Josh that he must be the thickest fella in the class if he's sitting beside Tom Callahan, and see how he likes that.'

Joe giggled and his confidence was restored. 'I don't care that you're not a doctor. I think you're really smart even if you're only a bus driver.'

Conor ruffled his son's hair and gave him a squeeze. 'Well, that's good to hear because I'm *way* too old and thick to have to do all that learning to become a doctor at this stage.'

CHAPTER 6

Conor picked Corlene up at the hotel, and they drove out into the countryside. Martin O'Donoghue lived in a train station that had been out of commission for many years now. He owned four miles of track, a goods shed and a ticket office, which he had lovingly converted into a really comfortable home. He was an expert woodworker, and he did every bit of the renovation himself.

Conor pulled into the track, the lovely cut stone of the platforms rising on either side. The place was magical. Martin had every conceivable plant and shrub growing there and knew the names and the medicinal properties of each. He was a tall, slim man with a head of brown curls and twinkling eyes that always seemed to be laughing at some private joke. He wore Birkenstock sandals all year and was bohemian in his dress, and he exuded a sense of being happy with himself and the world around him.

'Martin! How are you? Thanks for having us.'

'Ah, Conor, I'm delighted to hear something is being done with the old place. It's a shame to see it go to wrack and ruin.'

'This is Corlene Holbrooke, from Alabama. She's the other investor I mentioned. Corlene, this is Martin.'

Corlene took Martin in, and Conor could see her weighing him up into the two categories of men: the ones she would seduce and the ones she wouldn't. By the look on her face, Martin was definitely in the former category, though Conor found a less likely match hard to envisage. There was something attractive about Martin, though; even Conor could see that. He lived life on his own terms and didn't conform to what society expected of him.

'This is some place you have here.' Corlene looked admiringly at the pots of overflowing flowers all over the platform and how the track wound into a little copse of exotic-looking trees.

'Thanks. I love it. Now, will you have a drink?'

Corlene glanced at Conor. Martin was pouring himself a whiskey, and he'd placed some olives and nuts in a bowl.

'Well, I'm not much of a whiskey drinker…' Corlene began.

'I've a nice Rioja if you'd prefer?' He smiled, and Conor was amazed to see that Corlene was completely enthralled with him.

'Lovely.' She gave him a genuine smile as he handed her a glass of the ruby liquid from a dusty bottle.

'Conor?' Martin offered Conor some whiskey.

'No thanks, Martin, I've the car. I'll have a coffee, but I can make it myself.'

'Not at all. I've some nice stuff here. I got it from a Guatemalan fella who was over here learning about mushrooms. He brought me some coffee beans – they're delicious.' Martin surveyed the painted timber shelves in his kitchen, neatly packed with all sorts of exotic spices and ingredients.

As Martin ground the coffee, he answered Corlene's questions about the train station while Conor looked around. Martin had no TV but did have shelves of books and a big comfortable sofa that was positioned in front of a pot-bellied wood-burning stove. The furniture was all mismatched and covered with brightly coloured cushions and throws. The place smelled of sawdust and coffee and incense. Conor was particularly drawn to a colourful rug on the floor.

Martin noticed him examining it. 'I got it in Marrakech. The owner of the restaurant I was eating in had a bit of an electrical disaster and a big wedding due in the next day, so I fixed his dodgy wiring and he gave me the rug in return.'

Martin led Corlene to the sofa and sat himself on an old tea chest turned upside down and covered with a crocheted cushion. A fire crackled merrily in the stove. He handed Conor the aromatic coffee, and all three made themselves comfortable.

'So, Martin, Conor here tells me you know a lot about the history of Castle Dysert.' Corlene appeared fascinated by both the man and by the little world he had built for himself. In each nook and cranny, there was something of interest.

Martin shrugged. 'I suppose I do. It's a fascinating place.'

'What can you tell us?' It was clear Corlene was dying to hear the story.

'Well, it's a fairly typical story in much of it. The Kings were a wealthy family, made lots of money in coal over in the north of England, and so they bought Castle Dysert around 1860.

'The building itself was constructed sometime in the 1500s, one of the McNamara castles – they had loads of them. The O'Connors, the McNamaras and the O'Briens were the ruling chieftains around here, so every castle belonged to one or another of them.

'They went into ruin, of course, and it was a thing then for English gentry to have a big house in Ireland, and even by the standards of the time, Castle Dysert was an extravagant house. There are over a hundred rooms there over three floors, with an attic spanning the whole fourth floor, and the best of stuff went into it. The red sandstone that was used for the reconstruction of the façade was brought in from Italy, and the limestone for the decoration was all polished over in England. None of that is original – it was the Kings did all that front. It's such a beautiful castle, inside and out. Or at least it was at that stage – God alone knows what it's like inside there now. But in its heyday, the whole parish was on the payroll, between gardeners and domestic staff.

'Well, as was the case all over, the Kings had no regard for the local people, and they exploited them for labour and rent and treated them very harshly. If a man went onto their land and took a rabbit or a pheasant, they showed no mercy. So as you can imagine, there was no love lost between the Kings and the local people. After the revolution in Dublin in 1916 and the First World War, well, everything changed then. At the time, Grenville King and his wife Mary lived there. Both died of the flu in 1919. The younger children were all sent off to boarding school, all but the eldest boy, also called Grenville, who was fighting in the war. When he was injured and his war was over, he didn't go back to the family house in Yorkshire but came over here instead. This was the only home he'd ever known, I suppose.

'He brought his young wife with him, but he gave her a miserable life. After the trenches of the Great War, sure he was cracked as the crows. Drove them all daft with his antics, screaming and roaring at night and wandering around the place half-mad during the day.

'For example, he had connections in Africa and got all sorts of animals shipped over for hunting. He stocked the woods around the castle with warthogs and buffalo, and it's said that he had his carriage pulled by zebras – there's a photo in existence apparently of two zebras from Dysert standing outside the pub, tacked up to the carriage, while your man was inside having a few whiskeys. He was an awful man for drink, violent too, I believe, when he'd had too much. They had a lot to put up with in him. Sure nowadays he'd be getting psychiatric treatment for PTSD, but they hadn't a clue about that back then.

'His madness didn't stop him having issue, though, as they say, and that woman had her hands full with twin boys in 1917, a girl in 1920 and another girl in 1921. His wife was all right as they go. Constance was her name. I think most people felt sorry for her if anything, putting up with the carrying on of mad Grenville.

'Anyway, there was a lot of anti-British activity around here, and the houses such as the one owned by the Kings were targets. They were Protestant gentry who were seen as never having rightfully got the land in the first place. Independence was imminent, and people had a lot of old scores to settle with the likes of the Kings, who had exploited the people for generations. The IRA were busy raiding police barracks and making their presence felt, and so people were getting braver.'

As Conor had suspected she would be, Corlene was engrossed in the tale. Martin had a way of talking, slowly and with a musical lilt to his voice; his words were like vines wrapping the listener up in the story. Conor had seen him do it many times, but every time he was fascinated.

'A few local boys were in the IRA, and they worked for the Kings. I suppose their mothers put a bit of pressure onto them to do it, given that the King children were so small, but anyway they warned the family that the house was to be burned. IRA were burning every big house they could back then, determined to drive the landlords back where they came from. But it was often the case that the locals would have a bit of loyalty to the family, as some of them weren't bad at all. In fact, plenty of them were big supporters of Irish independence, but they were burned anyhow. The only difference was that some families got a warning, but many more did not.

'The story goes that Grenville King was given a note to get out, that the house was going to be torched, but him being mad or pig stubborn or something, he refused to listen. He never told his wife about the note, so on the designated night, they went to their beds as usual. Most of the staff were warned and so they slipped out, but the Kings slept as the castle was doused in petrol and set alight.

'The alarm was raised immediately, and the family got out, except for one boy, the eldest of the first-born twins, a lad called Grenville as well, after his father and grandfather before him. When Constance realised he wasn't there, she tried to get back inside, but by then the whole place was taken by the flames. The boy's twin, Samuel, told them that his brother couldn't sleep so he went to the playroom in the attic to play with his new train set. He was only four, the poor little lad, and while they got the rest of them out of the nursery, he wasn't there. By the time they realised it, 'twas too late.'

'And even the people who cared for those children, they just left them to burn in the fire? How could they do that?' Corlene was upset as well at the sad tale.

'You have to understand the times, though, Corlene. The local people didn't see them as children. They saw them as the next generation being moulded to be the next landlords, to continue the pattern. Getting rid of them meant it was over for good.'

'So what happened then?' Corlene was stone-faced.

'Well, after the fire, the house was not fit for living in, so the family did what they all did in the end and went back to England. They put a bailiff in charge for a while, but nobody went near the place so they stopped paying him. Grenville senior got put into a mental hospital and died not long afterwards. The wife remarried, some Scottish fella, and they took the children to live up there. Castle Dysert and all the land around it just went back into nature.'

Conor interjected. 'But it was lived in again since then, wasn't it?'

'Indeed. Samuel, the twin who survived, went to Australia in the forties. He was a young man then and had been stationed in Singapore, I believe, during the war. He took off for Australia and made a fortune in the opal business. He settled in a place called Lightning Ridge in New South Wales. Most of the opals had to be sent back to Germany or Hungary to be polished at the time, but he not only mined for opals, he also set up the factory to cut and polish the stones, so he made an absolute killing. He got married out there to an Australian girl.

'In the heel of the hunt, he came back to Clare, his pockets stuffed with money, and he was determined to bring Castle Dysert back to its former glory. He left when he was four, but he always told people he had memories of the place and that he never forgot his brother, his twin. So he landed back with his own children, two little girls, and they lived in a rented house here in Ennis while the castle was gutted and renovated. His wife, Beatrice, had no interest in houses, that was all him, but she loved horticulture, so she had all the plants she loved from home shipped over and planted the most amazing garden. My mother remembers her – they met often and talked about the medicinal properties of the different plants. My mother is a witch, you see.'

He dropped that bombshell in so casually, it took Conor a second to register it.

'A witch?' Corlene was rapt.

'A white witch, yes. So she and Beatrice King had a lot in common, as they both understood nature. They got to be friends, and my mother told her the house was haunted. But Beatrice was a practical Australian woman, used to living on the frontier, and she had no time for what she considered to be old nonsense.'

Conor moved forward in his seat. 'So what happened?'

'Well, Samuel was so excited to get the house back that he had it done just as it was when he was a child, except with all the mod cons available in the fifties. He was popular with the locals despite his lineage, and he employed all the local lads for the work. He'd buy them a pint in the bar on a Friday evening. His years in Australia had knocked the snootiness out of him. He was a man of the people and not afraid to get his hands dirty. He worked on the house himself as well – he didn't just stand by and watch.'

Martin took another sip of whiskey, clearly enjoying the effect his story was having on Corlene and Conor. 'Once the whole place was done, he paid off all the workers and gave them a nice bonus as well, and then he spent weeks working in the house by himself. Nobody could imagine what he was doing since the whole place was finished as far as anyone could see. His wife was in the garden most days, and the little girls were either with her or with a local lady they paid to mind them. Each night, he'd come out of the house and go back to where they were staying. After a few weeks, the family moved in, and there they lived happily for a spell. Local people worked there, and they all reported that Samuel and Beatrice were kind employers and very relaxed, nothing like his father and mother. The house was open and welcoming, and apart from the attic, people were free to roam round. The attic he kept locked. There was only one key, and Samuel kept it in his pocket. The story goes that he went up there occasionally himself but never his wife or the girls.'

'What was there? In the attic?' Corlene asked excitedly.

Martin smiled a slow, sad smile and calmly went on. 'I've no idea. Nobody does. The key was lost long ago, and when Samuel died and the daughters left, the place was just kind of left. He went up to the attic or the roof one night – nobody really knows – and threw himself off. They found his body the next morning on the stone patio. His wife was devastated. The girls were in their teens by then, I think. They went back to Australia with their mother, but a year later she was in a riding accident and they were left orphaned.'

'And the two sisters, they were…' Conor began.

'Samuel and Beatrice's daughters, yes. Charlotte and Sarah. They had nowhere to go, so at the age of eighteen and twenty, they came back to the only home they'd ever known. They moved into Castle Dysert and lived there together, never marrying, until the day that Charlotte died. She had cancer, and the poor woman must have had a very hard death. The local GP, the district nurse, home helps, they all tried to get in to see them, but they wouldn't open the door most of the time. People tried. I tried myself several times, as they'd let me or my mother in occasionally. When Charlotte died, Sarah was in the house with her, but she never contacted anyone. She was in there with her sister's corpse for a week or so, they reckon, judging by the state of the body.

'I went up after Charlotte's funeral to see if Sarah would let me in or just to check how things were going, and I saw her body on the stone patio, just where her father's had been years earlier. The poor woman must have thrown herself off the roof at the same spot.'

Martin paused and sipped his drink, and the three of them sat in silence for a moment.

'And now you two own it, so I wish you luck with it because very little luck was seen in that place over the years.'

'Are we being foolish to take it over? After everything that's happened there?' Corlene fixed Martin with her gaze.

'Well, that depends very much on your disposition, I think. If you believe that it's only a building and with new walls and wiring and paint it can be transformed, well, then that's what you think and good luck to you. But if you believe that there's more to life than what we see in front of our eyes, well, then it's hard to know.' Martin shrugged.

Corlene looked at Conor. It was clear to Conor that they were both thinking about the toy train noises they'd heard. They told

Martin about their visit to the castle that morning, and he didn't seem remotely surprised.

'"There are more things in heaven and earth, Horatio, than are dreamt of in your philosophy",' Martin quoted.

'Do you believe in all of that, ghosts and spooks and haunted houses?' Corlene asked.

'I do, I suppose. I've lived long enough to know we don't know much about the world we live in, or where we come from, or where we go when it's all over, but hand in hand with that, I'm a practical man. That old place could give you the creeps, though.'

Conor and Corlene shared a glance.

They chatted on for another while until Conor looked at his watch. He really wanted to get home before Ana went to bed.

'Well, thanks for all the information, Martin. We appreciate it. And we'll let you know how we get on.' Conor got up to shake the other man's hand.

'Well, it was nice meeting you, Corlene, and sure if you're going to be around these parts, maybe we'll bump into each other again. I wish you the best of luck with whatever you decide. I'll see you around, Conor.' He shook Conor's hand and walked them to the car.

Corlene noticed an old caravan parked beside the goods shed. 'Another project?' she asked, smiling.

'No, that's Pearl. I sleep there. I have a bed in the house, but I prefer the caravan. I like to sleep with my feet out the window, you see. The bed was designed for someone shorter than me.' He said it in such a matter-of-fact way that Corlene seemed unsure if he was joking or not.

CHAPTER 7

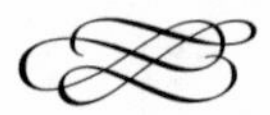

While it took a leap of imagination to see Castle Dysert as it was in its heyday, the architect, Daniel Coffey, a very trendy guy in his thirties with an irritating Dublin accent, was excited about the project. He showed them the plans that Samuel King had submitted when he returned to refurbish the castle in the fifties.

Somehow, Daniel had managed to unearth the original drawings by searching the archives of the Royal Institute of the Architects of Ireland and found the architect Samuel King consulted during the 1950s refurbishment. Though the man was long gone to his reward, the plans were still in his office, so Daniel drove down to Limerick to get them. His excitement was infectious. Conor had to admire his tenacity as he spread the blueprints across the bonnet of his large Jeep for Conor and Corlene to see.

There had been a huge maze the size of a football pitch on one side of the house, and a sunken garden on the other. The formal gardens, with rows of box hedging and a semicircular limestone amphitheatre, were directly in front. The back was just as impressive from the black-and-white photos Daniel had managed to find. Two sets of stables, a huge cobbled courtyard with a blacksmith's forge and twenty labourers' cottages led to a walled garden, woodland walks and an ornamental pond and fountain. To see the view out over the Atlantic to its best advantage, Samuel King had an artificial hill created behind the house into which he had set a hundred steps.

The very young and weedy-looking auctioneer introduced himself as Kyle Kinsella when he arrived twenty minutes late.

'I'm so sorry! I missed the entrance.' He looked mortified as he hurried up the stone steps and turned the enormous key in the lock. He shoved the door but nothing happened. He smiled nervously; the group waiting to gain access to Castle Dysert did not look like they had time to waste.

Daniel gave an audible sigh as Kyle slipped his Ray-Ban sunglasses up onto his head. The county engineer, John Gerrity, had by now arrived too, and he stood at the bottom of the steps with a face like thunder.

Conor felt sorry for the lad, who was clearly nervous about such a huge deal. The castle was sold but only subject to the engineer's report and planning permission for extensive refurbishment, and judging by the look of distaste on John Gerrity's face, his report wasn't going to be favourable. Conor knew John, as he trained the football team the boys played on, and he was not charming but was exceptionally reliable and straight as an arrow. Conor had warned Corlene not to try any of her charm stuff with him. He would probably report her for attempted bribery of an official of the state or something.

'Will we give it a shove, do you think?' Conor asked. 'I'd say the timber has swelled over the years and it's too tight for the frame.'

Daniel looked horrified – he was certainly not going to ruin his Armani shirt by shouldering a door – and John just stood there waiting.

'We could try.' The auctioneer looked doubtfully at the enormous door with its dragon's head knocker. The door furniture had once been polished brass but was now a tarnished greeny-grey.

'Grand so, Kyle,' Conor said. 'Here's what we'll do. I'll take a run at it and we'll see if that works, but if not then we can take turns. Right?'

Kyle just nodded. As he sized up Conor's very muscular and strong-looking frame, it was clear he doubted his own contribution to the endeavour would amount to much, but it was nice of Conor to include him anyway.

'Be careful, Conor. We don't have insurance yet,' Corlene joked.

'I'm sorry, what did you say? In order for me to do a survey, the building has to be fully insured. Under Section 5 of the Planning Act –' John Gerrity was about to leave.

'She's only joking, John. It's all done. I've spoken to them already, and we are on a temporary policy until all the reports are complete,' Conor reassured him.

'I'll need to see that,' Gerrity said humourlessly.

'No problem. It's on my phone here.'

Conor searched his emails and found the insurance confirmation. Corlene rolled her eyes at Conor while Gerrity checked the particulars in the email.

'Fine.' He handed Conor back his phone.

Conor charged at the door, thinking how odd it was that this was his second time doing this in two days. His shoulder ached from yesterday's efforts to gain access to the back, but there was nothing else for it. Luckily, the door gave way on the first shove.

They walked in gingerly as the unmistakable sound of scurrying and the overpowering smell of decay assaulted their senses once more.

Daniel looked enraptured. He ran his hands over the banister and scuffed the tiles with his shoes to reveal their true colour. He and Conor managed to drag a big table over to the shutters and stood on it to open all the windows, allowing the light in.

The entrance was breathtaking. A gigantic fireplace of Italian marble took up most of one wall to the right, while the staircase, a beautiful piece of craftsmanship, wound up from the left. There were squares and rectangles of lighter colour on the silk-covered walls where paintings had hung, now long gone – sold to keep the King sisters alive probably. Many of the pieces of furniture had been removed, but some of the larger and more unwieldy items remained.

Daniel enthused about the architectural features and the unusual pieces of furniture as they walked carefully around the entrance area.

'These families would have embarked on the Grand Tour, something young wealthy people of noble birth did for many years sometimes. They'd travel all around Europe and pick up all sorts of things to be sent back to their homes in Ireland or England that were to be used as symbols of wealth and evidence of travel. This, for example' – he placed his hand on a particularly horrid-looking gold standard lamp that stretched to well over eight feet in height and was all ostentatious decoration – 'is almost certainly early eighteenth century Italian, but there's stuff here from the Middle East and Scandinavia, and according to the records, there are even some medieval French tapestries. They may have been sold on the QT of course, but there's a good chance they're still here. To most people, they are just gaudy, moth-eaten or plain ugly in some cases, but to the trained eye, they are treasures beyond measure.' The condescension in his tone left them in no doubt which category they all fell into.

As they walked carefully up the stairs, Conor whispered to Corlene, 'Are you sure this guy is right for us? He seems like a bit of an eejit.'

'Trust me, he's a genius. He's an architect, but he also has the conservation credentials and his father is high up in the Department of Culture, Heritage and the Gaeltacht.'

Conor grinned. 'Listen to you with all your Irish language and culture.'

'Oh, honey,' she whispered, 'I'm virtually a local now. Anyway, I'm assured that he's our guy. He's a bit full of himself, but whatever. He's not our problem – this guy is.' She nodded at Gerrity, who was already measuring and inspecting.

For the next forty minutes, they were given a tour by Daniel Coffey, who Conor conceded had done his homework. Room after room was explored. Some had four-poster beds, complete with moth-eaten drapes, and there were several water closets. Some of the rooms had clothes hanging in the wardrobes, and there were pieces of crockery and china everywhere.

Conor took in the sheer size of the place and couldn't imagine the thinking behind choosing such a monstrosity as a family home. Many of the features, doors, shutters on the windows and furniture were not original to the house, as almost everything had been lost in the fire in 1921, but they were original to the time. Samuel King had taken no shortcuts when redecorating his family home. It was a weird mishmash of medieval, Edwardian and 1950s style.

In the dining room was a large seat that ran the length of one wall; Conor estimated it to be around twenty feet long. Daniel pointed out how the seat lifted up and underneath were lead-lined cases into which ice would have been placed for keeping wine cool. Several huge portraits, presumably of the family back through the centuries, remained on the walls, and Conor and Corlene both wondered why they hadn't been sold. The two sisters had rattled around this massive house, surrounded by priceless antiques and art, but by all accounts, they had barely enough actual money to survive. Conor imagined it was because, as the years went on, they became more and more reclusive, until eventually they had no contact with the outside world at all. Who would they sell to?

Daniel explained that he had discovered as part of his research that when the sisters first arrived back from Australia, two orphaned girls in their late teens or early twenties, they did a deal with an antiques dealer in Dublin. Daniel had found the bills of sale for several pieces.

This unscrupulous dealer offered them 500 pounds for a series of prints done by the famous Italian architects Marco and Pietro Senza. They did the deal, but the prints were grossly undervalued and the young women had nobody to advise them. The dealer, knowing their true worth, sold them within weeks of acquisition and turned an enormous profit. The prints, twelve in all, ended up in the hands of private individuals, but also in the Louvre, the Smithsonian and the National Gallery in London.

'If that happened once, it probably happened over and over,' Daniel said. 'They had no life experience – they were homeschooled by a governess and their father and mother protected them from everything – so they were very vulnerable when their parents died. Apparently, there was no contact with any of the other King siblings who lived in England, who would have been Charlotte and Sarah's aunts and uncles. They had disowned Samuel years earlier when he took a non-titled Australian wife and lived, as they saw it, as a savage in the outback.'

They hadn't by any stretch seen every room, but time was pressing on. Conor could see that John Gerrity was not there for a guided tour, no matter how enthusiastic Daniel was about lapis lazuli ground into paint to make it a vivid blue or original cornicing. Gerrity was not a man for aesthetics; he was a man who lived by the letter of the law and the building regulations. Where Daniel saw beauty and history and art, he saw danger, subsidence, dry rot, wet rot and bulging chimney breasts, and Conor could sense his frustration with being lectured on Louis XVI furniture when what he really wanted to do was inspect the property and file his report.

'Well, how about we leave you guys to your jobs, and Corlene and I take a stroll around?' Conor said. 'I know that you have a lot to look at, Daniel, and you're meeting the designer here next Thursday, I believe? How long will you need, John?' Conor was respectful and to the point.

'An hour,' Gerrity replied. 'I'll be able to speak to you in general terms then, but obviously the specifics will be in my report, which will be compiled within the week.' He didn't believe in small talk.

Daniel was clearly disappointed – he could have waxed lyrical for another hour or more – but he knew Conor made the decisions.

'Fine, let's meet here in an hour then.' Conor shook John's hand firmly, and Corlene followed him up the next flight of stairs.

'Nice work,' murmured Corlene as soon as they were out of earshot. 'That Gerrity guy was fit to strangle Daniel, and we don't need him in any worse humour than he already is.'

Conor just winked at her.

They went on, wandering from room to room, down corridors they hadn't explored the day before, and Conor started to see how beautiful the place could be if it were restored to its former glory.

'It's something else, isn't it?' They were in a room that was over the front portico on the second floor. 'This would be a lovely breakfast room, wouldn't it?'

'Y'know, it would. Let's tell that to Daniel.' Corlene made a note on her phone.

Six floor-to-ceiling windows allowed an uninterrupted view of both the gardens in the foreground and the bay behind. From this height, it was easier to imagine how the outdoor landscaping would have looked when Samuel and Beatrice lived there.

They never mentioned the train sound they heard or the conversation with Martin – they hadn't even discussed it between themselves much – but Conor got an eerie feeling in the house, especially as they progressed up to the third floor. It was so cold up there, much colder than the other floors. He told himself it was just his imagination working overtime and that he needed to have a bit of sense; still, the feeling lingered. He had told nobody, not even Ana, about the toy train sound. She had enough doubts about him working so closely with Corlene, and he didn't want to give her any more reasons to be against the hotel.

Corlene shuddered as they stood in yet another room, this time overlooking the stables and the courtyard. 'I think we can use this, the creepiness of it, as a selling point.'

Conor immediately resisted. 'No, we won't. Anyway, it's all in your head. Let's just market the place properly, as a fabulous hotel in a stunning location, and that will do. We can do all kinds of themes and all of that, but I don't think going on about hauntings is a good idea. It cheapens the brand, and anyway, it's a sad story. We want this to be a place people come to relax and be pampered, not to be scared half to death.'

'Hmm.' Corlene was non-committal and that worried him.

The hour passed quickly. A part of Conor wanted to go up to the attic to see what was there, but he didn't want to give Corlene any more ideas, and anyway, the door was locked. As they went back down, Daniel was holding court with John Gerrity once more, and if Gerrity's face was anything to go by, he'd had enough of the young know-it-all.

'In terms of furniture and so on, most of it is replica – the fire took most of the originals. But even so, I would imagine there are some nice pieces here that can be put back into the house once the work is done. As far as conservation goes, I'll liaise with the heritage people, but I don't envisage any real problems.'

'Maybe we would be more comfortable talking at the hotel in town?' Conor intervened, cutting across Daniel and quietly stamping his authority on the proceedings.

'That's fine,' said John Gerrity, relieved to see Conor back. 'The Old Ground? In twenty-five minutes?'

'That sounds good. Let me buy you lunch. We can hear what you have to say, and we're looking forward to your verdict.'

Corlene smiled as she and Conor walked to Conor's car. 'You see?' She nudged him. 'You are so much better at dealing with all sorts of people. You just made him feel like his viewpoint was the most important thing.'

'Well, it is, actually. If he's against us, we are rightly goosed,' Conor replied.

'Goosed, schmoosed. You underestimate me, Mr O'Shea. You forget I know people.' She grinned mischievously.

The lunch turned out to be a cordial affair, with everyone displaying various levels of enthusiasm for the project. Gerrity seemed to think the building was, at least on first inspection, structurally sound, and Daniel had a lot of ideas about restoration. Despite his earlier reaction to Daniel, Conor had to admit that the man knew his stuff when it came to period architecture, and his enthusiasm was infectious.

Finally, Gerrity and Daniel left, and Corlene and Conor spent the rest of the afternoon going over some figures and looking at the paperwork from the bank. It seemed to be all systems go.

Conor rang Ana, but she was in the car and couldn't really talk. She had to take the boys to football training and was going to a parents' association meeting afterwards.

'Dinner?' Corlene asked. 'Or are you going home?'

'I might as well stay. Ana and the lads are busy all evening.'

Just as their meals arrived, Ana rang back.

'Sorry, Corlene, I'm just going to take this, OK?' Conor stood and went out to the lobby. 'Hi, Ana. Everything OK?'

'Yes, I just was wondering where you are. We are home and you are still working?' She sounded a bit put out.

'Well, I was going over stuff with Corlene earlier. We met with the architect and the engineer. Now we're just having some dinner, and then I'll be home.'

'Who is "we"? You and the men from the building or you and Corlene?' Ana's voice was unusually hard.

'Me and Corlene. But as I said, I'll be home in an hour or so.'

'OK. Try to get home soon. Valentina is looking after the boys because I need to go to meet a social worker about the refuge. She has some women in Dublin who need a translator urgently.'

Conor sighed. He knew Ana was upset because he was with Corlene, but she was going to have to get used to it if this thing was going to get off the ground. 'Well, why don't you ask Valentina if she can stay over? I'm sure it won't be a problem, and then you can come and join us once you've finished. Will the meeting take long?'

'I don't know how long, Conor. Maybe... I will see. Look, I'll see you later, OK?' She hung up the phone.

Conor stood in the lobby, his phone in his hand, incredulous that Ana would behave like that. It was true that he'd been gone since early morning and it was around eight now, but surely she had to understand he needed to put the hours in? They rarely fell out, and they made up right away when they did, so he was mystified. He'd need to talk to her again, reassure her, but also make her understand that she was just going to have to tolerate Corlene and him spending time together.

CHAPTER 8

'So who's behind it?' Corlene asked when he came back to the table.

'Behind what?' Conor asked, confused.

'Well, somebody sure as hell doesn't want us to move on this, so they tried to spook us. You don't seriously think that there is some ghost roaming the corridors, do you? I had you pegged as smarter than that, Conor!' She punched him playfully on the arm.

'I never said I believed it – I just think it's interesting. But anyway, you're probably right. We're a superstitious bunch, us Irish.' He smiled.

'God, you are just gorgeous. I can't believe Ana got in ahead of me...' She leaned over and placed her hand on his.

He immediately pulled away. 'Enough.' He was serious.

She was a relentless flirt, but this had to stop. Anyone could see what she was doing and get the wrong impression. It could get back to Ana, and things were bad enough. If she did it again, he was going to say something to her, not in a jokey way like he usually did, but for real.

'OK, OK! We've got a lot of work to do to get this place up and running in six months. I reckon if we have enough bodies in there, it can be done. I must admit to thinking that Daniel was a bit of a big-hat, no-cattle kinda guy, but he's determined to get us one nice place there, and I reckon he's gonna do it too. I did a deal with him that if we turn the key in six months, it will be seriously worth his while. He'll be answerable to us, but I think making him the sort of project manager is a good idea – he's so psyched about the place and has all the right connections.'

'He's got a lot of enthusiasm, that's for sure, but look how he was with John Gerrity. I don't know, Corlene. He might have the whole place out on strike within a week.'

Corlene tapped her nose. 'And that, my darling Conor, is where you come in. That tour group all those years ago was the most muddled-up bunch of misfits I ever did see, and yet you managed to get us all going in one direction and not murder each other. And you've done it countless times since, I've no doubt, so just do your thing. I don't know how you do it, but you have that kinda emollient personality. Things just glide easier when you're there.'

'I don't know, but I'll do my best anyway.' He changed the subject. 'So how's Dylan?' He was annoyed about Ana and the way she had been with him on the phone, and he was all talked out on the subject of the hotel.

'He's great, so happy. He and Laoise are playing gigs at festivals all over Europe right now with a small backing band. They're playing in some really big venues, so it's making them some money as well, which is nice. Diarmuid and Siobhan have been so kind – they had us over to their house for Christmas and everything and the music was playing until the next morning once the whole family got going. Dylan really feels part of it, y'know? He loves Diarmuid – he's become the dad Dylan never had really.' There was a hint of sadness in Corlene's normally tough demeanour.

'Tell me to mind my own business if you like, but who is Dylan's dad?' Conor asked.

Corlene paused. Conor immediately regretted the bluntness of the question; he had no right poking into her private life like that. He was about to apologise when she began to explain.

'I told Dylan I never knew, that it could be any number of people, but that's not really true. I know all right, but he's no good. He wasn't then and he sure as hell isn't now. In fact, my mother sent me a message recently to say he'd been sniffing around, asking questions. Someone told him that I live here now, maybe he saw a picture of me and Dylan in that magazine feature a few months ago or something and is wondering, who knows, but it's a complication I could live without.'

Despite her constant flirting with him, Conor felt protective of her and Dylan. 'And you've said nothing to Dylan?'

'No. Everything is going so great with him, and he's so happy with Laoise and playing music. He doesn't need this.' She twirled the empty wine glass in her hands.

Conor thought about what he was going to say next. 'I don't know anything about it, but I wonder, if this guy wants to get in touch to meet his son, maybe they could have some kind of relationship? Dylan is old enough to decide for himself, and it might be good for him. I know my own father was a total disaster, just walked out and never looked back. I just can't ever imagine not being in Joe and Artie's lives no matter what happened with Ana.'

'No.' Corlene was adamant. 'Dylan doesn't need him and neither do I. My son is on the brink of his own life – he deserves all of this. God knows I was a crappy mom for most of his childhood, but he's happy now, and I won't let that jerk come in and ruin it. He can't bring anything but misery to Dylan, and I'll do what it takes to protect him.'

'What's his name?' Conor asked.

'Larry Costello.' She almost spat the words. 'He was the cool guy in our town, y'know? The guy all the girls wanted to be with. But when he found out I was pregnant, he didn't want to know, tried to say I was with so many guys it could have been anyone. But that wasn't true and he knew it. I was just a kid, seventeen… After that, I don't know. Maybe I should have had an abortion, but I just couldn't. It all seemed so unfair. It wasn't the baby's fault, so I kept him, but I wasn't ready to be a mom. I left him with my mother for weeks, months at a time, then moving him all the time… It wasn't fair. I'm trying to make it up to him now, and keeping that loser out of his life is one way of doing that.'

Corlene was upset, and she so rarely showed genuine emotion, Conor was taken aback.

'Excuse me… I need a cigarette. Will you join me?' Corlene pushed her chair back and left the table.

Corlene came across as a tough old bird, and she was in lots of ways, but she had really turned her life around, and this guy sniffing around seemed to really have rattled her.

She and Conor strolled outside without a word. It was a clear night. They sat down on a bench in a secluded part of the front lawn of the hotel, and Corlene lit a cigarette.

'I thought you'd given those old cancer sticks up?' Conor smiled to take the judgement out of his words.

'I did, but things have been a bit…well, a bit stressful lately. I don't need a lecture, thanks, if that's where you're going.'

'It's not, and I'm sorry about throwing my tuppence worth in earlier. It's none of my business.'

'Yeah, sure. Look, it's nice that you care. It's just I hate the thought of him showing up. He…he's really bad news. He'll charm the birds out of the trees, but he's a violent bully.'

Conor was surprised. From what she'd said inside, this Larry Costello sounded like the local hero that all the girls wanted. 'Did he hurt you?' he asked gently.

She looked him square in the face and took a deep breath. 'Everyone wanted to go out with Larry, but not me. I just wasn't into that jock thing. But he liked me, and I turned him down in front of everyone. He was so mad. Anyway, that night we were all at a party out at the creek, the summer before our senior year and I had to pee, so I did like everyone did, went in the bushes. He followed me, and… he raped me. Dylan was the result.'

Conor was shocked and saddened to hear her story. She was just a kid, as she said, and to be attacked like that… Well, he'd never understood men who could do that.

'Ah, Corlene, I'm so sorry that happened to you. No wonder you don't want that animal anywhere near you or Dylan.'

Tears were pouring down her cheeks. Conor had never seen Corlene like this, and his heart melted. He put his arm around her and drew her close to him. She turned into his chest as she cried softly. For a long moment, he said nothing, just rubbed her back until the sobs subsided.

'We can talk about it, if you like, or if you'd rather not, that's OK too. Whatever you want,' Conor said gently.

'I thought I was over it, you know? It was years ago. I have so many regrets, but Dylan's the one great thing in my life, the only thing I'm proud of really. So it's complicated. Afterwards, I felt so ashamed, so disgusted with myself, though I could have done nothing to stop it. None of it makes any sense, but that's how victims feel, like they are to blame or something.' She took another cigarette from the pack and lit it.

'But you know that there is only one person to blame, and that's him. You need to believe that, Corlene.'

'In my logical head, I do, of course I do, but something like that... It plays tricks on your mind, you know? It affects people differently, I guess. People go one of two ways, it seems. They either hate to have anyone near them, become recluses or nuns or something – that wasn't me – or they become kind of promiscuous. And I was. I've had a lot of men in my life, and I put them before Dylan. Those men were often not good people, but I just thought on some subconscious level that it was all I deserved. It was like I was disconnected from my body, like it wasn't worthy of being loved and cared for because it had somehow betrayed me. I know this must sound crazy, but that's how it is. I've been seeing someone, a therapist here in Ireland, and it's been great, you know, taking all this stuff out from where I've buried it and dealing with it. I was so young, and I believed certain things then – it must have been my fault, I must have said or done something to make it happen. And now I'm trying to process it in a better way, but it's not that easy.'

Conor had never seen Corlene like this, honest, vulnerable. It made him understand her behaviour a little more, and he realised that behind the confident, almost sexually aggressive façade was a very damaged woman who deserved better. 'I can't imagine how hard it is, and I'm so sorry you had to go through that. There is no excuse ever for a man to treat a woman like that. It's such a heinous crime, to violate someone, and the scars must be so deep. And yet look at how strong you were. You talk about all the mistakes you made, but what about the fact that you raised a fine lad all on your own? And sure, you beat yourself up because you weren't the best mother all the time, but you loved him and took care of him as best you could in the circumstances. And he survived and is a great person. In recent years you have got so close. He loves you very much – anyone can see it. My old man just took off, leaving my mam with me and my brother to rear, no help, no money, nothing. He was a useless parent, but you are nothing like that. You're a good mother, a good friend and a brilliant businesswoman. You have nothing to fear from that man because you have people around you and Dylan who care about you both very much. You're not on your own.'

They sat on the bench in silence, her head still on his chest.

Minutes passed, and then Conor glanced to the entrance of the hotel. He spotted Ana sitting in her car in the car park, watching the scene before her. She must have finished her meeting and come to join him.

He mentally cursed her timing. He knew how this must look. Before he had a chance to go to her to explain, she turned the key in the ignition and drove away.

CHAPTER 9

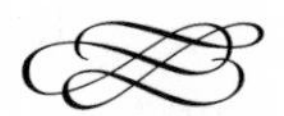

Conor ate his breakfast in silence. He'd wanted to talk to Ana last night when he got home, but she pretended to be asleep. When he tried to wake her, she said she was tired and for him to let her sleep.

He knew she was upset with him. If she would just let him explain, everything would be fine, but he'd never seen her like this. Apart from the scene last night, she had no reason to be suspicious of him and Corlene. Part of him was angry that she wouldn't even give him a hearing. He had never once in the years they were together given her any reason to be jealous. He loved her and the boys with all his heart, and the idea of cheating on them was so alien to him. Yet she seemed to believe him capable of it. It was only five thirty in the morning and she and the twins were still asleep, but he clattered around the kitchen making coffee and toast. Maybe if she heard the noise, she might come down to say goodbye. He realised how childish he was being, but he'd never gone off on a tour, no matter how early, without her making him breakfast and kissing him goodbye. This felt all wrong.

The timing couldn't be worse. He had to pick up a short tour in an hour, one he had been committed to since last year. He'd tried to get someone else, but the tour operator pleaded, as the clients were a large corporation in the States and they'd taken many tours with Conor in the past. His former employers were understanding about him wanting to leave, though they were sorry to lose him. They'd even promised to send some business his way when the hotel was up and running, so he wanted to keep on the right side of them. And so reluctantly he'd agreed to do the tour.

As he sipped his coffee, he heard feet on the stairs, and then his two tousle-haired boys burst into the kitchen. With their blond hair standing on end and their matching Angry Birds pyjamas, they looked so gorgeous. Conor's heart hurt at the thought of leaving them. This hotel was such a fantastic opportunity. He could have a proper family life and be there for his sons in the way his own father never had been. If only Ana could see it for what it was.

'Good morning, men.' He smiled and they ran to him, climbing onto his lap.

'Why're you up so early, Daddy? Artie can read the clock, and he said it was only eleven past four.' Joe deferred in all matters mathematical to his brother.

It amazed Conor that there was no jealousy between them. Sure, they had the odd squabble over a toy or something, but it was as if Joe accepted Artie was the smart one and so his word was law.

Artie grinned. 'Quarter past five, Joe. 'Member, the big hand was on three and the small hand was just past five.'

Artie was so patient and generous. He didn't lord his superior skills over his brother and was always quick to point out Joe's achievements to their parents.

'I've got to go to work. Don't you remember I told you yesterday? But it's only for a few days and then I'll be home again.' He hated to see the sadness on their little faces.

'I don't like it when you have to go away, and Mammy said you work now at the new hotel so you don't have to go anywhere and stay in faraway places without us.' Tears were in Artie's eyes, and Conor's heart hurt.

Conor held his sons tightly and kissed their heads. 'And that's true, but I need to do this one tour because the people who booked it asked for me specially. And they are going to bring lots of people to our new hotel, so we need them not to be cross with me. Because if lots of people come to the castle on their holidays, then I'll be able to work there and come home every night, and we'll be able to go swimming and play football and everything every day. So I need you to be big brave lads and mind Mammy while I'm gone and be very good. And, Joe, you must do the best job you can with your lessons, OK? And, Artie, you must both keep your room tidy and clear the table after dinner, and don't be leaving everything around for Mammy to pick up, all right?'

They nodded earnestly.

'We'll be good. How many sleeps before you're back?' Artie asked.

'Five sleeps.' Conor smiled at their measurement of time. It was always the same, how many sleeps to the birthday, to Santa coming, to a holiday.

The flight was due down in Shannon in an hour, so he'd have to get cracking. He hugged the boys once more, then gave them some cereal and juice and told them to be quiet and not to wake their mother, though he knew she was probably awake but choosing not to come down.

He glanced at his watch, an antique Ana had bought him for his birthday last year. It was engraved on the back, with simply 'I love you, A x', and he treasured it.

This was stupid. He bounded up the stairs. He went into their bedroom, where Ana was still in bed. 'We have to talk, Ana, and I'm leaving in fifteen minutes,' he began.

'We do not have to talk. I see enough with my own eyes last night.' She spoke quietly, never turning.

He sat on the bed and touched her shoulder, and she almost flinched. His heart sank. She'd never reacted to him like that before. 'Ana, come on, nothing was going on – of course it wasn't. She was upset about Dylan and left to have a cigarette, and I went with her to check she was OK...'

Ana sat up and turned to face him. 'Always I tell you she looks at you like she want to – I don't know how – like she wants to eat you up, and always you say it is not a worry, nothing is there, only from her side. But a married man with a family does not do what you do last night with another woman. You know that too, Conor – don't pretend that you don't. She wants you, always she has, and now she is closer. Maybe nothing happen, maybe you don't kiss her yet or take her to bed yet, but –'

Conor felt himself getting cross. 'So that's it, is it, Ana? You don't trust Corlene and suddenly I'm having an affair? That's a big leap to make. You're being ridiculous and childish, and you won't even let me explain. Even if she was interested in me – which she's not, not really, it's just messing – I can't believe you don't trust me enough not to cheat on you.'

Fury and pain flashed in his wife's eyes. 'So I am being childish now. I come to a hotel at night and my husband is alone in the dark with another woman in his arms, and I'm being childish? Go to your tour, Conor. Maybe Corlene can come to see you in the hotel, make you feel better about your childish, ridiculous wife.'

'Oh, for God's sake, this is so stupid! You –'

'Dad? Why are you shouting at Mammy?' Artie was standing in the doorway, tears in his eyes.

Instantly, Conor felt awful. He'd never wanted his kids to see their parents arguing like this. Before he had a chance to say anything, Ana got up and soothed Artie, taking him back downstairs.

'I wasn't…' he began, but they were gone.

His bag was in the car already, so he left without another word.

He picked the tour up and transferred them to Killarney. He was in an absolutely foul humour, and while he tried to be his usual cheerful self, it was a struggle. The group of golfers was luckily not too interested in history or stories of the country, and they'd taken an overnight flight so many of them were snoozing, which saved him having to entertain them. He checked his phone every few minutes. He'd texted Ana from the airport to tell her he was sorry, that he loved her and only her, but she didn't text back.

That night, after having taken his group to play golf in the afternoon, he lay on the bed in his hotel room, flicking channels, settling to nothing. He'd called home and Joe answered; he'd got some kind of revenge on the horrible Josh Harrington so he was anxious to tell Conor all about it. Then Artie came on the line, and Conor thought he sounded a bit down. He wished Artie hadn't walked in on him and Ana arguing that morning – it must have been such a shock for the poor lad since they so rarely fought.

'You OK, Artie?' Conor asked.

'Yes, I just don't like it when you and Mammy fight.'

Conor sighed. 'I know, pet, and I'm sorry we had a fight, but it's not anything bad. You and Joe have fights all the time, don't you, and then you make it up again?'

'I want you to come home. I hate it when you're gone, and Mammy is really sad and cross. She gave out to us for just playing with the Lego, and we weren't doing anything bad. She's in a really grumpy mood.' Artie was upset, and Conor wished there was something more he could do. He was the more sensitive of the twins; Joe was more resilient.

'I'll be home in five sleeps, and how about I bring you a present?' Conor felt awful. Now he was the kind of father who bribed his kids.

Artie said nothing, so Conor tried again. 'Ah, come on, Artie. *Babusya* and *Didus* are coming soon, and I bet they'll be delighted to see you all. Put Mammy on the phone and you'll see we're fine.'

He heard muffled voices, and then Artie came on the line again. 'She says she is too busy to talk to you.'

Conor hated to hear the pain in his son's voice and felt angry at Ana for using the boys like this. 'That's fine. Tell her I'll call her later, OK?'

'OK.' Artie sounded even younger than he was on the phone. 'Good night, Daddy. I love you.'

'I love you, Artie, and tell Joe I love him too. I'll talk to you tomorrow.'

Artie hung up, and Conor sat on the bed, looking at his phone.

Then a text came from Ana. *Please, just let me alone now. We'll talk when you come back home.*

Conor threw the phone on the bed in frustration. She'd never sent him a text without a kiss in it before.

He went down to the hotel pool and swam fifty lengths. Each stroke helped to ease the aggravation he felt.

CHAPTER 10

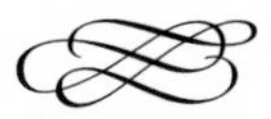

After swimming, Conor was starving, so he went to the hotel bar for something to eat. As soon as he'd ordered, he sat down and took out his phone again. He had just begun another text to Ana when he heard a voice he recognised.

Mad Mike Murphy was standing over him, pint of Guinness in his hand. 'I thought you were gone and too good for us, buying some fancy hotel up near you? But here you are down with the plebs again?'

At the bar were two other drivers Conor knew, who raised their hands in a wave. They were probably delighted to be relieved of Mad Mike's irritating company for a few minutes. Mike was the very last person on earth Conor wanted to talk to right then, so Conor stayed focused on his phone. 'I've some work to do, Mike, so you might leave me to it.' He didn't even make eye contact.

'Ha! Work – is that what you call it?' Mike sat down beside him, landing his pint on the table in front of Conor. 'And what's this I hear about yourself and some Yank having romantic dinners above in the Old Ground the other night? I thought you were all loved up! Ha, ha! There you are now. Who'd have thought the saintly Conor O'Shea is a normal man with normal appetites like the rest of us, huh?' Mike punched Conor jokingly on the shoulder.

The waiter arrived with Conor's food, and he sighed; Mike was not going to leave.

'Could you bring it up there, please?' Conor asked, indicating the bar. 'I'm going to join my friends.' He stood and went to where Shane Healy and David Kelleher were sitting. 'Mind if I join you, lads?' he asked wearily.

'Not a bother, Conor. How're things?' David was an older man who had served all his career in the Guards, and then his wife died six months after he retired. He drove tours for something to do. Conor had always liked him. Shane was a younger lad, and Conor had only met him once before in the company of a group of drivers at one of the many tourist stops around the country – he couldn't remember where.

Mike was flirting clumsily with a young waitress, holding her arm while he told her some stupid story. She looked really uncomfortable, but the bar manager was too busy to come to her rescue.

'God, he's a right gobshite, isn't he?' David rolled his eyes. 'He had the head bored off myself and Shane here with the last half an hour.'

'He's that, all right.' Conor sighed, then tucked into his dinner.

The food was probably nice, but it might as well have been sawdust. If he hadn't been so hungry, he'd have gone up to his room, but maybe a bit of company was what he needed instead. David and Shane chatted easily about the tours they were on.

Conor glanced over at Mike again, and this time the man had his hand on the young woman's shoulder. She was holding a tray of dirty glasses and seemed powerless to get away. An older, more confident woman would have told him to shag off and leave her alone, but this poor kid seemed rooted to the spot.

Conor put down his knife and fork, stood up and walked over to Mike and the young woman. He removed Mike's hand from her shoulder. 'She's busy. Leave her alone,' Conor said quietly. He smiled at the waitress, who couldn't have been older than eighteen, and she looked very relieved.

'What the hell has it to do with you? Myself and Marta here were just having a chat, and –'

'You were talking *at* her, and you were annoying her, and you were touching her without her consent. She has work to do, and I'm fairly sure she has no interest in listening to you banging on and on with some kind of old rubbish that isn't even true, so leave her alone.' Conor's voice was cold.

He'd sat and observed Mike's antics and many more like him for years in the tour business, and he wasn't going to ignore it ever again. Ana often told him of the sexual harassment she'd had to endure when she was a waitress at the Dunshane Hotel where they met, and hearing Corlene's story the other night just made him want to punch people like Mike.

Marta practically bolted away, and Mike puffed up in indignation. 'Who the hell do you think you are? I…I was only –' he spluttered, incensed.

'You were sexually harassing her. God almighty, do you not see what you've become? She's young enough to be your granddaughter, and she's a lovely young woman – what on earth are you thinking? Mags has stayed with you all these years, though for the life of me, I can't see why. But she did, and she raised your kids more or less on her own, and this is how you treat her? Would you ever grow up and don't be making a total show of yourself every time any female is within fifty yards of you?'

'Ha! This from you, knocking off some Yank, and you married to a wan half your age? You've some cheek, you…you –'

'It's true, Anastasia is much younger than me – and I'm well aware of the age difference – but she loves me and I love her. And I respect her. That Yank, as you call her, is the other owner of the hotel, so we were having dinner to talk about the business. I have never cheated on Ana nor would I ever, so your gutter mind can think what you like. Frankly, your opinion of me is irrelevant. But if I ever see you harassing a woman like that again, I'll give you such a clatter, it will knock you into the middle of next week. Do you hear me?'

Conor was not a violent man, and yet here he was threatening to batter Mad Mike. He knew it was just all the frustration he was feeling about Ana and Corlene and everything, but it felt good. Mike knew he meant it too. Mike was small and fat, and Conor would have loved to have hit him a box into his stupid face.

'Lads, let's settle down, will we?' David put a hand on each of their shoulders.

'I won't ever sit with him again,' Mike said sullenly, and David suppressed a smile. Mike sounded like he was four.

'Fair enough, whatever you like. Now, Conor, your dinner is getting cold, so you better sit down and eat it.' He led Conor back to the bar, and Mike stormed off in a huff. David's years as a police officer had taught him how to defuse potentially difficult situations.

Shane's phone rang and he went off to take the call, and Conor ate his meal in silence, still seething.

'Will you have a pint?' David asked.

Conor didn't drink when he was driving normally; he wasn't a big drinker anyway. But when he did have one, it was a glass of wine or two over dinner with Ana.

'Thanks, I'll have a pint of Guinness.' He sighed. 'Sorry about that. I shouldn't have kicked off at him like that in front of everyone, but he's such an eejit and that young woman was half scared of him. He's probably out leaving the air out of my tyres as we speak.'

David called for the drink and turned to Conor. 'Yerra, he hasn't the guts to do that. He's afraid you would give him a hiding. You looked back there like you just might. Nah, he'll get over it. Fellas like him never learn. He had it coming. So how are you doing? I haven't seen you around for a while.'

Conor and David chatted amicably for a while, Conor telling him about Castle Dysert and all the plans he and Corlene had for the place.

'It sounds great. I'm looking forward to seeing it.' David sipped his pint.

Conor thought for a minute. 'David, can I ask you something?'

The older man turned to him. 'Sure, what is it?'

'You were married to Eileen for a long time, weren't you?' Conor was slow to discuss his private life with anyone, but he really needed some advice and David was a very steady, solid kind of guy.

'Forty-two years,' David said quietly, the pain of her loss still in his voice.

'And did you fall out much?' Conor had realised as he swam that he had no real experience with marriage. Maybe fights like this were normal. His mam had been on her own all her life, and he hadn't had a serious relationship since Sinead left him. He had loads of women friends, some even more than friends over the years, but he'd never really let anyone get close enough to consider it a real relationship before Ana.

David seemed to sense that it wasn't a general enquiry. 'Yerra, we did from time to time, usually about me not being there. When the kids were small, I was working my way up the force, getting promoted and all of that, so I worked long hours. She was stuck at home with three small children, then three bolshy teenagers. 'Twasn't easy, I suppose, and when I'd come home, I'd be so beat out tired that I wasn't a whole pile of use to her. That was the main thing we fell out over.' He stopped and waited for Conor to speak.

'Ana isn't talking to me. She thinks the woman I'm working with to get the hotel up and running has designs on me or something. I've never done anything to make her think I'd cheat on her – I'm not like that clown Mike – and yet she thinks I would.' He blurted it out, as he needed to understand what was going wrong in his life. It all seemed so complicated. He couldn't tell Ana the reason Corlene was the way she was; she'd told him in confidence, and it was her story to tell, not his. But if Ana knew, maybe she'd be kinder. She worked in the refuge, helping women who were victims of abuse, trafficking and all the rest of it; if she knew Corlene was just like the women she had such compassion for, things might be different.

David thought for a moment. 'Does she work? Outside of the home, I mean?'

'No. She's a teacher, but she went to university in Ukraine so her qualifications aren't recognised here. She looks after our twins, Joe and Artie – they're almost seven.' Conor smiled at the thought of the twins.

'Well, Conor, I know, like myself years ago, you're out trying to make a living, to look after your family. And I'm sure your wife knows that you're not the type to be off chasing women behind her back. But it's hard on mothers. It's great for a family if the mother can be at home. It's the best thing for the kids, and if we're honest, it's great for us men too. And she is probably all about the activities and the friends over to play and all of that. My Eileen was the same. But making dinners and picking up crayons and driving all over the place dropping and collecting kids to things is not exactly stimulating, you know. And then we come home and are tired and just want to throw ourselves down in front of the telly. It can't be easy for them.'

'I know, but that's exactly why I'm taking this opportunity – so I won't be on the road, away for weeks on end, leaving her at home with the lads on her own. We're bringing her parents over from Kiev to stay with us, and so if I'm home more and her parents are around to help with the boys, she'll have more time for herself. But if it's going to work, I have to be in partnership with this American woman, and Ana can't stand her.'

'It's a tricky one, Conor, and I don't envy you, I honestly don't. It is true, though – happy wife, happy life. She's your priority, and I'd say do whatever it takes to put things right with her. If I had my Eileen back, I'd make sure we didn't waste one second fighting. Life's too short.'

Conor finished the pint in one gulp and stood up. 'Thanks, David. I appreciate the chat. You're right. I'll fix it. See you in the morning.'

'Night, Conor. And here, if you meet Mad Mike, don't hit him, will you, no matter how tempting it is to wipe that lecherous smile off his face. That eejit would sue you, and you've enough to deal with.' David grinned and patted Conor on the shoulder.

'I won't.' Conor smiled.

As he walked out, he saw the manager of the hotel, a man he'd known for years. 'Hi, James. Listen, just a quick word.' Conor led him to a quiet corner of the lobby.

'Is everything OK, Conor?' James was eager to keep Conor happy, as his company brought a lot of business to the hotel.

'Fine, fine. But you know Mike Murphy, the bus driver?'

'Mad Mike? Yes, I know him.' James's tone indicated he held Mike in no higher esteem than Conor did.

'Just tell the women on the staff to keep an eye out for him, especially the younger ones. He's been harassing one of the young waitresses in the bar, and he's always the same. The poor woman couldn't get away from him. Maybe a word from you that they don't need to put up with that kind of behaviour and they should report anything like that to you would be a good idea. If there's anything, you can ring Josephine Hilser. She's the tour operations manager for the company Mike's driving for, and they'll deal with him. I'm going to speak to her myself about his carry on, as I know her well, so she'll know what it's about if you do need to ring her.'

James smiled gratefully. 'Thanks, Conor. He is a pest, but to be honest, we need the business, so I was loathe to complain to the company. But you're right – he's always doing it. We had a particularly nasty incident with him last year, so I will ring Josephine myself and make a complaint.'

'Do. Goodnight, James.' Conor went up to bed feeling that at least Mad Mike Murphy might get his comeuppance at long last.

Lying in bed, he texted Ana. *I know you are angry at me, and you are right to be. I know how it looked, but I SWEAR to you I have no interest in Corlene or anyone else. You're my whole world, and I love you with all my heart. I miss you, my darling Anastasia. xxx*

CHAPTER 11

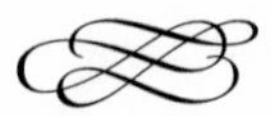

The building went ahead as Corlene predicted, with incredible speed, and when Conor went there every day to check on progress and attend to administration, he was stunned at how much work was done. Daniel was the site manager, insisting things be done faster and better all the time. The bonus that Corlene offered must have been fairly substantial, and it was certainly doing the trick.

He walked in the gardens where the tropical plants Beatrice King took from Australia all those years ago were now flourishing again, since the bindweed and briars that were choking them were removed. There was a team of gardeners working on the space, and though Conor knew very little about horticulture, he could see how much progress was being made.

He spent time every day roaming the extensive grounds, wishing Ana was with him. He wasn't used to a desk job and the office made him a little stir-crazy, so he needed fresh air. They'd patched things up when he came home from the tour a few weeks back, but things were not as they were. He wished he could get their relationship back on track, but he just didn't know how. Her father and mother had arrived, and Artur was happily getting stuck into the many tasks that needed doing in the hotel. Daniel and Artur had some kind of way of communicating, and only God knew how, but it worked. Tradesmen of all descriptions teemed throughout the building, and the whole place was a hive of activity.

Danika helped Ana with taking care of the boys, and while having her parents there was nice for Ana and the boys, it meant he and Ana didn't have much time alone together. He longed for a proper talk with her, not even about Corlene or the hotel but just about them and how things were.

He'd been in Dublin last week doing a round of interviews on TV and radio that Corlene had set up, and then they'd recorded an ad for Facebook. In it, he was walking along the shoreline talking about Castle Dysert's location on the Wild Atlantic Way. He felt a bit foolish because the script was overly romanticised, but Corlene assured him it was, as she called it, clickbait for Americans. She'd had the social media gurus in Dublin target the ad at females in the US aged between twenty and seventy years of age. She'd called him this morning to say the video had been viewed 500,000 times in the last week and that he had some huge number of 'likes'. She tried to tell him about all the comments to the effect that if Conor himself was part of the package, they'd be on a plane in a shot, but he cut her off. He didn't need to hear that.

Laoise, Dylan's girlfriend, had texted him that morning. I never had you down as a sex symbol, but the silver fox is breaking the internet!!!

Several people had mentioned the ad and the interviews to Ana, but she hadn't watched them yet. He didn't give a damn about all of that; he just missed her so much. They slept beside each other every night, but they'd not made love in weeks – another first.

Conscious of what David had said, he tried to help out as best he could, but since he couldn't speak Ukrainian, he felt he was in the way. The twins spoke to their grandparents fluently, and he really felt outnumbered in his own home. But there was nothing to be done about it.

There was something very wrong with his marriage, and he wished he knew how to fix it. It wasn't just the stupid thing with

Corlene, though that certainly was the start of it; he also felt Ana wasn't happy. Corlene would be just the person to talk to about it to get some advice, but he didn't dare; if Ana thought he'd spoken to Corlene about them, she'd lose the plot completely.

As he walked the grounds every day, he thought about how he kept himself distant from people in the years before he got married. He was friendly and all of that, had friends and had had a few girlfriends, but he never let anyone in. Ana was the first, and still the only person who knew the real him. Now that they were in trouble, he had nowhere to turn. He thought about ringing David, but he stopped himself; it was fine in the moment that night, but he couldn't just open up to him like that over the phone. He wished he had a woman friend, someone who knew both of them and who might know what he should do, but there was no one.

They were normal on the face of it. He didn't think the kids suspected anything was wrong, and they were so busy with school and sports and having their grandparents in the house, they didn't have time to notice.

Most of the time he was out of the house. When he was home, Danika was always trying to make him food. He knew they felt awkward speaking Ukrainian around him, but it was either that or silence. It was easier on them if he was out. The boys were mad to come up to the site, but there was so much dangerous equipment there that Ana said she would be worried. He promised them he'd take them up soon when the work was further along. He still took them hurling and to football training, and he did as much of the dropping and collecting as he could.

He had a lot of media engagements, as well as meetings with operators, tour companies and corporate agents who were interested in using the resort, so he was kept very busy. He and Corlene spoke on the phone most days, but she was back in Dublin thankfully, so at least her presence wasn't antagonising Ana.

He considered going on another tour; he was always in demand. A lot of the interviews he could either do from the road or arrange them to fit in with his schedule, and Daniel had the whole renovation thing under control. He'd get out from under Ana's feet. Maybe if he was away, she might miss him enough to come back to him. She might even come to one of the hotels like she used to. Danika and Artur could mind the boys.

He returned from his walk and entered his new office on the ground floor. It was a gorgeous room, with three bay windows overlooking the lawns out front. His desk, chair and filing cabinet were all antique, sourced by Daniel, who insisted that all fittings in the public areas be contemporaneous with the era of the house.

He was just about to respond to the many emails in his inbox when there was a knock on the door. He looked up. 'Come in.'

Ana entered, a picnic basket over her shoulder. 'I thought we could have some lunch together? I made your favourite sandwiches, and Mama sent some cake.' She smiled shyly.

Conor came out from behind his desk and crossed the room. 'I'd love to.' His voice was hoarse with emotion.

They stood there, space between them for a second or two, then she moved forward, and as she did, he put his arms around her. They said nothing but stood, clinging to each other, and Conor felt he could breathe for the first time in weeks. It was going to be OK.

They had lunch on a rug she'd brought, with builders milling around them. One or two of them smirked to see the boss all loved up with his missus, but Conor didn't even notice. He was just so glad Ana seemed happier and things were going back to normal. They chatted about her parents, and about how, however much she loved them, it was still hard to get used to living with them again. Then they talked about Joe. Ana was really worried, much more than Conor had realised. He still thought she was overreacting, but he decided not to voice that opinion. Instead, he suggested they set up a meeting with his teacher.

After lunch, they went for a walk and he showed her all the progress. He reached for her hand and was relieved when she squeezed his as they strolled along.

They stopped to admire a luxurious creeping plant that was winding its way up one of the gable walls of the castle. It had elegant pointed leaves, and the flowers hung, lilac and so fragrant. He picked one of the hanging flowers and smelled it.

'Beautiful, yes?'

They turned to find a man of about thirty standing behind them. He had jet-black hair, dark eyes and skin the colour of caramel. He was lithe and wiry, and Conor thought he looked like one of the Romany people. His shorts and T-shirt were filthy; he was obviously one of the gardeners.

'It is. What's it called?' Conor asked.

The man smiled. 'Wisteria.' His accent was foreign as Conor expected, Eastern European possibly.

'It's so lush. I don't remember seeing it here before, but I imagine it must have been?'

'Yes, it was. Like so much of the garden, it was covered with weeds and briars. A little cutting back and it is like revealing a masterpiece. The original gardener was an artist. Not just the array of plants, but the way they are set, like a painting.' The man sat on an old stone bench and took a flask out of a bag he was carrying. 'You want a coffee?' he asked.

'No, thanks, we've just had some. I'm Conor O'Shea and this is my wife, Anastasia.'

'Conor the boss? I'm Nico Sokolov. Corlene hired me. I'm the head gardener. I came three weeks ago to start everything off, but you were away. Then I had to go to Durban to finish a job there. Now I'm back full time. Nice to meet you at last.' He held out his hand and Conor shook it.

Corlene had mentioned she'd hired some garden expert, so this must be him. Conor didn't know what he expected a world-renowned horticultural restorer to look like, but this guy was not it.

Nico went on, turning his attention to Ana. 'Anastasia? Not an Irish name?' He smiled.

'No.' Ana smiled back. 'I'm from Ukraine, Kiev, but I live here now ten years.'

'*Prijemno poznajomytusia.*' Nico leaned over and shook her hand.

Ana was taken aback; she'd obviously not expected him to speak her language. He looked more Mediterranean than someone from her part of the world.

'*Vy rozmovliajete Ukrajinskoju?*' She smiled again.

'A little. I used to have more, but I lost it. I learned it from my grandmother – she was from Odessa.' He grinned. 'So now I know the boss and his wife.'

He drank his coffee and then offered first Ana and then Conor a cigarette.

'No, thanks, not one of my vices.' Conor shook his head.

'I'm always trying to quit, especially here. Back in Russia, everyone smokes, so it's not a problem. But here, not so much.' He lit the cigarette and exhaled the pungent smoke.

'How long have you been here?' Conor asked. 'Your English is perfect.'

'Just a few weeks, but I travel a lot. When gardens all over the world get into this kind of state, they call me and I revive them. I'm a sort of plant paramedic.' He chuckled, a low growly sound.

'So you haven't moved here then?' Conor was fascinated. Usually the immigrants he met were moving to Ireland in search of a better life.

'No, but I will be here for perhaps one year, as this is a big job, so much to do. I have come from the United States, where I was working in Greenwood Gardens in Essex County, New Jersey. Before that I was in Durban, the job I told you about – the owner knows Corlene and she hired me. Before that I was in Wrest Park in England, Bedfordshire. So you see, I move around a lot. I speak English now more than Russian. I don't get to speak my language so much any more.'

'Do you miss home?' Ana asked.

'No. Nothing to miss. My parents are dead. I was an only child and grew up in an ugly apartment in Moscow. I won't ever go back, not if I can help it.' He stubbed out his cigarette and rose from the seat. Conor sensed he didn't want to talk any further about Russia.

'You're doing an incredible job, but there is so much of it,' Ana said.

'How many gardeners are here?' She looked around in awe at the scale of the task ahead.

Conor imagined it must have taken a lot of grafting to even clear the briars, let alone start gardening; yet in a few weeks, ponds with trickling fountains were in operation and beds of brightly coloured plants lined the pathways, which were now all power-washed and clean.

'Well, I am in charge, and there are about ten others. We also employed some kids from the local town for the cutting at the beginning. That's one of the nice things about gardens – though it takes patience to let things grow, you can make huge advances in a short time when you cut back.'

'I can see that,' Conor said. 'I haven't a clue. We didn't have a garden when I was a kid, and now I cut the grass and that, but Ana here does the planting.'

'Well, if you need any help, you know where I am.' He smiled at Ana.

'Actually,' Ana said, 'why we don't make a barbeque at the weekend? I can show to Nico my bad gardening, and my parents would much love talking to someone not me. The boys would love it, and they could have some friends over.'

'Sure.' Conor was delighted to see her enthusiastic about something.

'Are you free on Sunday?' Ana asked Nico.

'Of course, thank you,' he replied.

She sent him a dropped pin of their address to his phone, and Conor listened to them naturally slip into their own language again. He felt a pang; Nico seemed nice, but another Ukrainian speaker in his life wasn't what he needed.

As he and Ana strolled on, they chatted more easily than they had in weeks.

'I will make invite to Valentina. I think she might like Nico, and she has not ever even gone on a date since that awful husband was put into the jail. She need some fun.'

Conor was relieved to hear his wife's enthusiasm for inviting Nico was as a potential match for her friend. 'Good idea,' he said. Maybe things really were going to be OK after all.

As he walked Ana back to the car, he pivoted and led her into a copse of trees, away from all the hustle and bustle of the castle. They walked in the woods for a few minutes until all they could hear was the breeze rustling the leaves and an odd bird.

They stopped, and Ana stood with her back against a tree. The light dappled her face as the sun shone through the canopy of leaves.

'Thank you for lunch and for coming to see me.' Conor spoke quietly, his face close to hers.

She slipped her arms around his waist and drew him to her. 'We are OK.'

He couldn't tell if it was a statement or a question, but he was just glad to hear her say it. 'We are rock solid, you and me, Anastasia O'Shea. I'll never let anyone or anything come between us.'

He bent his head and kissed his wife properly for the first time in so long, and she responded eagerly. He felt her hands under his shirt on the skin of his back, and he held her tighter as on and on they kissed.

CHAPTER 12

'Thanks for coming, Mr and Mrs O'Shea,' Miss Carney said. 'Please take a seat, and I'll just go and get Joe's file. And can I say what an honour it is to meet you, Mr O'Shea. I've seen you on TV and of course the ad – it's gone viral, hasn't it? Nearly a million views the last time I checked. Imagine someone local breaking the internet! Everyone is so excited about the new hotel and everything...' The teacher was gushing, and Conor cringed.

Ana was stone-faced. Even though communication was better between them, things were still strained at home. Danika was driving Ana mad, changing things around and fussing over everyone. She was just trying to be useful, but it was grating on Ana. Artur was gone from dawn to dusk; Conor had never seen a man work so hard. He seemed determined to earn his place on the workforce, and while his English was virtually non-existent, he carried a dictionary in his pocket.

'Just Conor and Ana is grand. We don't really do the mister and missus thing,' he said.

The teacher, who Conor judged to be in her twenties, coloured with delight. 'Of course, Conor...and Ana. I'll be back in a moment.'

They sat in the bright, sunny classroom where their boys spent their school days. He squeezed her hand, and while she didn't pull away, she didn't react either. Conor hoped it was just because she was worried about Joe. Danika spoiled the boys, which was also irritating Ana. It was fine when they saw their grandparents on holidays, but Ana felt it was undermining her everyday routine when her mother gave in to their every demand. At night, she complained to him, but he wasn't sure what to say. After all, Danika was Ana's mother and her heart was in the right place, so he usually listened but remained non-committal.

He looked around at all the artwork and posters and toys; it was so different from the schoolrooms of Conor's childhood, so much more colourful and child-friendly.

Miss Carney came back in and sat beside them, opening a file with a variety of test scores and samples of Joe's work. She went through each item, explaining what it was. Conor could feel Ana bristling beside him. She was a teacher herself, and he knew she felt patronised as Miss Carney gave them a layman's guide to their son's progress. The fact that she addressed everything to Conor wasn't helping.

'So I know you are a little concerned about Joe?' She looked so young she could have been a schoolgirl herself, but despite her ditziness today, she was a brilliant teacher and the lads loved her.

'Yes. We don't...what is word...side in side' – Ana's brow furrowed as she tried to think of the term – 'compare them. They are totally different boys, but Joe seem to have much more troubles with his schoolwork than Artie, and we think maybe there is problem, perhaps dyscalcul...?' Ana stumbled on the unfamiliar English word.

Miss Carney looked up at both of them and smiled. Conor knew she didn't mean to be condescending, but he realised that was how Ana saw it.

'Joe is a wonderful boy. He's very athletic and socially he mixes very well. Undoubtedly, his scores in maths and reading are below his brother's, but then Artie does exceptionally well. I would say Joe is a little below average, but not worryingly so. See here.' She showed them a graph of attainment scores for the twins' age in numeracy and literacy and plotted where Joe was in relation to the norm, and as she said, he was slightly below the middle.

'So as you can see, Joe is in the forty-fifth percentile. That means that –'

'I know what it means.' Ana took the graph from the teacher and studied it.

'So we shouldn't be worried?' Conor asked, trying to compensate for Ana's snappiness. 'Or what should we do to help him?'

The teacher turned to Conor. 'Well, not worried, but I suppose if he got a bit of extra help at home? I know it's so difficult when someone else in the family does it all effortlessly, but even if you could spend half an hour a day, he would come on, I think. If you like, I can speak to the principal and we can arrange to give him some one-to-one lessons here with the resource teacher. We don't have the funding to give him more learning support than that since he doesn't present with a specific educational need, but he definitely could benefit from more individual attention.'

'Well, I doing his homework with him every day, and Conor, he help him too, so I do not think that is all he need,' said Ana. She was getting upset. She obviously saw the teacher's comments as offensive, which wasn't like her at all.

'I don't think Miss Carney is suggesting we –' Conor began.

'I know what she is saying, Conor. I understand enough. We don't spend enough time teaching Joe, and now he is below the others and we must do more,' Ana snapped. 'In Ukraine, I was a teacher, and I think Joe has this thing...this...' She was getting frustrated and English words escaped her.

'Dyscalculia,' Conor prompted. 'I know you do, but I just think he's like me – he will learn when he sees a practical application for it. He picks up plenty when he's interested. Miss Carney's right. We'll just do a bit more with him at home and –'

'And you know this because of your life as a bus driver? I am a teacher, Conor, and I am Joe's mother. Why won't either of you listen to me?'

Before Conor even had time to get up, she was gone.

'I'm sorry about that,' he began. 'My wife is under a lot of pressure at the moment. Her parents are staying with us and I've been very busy, so she's had a lot on her plate. She didn't mean to...'

'It's fine. I didn't want to suggest you weren't doing a great job. They are wonderful little lads, but some kids just need a bit extra, that's all. Look, why don't you give me a call next week and we can talk some more – maybe after school or some evening we could meet?'

Conor wasn't stupid. He knew a come-on when he heard it. He ignored the suggestion. 'My wife and I will talk, and we'll let you know what we're going to do. Thanks for all you do for our boys, though. We really appreciate it.'

Conor walked outside to find Ana standing beside the car. He opened it from the other side of the car park using the remote, and she got in. When he got into the car himself, he didn't turn the key; instead, they just sat there, trying to formulate the right words. Ana stared intently out the passenger window, facing away from him. Eventually, she spoke. 'Can we go? I need to get back to collect the boys from Ian's house.' She was close to tears; he could hear it in her voice.

Conor said nothing but took out his phone and scrolled for Ian's mother's number. 'Hi, Deb, Conor here. Could you hold on to our lads for another bit? Myself and Ana have just got a bit delayed and won't be back until around seven.'

'Sure, Conor, no bother. I was going to give them their tea anyway. Swing by and collect them whenever. They're out kicking a ball all evening anyway. I've hardly seen them.'

'Thanks, Deb. We'll see you soon.'

He hung up and turned to face Ana, who was still staring out the window. 'Will we go for a walk, or a drink, or will we just sit here?' he asked gently.

'I need to get back, Conor. My parents –'

'Will be fine. They know where we are. Danika will ring if there's a problem, and we need to talk.'

She sighed a ragged breath and he waited. If she refused, he was going to insist. This couldn't go on.

'OK. Let's go for a walk then,' she said eventually.

He drove out of the schoolyard and headed towards Castle Dysert. He knew for sure they wouldn't run into anyone there. The days were getting longer now, dusk not falling until after nine at night. The workers were gone for the evening, and the makeshift car park was empty except for one van and a lot of earth-moving equipment.

He led her down the path they had taken the other day that circled the pond, now complete with big lily pads and a huge stone dragon on a plinth in the middle pouring water from its ferocious jaws.

'It is beautiful. So much different,' she said, but her voice sounded leaden.

'It is, isn't it? Hard to believe it was all here, hidden by years of nature uninterrupted by humans.'

They walked along the path all around the circumference of the pond until they came to the stone bench. He sat down and patted the seat beside him. She joined him, and instinctively he put his arm around her shoulders, drawing her close.

'I'm sorry I didn't take your side back there. I should have. If you think Joe needs an assessment from a psychologist or whatever, then that's what we'll do. You're right – how would I know? You're the expert.' He said the words quietly.

'She was flirting with you.' The words fell from her lips.

Conor had brushed off her worries before and it got him nowhere, so this time he took a different approach. 'Yeah, I know she was. It's that stupid Facebook thing. This never used to happen, so it's not me. After you left, she asked to meet me some evening and I told her that you and I would decide what we wanted to do about Joe and let her know. Like I said, nothing, nobody – I don't care who they are – will come between us.'

She didn't reply, but she didn't move either. Even though things were better, they had never again discussed the night she saw him with Corlene.

'That night you saw me hugging Corlene, it was just a friendly hug,

I swear to you. Dylan's father is sniffing around. He saw Corlene in some magazine or something and is apparently trying to make contact. She told Dylan she never knew who his dad was, and now she's afraid that this guy, who is a total loser apparently, is just going to show up and take Dylan from her. She got upset and I followed her out. She was crying, so I gave her a hug. That was all there was to it, I swear to you. I have never looked at anyone else, nor would I.'

'I know. Sorry. I should not have gone so crazy.'

Conor's heart sank. It wasn't just Corlene, as he had suspected; there was something else wrong. 'So what's the matter, pet? You seem so sad and exhausted these days. Is it your parents – is it too much?'

She turned and faced him, crossing her legs. 'I don't know, maybe. I just feel like…I don't know…like nothing I do matters. Every day, the same thing – cooking, cleaning, taking care of the boys, and now my parents. I just feel like that is all that I am, nothing interesting, just a mother. And now I'm not even good at that. That child teacher telling me that my boy needs more attention – it was just too much. I feel like I'm a terrible mother and a difficult wife. I know everything you do for us, and for my parents as well, and I should be grateful, but I just feel –'

'Ana, what are you on about? Grateful? Why the hell should you be grateful? Look, I know – well, I don't because I never did it, but I can imagine – that it is so boring and repetitive being at home all day. I get it. Like back there, that kid of a teacher telling you stuff about your own son, stuff you were doing while she was in her pram, it must be so hard.'

'Exactly. I feel like I am lost, just Joe and Artie's mother, your wife, my parents' daughter. I love you all, but there is no me any more.' A big fat tear ran down her beautiful face.

Conor wanted to scoop her up in his arms and soothe her pain away, but that wasn't what she needed. 'What can we do? How about you get a job again? We'll get someone in to take care of things at home.'

'No. I can't do anything here with my education because my English don't work enough, good enough, and I don't want to work in hotel or shop or something. Anyway, *Tato* and Mama need me, and the boys too, but I just wish…'

'What do you wish, Anastasia?' He rarely called her by her full name, and when she heard it, she gave him a weak smile.

'I wish… I don't know. I can't wish to be young and with no cares again because then I won't have you and my children, but I wish I could feel like me again. I know I am being pain. I'm sorry. I just can't… I know it's stupid. Valentina say to me, look, you have everything, house, kids, husband, and now your parents safe and well, and still you not happy. I don't know what is wrong with me, but I am so sad all the time. And then imagining you and Corlene. She is so beautiful with all make-up and lovely clothes, and I look so crap.'

Conor dismissed every thought that came into his head as a stupid thing to say. Eventually, he spoke. 'I love you more than anyone on this earth, and your happiness is so important to me. You're stunningly beautiful, by the way, and Corlene is, by now, at least seventy percent silicone. Every bit of her has been nipped and tucked and puffed up and sucked in – the hair, the teeth, the whole lot is fake. So if you ever compare your natural gorgeousness to her again, I'll have to get your eyes tested.'

He grinned. 'Look, Ana, don't mind her or that Miss Carney. They are nothing to do with us. I want to make you happy again. I want to see that beautiful smile every morning when I wake up beside you. And whatever that takes, we'll do it. OK?'

'Maybe I just need to stop being stupid and smile…' She smiled sadly.

'No, you're not stupid, but maybe you need to see the doctor or a therapist of something. I'll come with you if you like?'

'Maybe. We'll see.' She smiled again but it never reached her eyes.

He took her hand and they walked all over the estate, and as they walked, they chatted quietly about her parents, about Joe and the school and even about their lack of intimacy. After an hour, Conor felt lighter than he had in weeks. Eventually, as the sun was sinking over the Atlantic, they were back outside the castle.

'I have a key. Do you want to see inside?' he asked.

'OK, but is it safe?' Ana held his hand a little tighter.

'Yeah, it's in remarkably good shape considering. Daniel is driving everyone daft restoring things – he won't let the builders demolish anything. Come on, let's see the progress. I know you've not been upstairs before, but the state of the place before the work started… Well, it was seriously creepy. Now it's all bright and open and a hive of activity.'

They walked up the steps, and Conor opened the door with the key. An almost invisible lock had been inserted into the original door for security, but Daniel was determined to keep the original door furniture exactly as it was. They still had the huge brass front door key, but that lock was no longer used. The knocker and letterbox shone in the late-evening sun, having been polished constantly for weeks to remove the tarnish of years of neglect. The door swung open easily.

'They had to take this door off and plane it down. The first time I had to run at it and shoulder it open.'

The hallway was transformed. The original tiles shone black and white in a geometric pattern, and the banister was rich and burnished. A very ornate chandelier hung thirty feet from a chain that stretched up to the ceiling above the balcony. He showed her his office, the ballroom and the kitchens, now all stainless steel and twelve-ring stoves.

'Will we go up? Daniel is working on this floor by floor, so they haven't started working on the top floors yet. They need the ground floor perfect for the TV crew who are arriving next week, so they've just been focusing on that. The second floor has been cleared of furniture and they're starting on it next week. The third floor and the attic have had nothing done. Daniel said he tried to get into the attic but none of the keys fit. The door is from the 1800s, so he's getting a locksmith down to try to open it rather than break it. The builder and himself nearly came to blows over it, like they do around fifty times a day. I just stay out of it unless it's looking like a blood injury.' Conor chuckled as he led her up the stairs.

The landing was full of boxes of tiles and tubs of paint and all manner of decorating paraphernalia. The entire house smelled of paint and drying plaster. The windows had been cleaned by an expert company that specialised in maintaining old water-balanced glass, and they could see the ripples. Daniel had explained to Conor at excruciating length that Samuel King must have sourced the Georgian glass in the fifties and replaced the panes cracked in the fire with original glass rather than replicas. The attention to detail Daniel showed was truly astounding. Virtually everything was original to the period if not to the house. Anything remotely salvageable was sent out for restoration and would be shipped back in time for the opening, he assured them.

They wandered up to the third floor, which was entirely empty. Decorating had not even started on that level yet. The views out to the sea were spectacular, and Conor explained to Ana that this was where the suites would be, the really high-end accommodations. At the end of the main bedroom corridor, there were three small steps with a smaller door at the top.

'That's the attic, the door the builder wanted to hack down. Daniel practically had to chain himself to it to stop him. Apparently, it was where Samuel King spent most of his time when he lived here.'

Conor approached the small door that was barely big enough for an adult to go through. It was in the shape of a gothic arch and seemed to be made of oak; it had darkened to almost black with age.

'But didn't they try all of those keys already?' Ana asked as Conor pulled the master keys from his pocket and inserted the smallest key he could find into the lock. It wouldn't fit.

'Yeah, but I thought I'd give it a go.' He shrugged. 'Now that we're this far, I want to see it for myself.'

'It's a huge lock for fitting the small key. Maybe try the big one for the main door? Not the one we just use, but the one from long ago? Maybe he don't copy that one because they don't use it any more now they have the new lock.' Ana was kneeling on the top step, trying to peer through the keyhole.

'It's worth a shot, I suppose. I think that's in my office. I kept it to put in a case over the door, another of Daniel's ideas. In fact, he was going to have all the room keys attached to a replica of that huge thing, a kind of novelty. Will I go down for it?'

'Let's try anyway. Maybe it will work.'

Conor was happy to see a spark of enthusiasm in her eyes, and he bounded down the stairs. He had not heard the toy train sound again since that first day and had managed to convince himself it was nothing.

He found the key easily in a desk drawer and came back up. He handed it to her, and she inserted the five-inch-long key into the lock and turned it. It clicked easily, and they looked at each other with excitement and alarm.

'I don't believe it. I'd never have thought of it in a million years.'

'Will we go in?' Ana asked.

'Well, nobody has for God knows how many years, so I've no idea what's in there, but I'm game if you are.'

CHAPTER 13

Ana stood back to let Conor go first, suddenly frightened of what they might find. He had to duck his head to get through the door frame, which was much shorter than he was, and he led Ana behind him by the hand.

They stood and gazed around at the most beautiful room. It was an Edwardian playroom, with two large windows as well as a huge skylight. Even though the glass needed to be cleaned, what remained of the evening sunlight shone through. On the floor were two doll-houses, an ornately painted large rocking horse with what looked like real hair in its mane and tail, and a large wooden box full of jungle animals. Other chests with what seemed like dressing-up clothes, model cars and vehicles of all kinds were on the other side of the room, and against one wall was a huge bookcase filled with children's books. Jigsaw puzzles were stacked neatly on another set of shelves, along with toy soldiers and dolls. A large couch in the corner was home to several teddy bears of all shapes and sizes, and there was a child-sized table with four painted chairs, complete with pencils, paper and paint. A large porcelain sink stood in the corner, on the draining board of which sat a glass jar containing paintbrushes. There was even a toy motorcycle, leaning sideways on its stand, that a child of four or five could ride.

The really weird thing was that there were no cobwebs. Conor remembered the kitchen that first day, festooned with them, and the rest of the house too, but in here, nothing. No cobwebs, no dust – it didn't even smell musty. And the room was freezing cold, much colder than the landing outside.

As they stood there taking it all in, they noticed a track running around the entire floor of the large room. It weaved under the table, around the leg of a chair, beneath the couch and along the skirting board. On it was a beautifully painted little toy train. Conor felt his heart speed up. He had dismissed the sound he heard that first day, but now that wasn't so easy. Martin's words echoed in his ears – Grenville King had gone to play with his new train set the night of the fire.

'It's so…I don't know… It is lovely but also so sad. I don't think any child played here. Maybe we should bring Joe and Artie. They'd be so amazed at all these old toys.' Ana picked up a doll. Her clothes and hair were perfect, as were all the teddies, and nobody had ever drawn a picture with the coloured pencils.

'I don't think so, as it's probably dangerous. And it's a bit creepy, don't you think? It would give them nightmares. This must have been what Samuel was doing all those years up here.' Conor had told Ana about the history of the house and the suicides of Samuel and his daughter.

He pointed to the only adult-sized piece of furniture in the room, an old green armchair. Unlike the rest of the things in the room, it was battered and well worn; springs poked through the fabric, and the arms were shiny from use.

'Did he kill himself up here, do you think?' Ana swallowed and shuddered.

'I don't know. He was found below on the patio. Let's get out of here – it's giving me the creeps. Though once Daniel gets his beady eyes on this lot, he'll be beside himself with excitement.'

'You're right about not bringing our boys here. This is a place not for a living child. Can you feel something here, Conor?' Ana asked. 'Something… I don't know how to say it. Something kind of…'

'I don't know. It's so strange being in here after all these years, and the circumstances were so sad. I just think it's a lonely place and maybe it's best dismantled. God knows it didn't bring the man who put it together any joy or peace.' He considered telling her about the train sound but dismissed the idea.

'Yes, you're probably right. Let's go. I want to see the boys.'

Conor smiled and nodded; he knew exactly what she meant.

'This place is too much sad. They are so alive and full of energy, not like this dead place.'

Ana went to the door and down the three small steps, anxious to get away from the creepy playroom. Conor followed her, just as glad to get out of the eerie room. He closed the door behind him, then followed Ana down the main staircase.

As they pulled the huge front door shut, they started with fright when they heard footsteps on the gravel behind them. Conor whipped around to see Nico standing there.

'Ah, it is you, Conor. I was worried we had a burglar. I was in the rose garden and saw a figure pass the window on the stairs. Though now that I am here, I am armed only with this trowel, so I don't think I could have done much.' He grinned cheerfully.

'I'd say that Russian accent would scare them off. Sure weren't all the baddies Russians in the films? Well, they were when I was a kid anyway. It's probably someone else now.'

'*Priyatno poznakomit'sya*.' Ana smiled and shook his hand. 'Don't worry, Conor, we'll speak in English. It is bad enough to have your house filled with Ukrainians.'

'Oh, the more the merrier. Are you only knocking off now, Nico?' Conor checked his watch. 'It's ten to eight.'

Nico laughed. 'You Irish with your going home in the middle of the day. I can't believe it when I got here, five in the afternoon, everyone gone. Hours of daylight left, but no, everyone gone.'

Ana laughed as well. 'Yes, they don't have the communist working way. Too much time for going in the pub.'

'Oi! When was the last time I went to the pub? I don't know about all this, you lot ganging up on the poor old paddies.' Conor pretended to be hurt.

'We are just jealous, Conor, of the Irish cheerful disposition. Stalin made sure there was plenty of misery left in his wake to keep us in desolation for generations to come. So yes, I am just finished, and now I will go to my hotel and have a shower and eat some dinner and go to sleep. This is my life.' Nico shrugged.

'Well, it doesn't have to be all work and no play,' Conor said. 'We're seeing you on Sunday, right? It looks like this nice weather will be around for another few days. I'm in charge of the barbeque, so drink a lot of beer – it helps with the taste,' he joked.

'My parents are looking forward to meeting you to talk to someone other than me. My friend Valentina is coming too – she's from Siberia.' Ana seemed happier, and Conor began to feel a ray of hope. Maybe things were going to be OK after all.

'I'm really looking forward to it. See you then.' Nico waved and walked towards his car.

Ana slipped her arm around Conor's waist, and he put his arm around her shoulders as they went to collect their boys.

* * *

THE BARBEQUE WAS A GREAT SUCCESS. Valentina was delighted to meet Nico and gave Ana a thumbs-up behind his back as he was deep in chat with Danika. Artur seemed less enthusiastic, but then Nico was Russian and Artur a patriotic Ukrainian, so Conor put his reticence down to that.

Also, Artur was in no rush to speak Russian. He loved practising his English and was improving daily. He asked lots of questions and wrote down words he learned in a little notebook he carried with him everywhere.

Artur helped Conor with the steaks, burgers and sausages, and Danika had made lots of salads and bread. As the two men manned the grill, Artur spoke. 'Tomorrow, Danika and me, go Galway. In bus. Is OK?'

Conor was surprised. Artur worked every day, many more hours than he was contracted to do, and he'd never expressed any interest in a day off.

'Of course it's OK, but do you want something there? I could drive you if you like?' Conor spoke slowly.

'No. Thank you. Danika and Anastasia, two women, one kitchen.' Artur made a gesture of banging one fist off the other and smiled.

Conor laughed. His father-in-law didn't say much, even in Ukrainian, but he noticed everything. He knew mother and daughter needed a break from each other.

'No problem. I'll drop you to the bus in the morning.'

'Yes. Good. Thank you.' Artur flipped a burger, nodding his satisfaction.

The boys had lots of friends over, so there was a huge football match on the lawn, dads against boys. Artie and Joe came and begged Conor to play, so Artur took over the barbeque. As Conor jogged to the lawn, he noticed Ana deep in chat with Nico. Valentina stood alone, looking a bit lost. Ana was laughing at something Nico said, something she rarely did these days. Conor was glad to see her happy but wished it wasn't a handsome young Russian who was the cause.

He dismissed the thought. He'd berated her for being jealous of Corlene, and here he was doing the exact same thing.

Artur called Valentina to help him, and she seemed grateful to go. Her awful ex-husband was serving a long sentence for human trafficking, and Conor remembered well the night it all came to a head. They were on a tour with him, and it all came out. He had to intervene and got himself a punch in the face for his trouble from the disgruntled husband who claimed that Valentina was his property. Ana had been invaluable that time. Valentina spoke very little English, and Ana could translate and also be a friend to her. Valentina spent some time in a women's refuge, where she soon realised that this was an international problem. Women and often girls were lured away from poor countries with promises that they would have a much better life by unscrupulous people. Once they arrived in Europe or the States, they were trafficked into prostitution. Valentina met so many like herself, and she resolved to stay and help. She and Ana worked really hard at fundraising as well as raising awareness of the plight of these women. Now that Artur and Danika were settled in, he hoped Ana could go back to giving more time. She loved the work there, but in recent months she had to cut back, what with him being away and the boys having so many things on all the time.

He returned his attention to the match, which the boys were winning twelve to nil. He tackled a small red-haired boy and shot at the goal, scoring. Cheers from the dads and theatrical groans from the boys were halted by Artur and Valentina calling everyone for food in strongly accented English.

Valentina tried to catch Nico's attention over the salad table. He was polite and friendly, but within moments he was once again at Ana's side.

Conor took his position beside his father-in-law, dishing out meat. The two men worked happily alongside each other. Once everyone was served, Conor got two cold beers and handed one to Artur, who accepted it gratefully.

'This Russian, he no good,' Artur remarked.

Conor was taken aback. Normally, Artur was very mild-mannered. 'Nico? Ah, he's OK. Ana thought he might like Valentina.' Conor spoke quietly.

'Not Valentina, no. Ana. Careful. Look.' Both men looked over to where Ana and Nico stood at the edge of the garden. Despite Artur's poor English, Conor knew exactly what his father-in-law meant. He saw the same scene he'd witnessed several times that afternoon – Ana and Nico chatting and laughing. Nico was leaning down to tell her something into her ear and had his hand on her shoulder. The body language suggested an intimacy that Conor didn't like. Maybe Artur's distaste for the man was not solely based on his dislike and distrust of all Russians.

CHAPTER 14

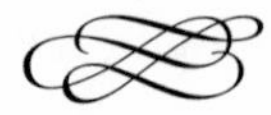

The weeks flew by as a flurry of work was done on Castle Dysert. Corlene set up more television and radio interviews for Conor, not just in Ireland but in the US as well. The boys were thrilled to go into school to talk about their dad on the telly, and all the drivers and guides Conor ran into from time to time gave him a terrible slagging over it, but he laughed it off. The Facebook campaign had resulted in almost full-capacity booking of the hotel once it opened, so both he and Corlene were delighted with how it was all going. They'd even managed to secure the wedding reception of a member of the Irish rugby team, and the publicity from that was very welcome.

Corlene was staying at the Old Ground until the opening, so Conor saw her almost every day up at the castle, albeit briefly. She was like a dynamo, constantly running and racing and getting so much done. Some of the workmen made the mistake of flirting with her and were given short shrift; Corlene, it seemed, had no time for men any more. They were the means to an end for so long, but now that she had that end herself – money – she had no further need of men. She wanted to up the ante on the Facebook ads, and she even suggested Conor wear an Aran sweater, but he absolutely drew the line at that.

'Ah, will you go on away with yourself, trying to turn me into some kind of a mad leprechaun. You know well how I feel about all that paddywhackery, and I'm not doing it.' He laughed at her suggestion, but he wasn't going there.

'OK, OK, no knitted sweaters. But I keep telling you, you're a hit! They just can't get enough of you. It's like those coffee commercials years ago, remember? There were several commercials, but they were all one story with this hunky guy and this girl?'

Conor had no idea what she was on about.

'Whatever, it doesn't matter. The point is they love this humble hunky Irishman talking about taking this beautiful old castle and grounds and restoring them lovingly in complete compliance with all the rules and laws and all of that. You know what to do, and you are doing it beautifully, so quit your whining.' She patted him on the cheek. 'You love it really.'

Conor chuckled good-naturedly. 'I'm not whining, but I'm just telling you I'm not going to turn myself or this place into some kind of plastic paddyland. We have a wonderful product here, amazing history, the works, so we don't need to go down the green shamrocks and leprechauns route.'

'OK, OK. But we will do another Facebook ad campaign, right? I suppose you won't do it with your shirt off?' she asked, her eyes wide and innocent.

'You suppose correctly,' Conor said dryly.

'The place is looking fabulous, though, isn't it? I can't wait for Dylan to see it. There's a TV crew coming tomorrow – you know that, right? So if you can take them around and do a little interview afterwards, please?' Corlene made a pleading silly face. 'The woman who's coming, I told her how hot you are, so she's dying to meet you.' She winked. 'Also, Conor, I was thinking, and don't blow this out of the water before you at least consider it, but I really think we can go with the whole haunted thing. It would be such a great selling point, you know, the tragic history, a little boy burned to death, the train sounds. We could –'

Conor raised his hand to stop her talking. 'Absolutely not. I've told you before, and I'm not changing my mind on this no matter what you say. Firstly, because it's just not true. That sound we heard could have been anything, and there have been hundreds of people in and around the castle since and not a whisper. And secondly, it's a really tragic story and we don't want the hotel associated with something like that. Ana and I would not take our lads to a hotel where a child died. It's a horrible idea. Finally, we have the goodwill of the people in the area. I know for you this is all ancient history, but here in Ireland, feelings about that time still run very deep. I don't know who burned the castle, but someone round here does, and it was somebody local. A person living today, maybe even working here, his or her grandfather or great-grandfather could have done it. So you need to trust me on this – these things are best left in the past.'

'But –' she began.

'No buts, Corlene. I go along with lots of your madcap ideas, but I'm adamant on this. You got me on board because I know this country, so just accept that I know best on this one thing, OK? I don't want you discussing it with anyone either. Can we agree on that?'

'Fine.' She clearly wasn't happy. She was used to getting her own way, but she knew Conor well enough to know when no meant no.

They hadn't again discussed the night she cried – something told him she would hate for him to bring it up – but he'd heard from Laoise that some guy had sent Dylan an email, claiming to be his father. Dylan wasn't going to just leave it, and the whole thing was going to blow up in Corlene's face if she didn't at least have a conversation with Dylan about it. But the subject was a no-go area.

Conor considered warning her that Costello had made contact, but he decided to stay out of it. It was between Corlene and Dylan, and he had enough problems of his own without inviting Corlene's thorny past into his life as well.

Anyway, as far as anything other than work was concerned, he was giving her as wide a berth as was possible in the circumstances.

Things were better with him and Ana and she seemed a bit brighter these days, but it wasn't the way things were. Things were almost back to normal in the bedroom as well, but he always had to instigate it, whereas before she seemed as interested in sex as he was. She was often asleep before he went to bed, and as for having privacy anywhere else, well, the house was like a train station these days.

The boys were on holidays from school and had friends over all the time in the afternoons, so there seemed to be an endless stream of boys in soccer shirts needing to be fed. Danika and Artur were there too, and when Artur wasn't working, he was to be found in the guest bedroom learning English on the internet. Ana offered to teach him, but he insisted she had enough to do with the lads, so he was doing it mostly on his own but with some assistance from Joe of all people. Joe was a dinger on the computer, so he helped his *didus* download the course he bought and set up his microphones and everything. Conor could have done it in half the time, but he let Joe at it; it was good for him to feel smart at something. Artur was taking his new role very seriously and had noted down the serial numbers of the various machines used at Castle Dysert, from lawnmowers to coffee machines, and was, with Joe's help, sourcing Ukrainian versions of manuals. Where it was impossible, Joe and Artur were reading the English versions slowly and translating. Conor watched them from the garden as he was cutting the grass, their two heads bent over the computer in total concentration. It was great to see. Conor could see himself in Joe so much, especially as a kid.

He'd spent all his time in Joe Kelly's garage, messing around with cars and eventually serving as a mechanic. The schoolbooks never attracted him much, but he loved getting things to work that were broken. Artie was an academic like his mother, so bright and sensitive, whereas Joe was a bit more rough and tumble.

* * *

THE FOLLOWING day dawned bright and clear, and Conor was up at the castle by seven a.m. The TV crew would arrive by eight and everything had to be ready. Nico had made sure the gardens looked spectacular, and the whole ground floor was looking beautiful. Daniel had sourced a huge oak desk that would be used as the reception, and the floor had been sandblasted to remove years of dirt and then waxed to seal the porous tiles. The banisters were polished till they shone, and a huge gilt mirror hung over the ornate fireplace, giving the impression that the already huge area was even bigger. On either side of the fireplace were a pair of Edwardian wingback chairs, upholstered in gold brocade.

Conor did a few last-minute checks with Daniel and Artur, whose main job today was to ensure that the workmen, who were working on the top floor now, stayed out of sight. There was a back staircase down to the kitchens in the basement, so it was easy to keep them away from the front hall.

Conor was about to enter his office when Daniel crossed the reception.

'Conor, have you a minute?'

'Sure, come on in.'

Daniel sat down on the seat opposite Conor's desk. 'I was thinking about the playroom. I know you want it dismantled, but I really think we could make an amazing feature of it. The stuff in there is so unusual – much of it was antique even when it was bought in the fifties. I've been doing some research. Samuel went to such lengths to source the toys, so maybe we could make a modern playroom on the third floor, PlayStation, Lego, all of that, but I really want to keep the attic one as it is.'

Conor looked at the eager young architect in front of him. He was a bit pushy, no doubt about it, and when he got going about original cornicing or window reveals, he could talk for Ireland, but it was just that he was so enthusiastic about the project. Conor bowed to his superior knowledge on most things, but he had a gut feeling about that playroom. He wanted it gone.

'I know how you feel, Daniel, but I think we should dismantle it. It's just too…I don't know…macabre or something. Samuel probably threw himself out of the window up there, and his daughter most likely did the same. That little boy burned to death in there as well. So no. Box it all up and sell it. God knows we've bought enough antiques, so it would be good to recoup some of that money.'

Daniel looked like he was going to argue, but Conor just stopped talking and looked directly at him.

'OK, you're the boss, but I think it's a mistake. Oh, another thing – the plumbers have been over and over the whole system, but they're having serious trouble with the heating on the third floor. I think we need to bring in some specialists because something's not working and the lads here are stumped.'

Conor remembered how cold the attic was the day he and Ana went up there; there was a discernible temperature difference. He wondered if the attic and whatever was going on up there was the reason, but he dismissed the thought immediately. There must be a technical explanation for it.

'Well, bring in whoever we need. There must be a reason and we need to find it, and time is not on our side. We can't have the most expensive rooms in the place freezing cold.'

'Right, will do. And you're sure about the playroom?' Daniel had one last go.

'Certain. Have it boxed up and taken away, today if possible.'

Before Daniel could object, Artur popped his head around the door. 'They here. Television.'

'Thanks, Artur. I'm on my way.'

The area outside the castle was a flurry of activity, with cameras and other equipment everywhere and electrical cables running in every direction.

A big scruffy man introduced himself. 'Nice to meet you, Conor. I'm Teddy O'Connell, the producer. So if you could just show our cameraman around, we'll get some shots of the grounds and the gardens and the view over the ocean, and then we'll go inside, where we'll do the interview. How does that sound?'

Conor knew it was a coup for Corlene to have secured an interview on the national broadcaster, and it was going to be shown on

PBS in the States as well, so he was determined to really sell the castle as a unique holiday location.

'Absolutely, no problem. We can start in the rose garden. It's been brought back from near dereliction by our garden restorer, Nico Sokolov, and it really is a wonder to behold now. The last family to own the house privately was the Kings, and Mrs Beatrice King was a brilliant gardener as well as a garden designer, so we're doing all we can to restore it to its former glory.'

Once he'd shown them all there was to see outdoors – and thankfully the weather behaved – he took them into the downstairs drawing room, which would be the main dining room once the hotel was up and running. Floor-to-ceiling French doors opened onto a verdant green lawn surrounded by box hedging and rose bushes, beyond which the ocean met the sky on the horizon. The room itself had painted panels on the walls depicting scenes from the outback of Australia and were of course a talking point as the crew gathered in the room. Conor explained the Australian connection, the opal fortune and how benevolent that generation of Kings was to the people of the local area, omitting any comment on the behaviour of their antecedents.

CHAPTER 15

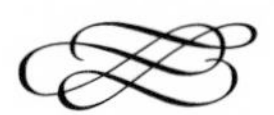

The crew had set up the interview area while Conor was in the garden. Sitting on one of the chairs having her make-up touched up was a woman he recognised.

Moira Delaney was a national treasure and everyone tuned into her show, not least because she was easy on the eye. Her quintessential Irish look went down very well in America too, with her flaming red hair, green eyes and curvaceous figure. She was a native Irish speaker, and there was something wholesome about her. She seemed to be able to extract the most incredible confidences from the guests she interviewed. She'd recently been all over the papers after a very public break-up with a notoriously philandering property developer. She had the sympathies of the nation, which she used to her advantage when getting to the juicy bits of a story. Conor knew he'd have to be careful; the temptation to get into the sordid past of the house was going to be too much for her, so he'd have to steer well clear of those kinds of questions.

As he walked in, accompanied by the producer, Moira stood up and approached him. She looked polished and impeccable.

'So we meet at last, the famous Conor O'Shea. I've heard a lot about you, and, well, that ad, what can I say…' She beamed.

The incongruity of one of Ireland's most well-known faces telling him he was famous was not lost on Conor. He smiled. 'Well, I'm certainly not famous, and you can only have heard about me from Corlene Holbrooke, so I'm worried.'

She laughed. 'She speaks very highly of you, don't worry. I met her at the races a few weeks ago. She told me I had to come down and meet you, so here I am. And what an amazing place. I've been down this way a few times, and to be honest, I never even knew this place was here.'

'Well, it was so overgrown that it's understandable. Yes, the work that's taken place over the last few months is nothing short of miraculous.'

'So, Conor, Moira, if you're ready, we'll get going?' Teddy had appeared at Conor's elbow. 'Conor, if you can just take a seat, we'll get some make-up on you.'

This part had been a revelation to Conor. He never knew that everyone on TV wore make-up, both the men and the women. He went home after the first interview and told Ana and the boys that he'd been wearing it, and they found it hilarious.

He tried not to wince as the make-up artist did her job. How women put themselves through this palaver every day was a mystery to him. He hated the feel of it on his skin and couldn't wait to wash it off.

Moira did her introduction to the camera as Conor watched; she was a natural. After a few preliminary questions, she said, 'So, Conor, can we talk about the Kings and the history of the house?' Her smile was radiant.

'Of course, Moira. Beatrice King really did an incredible job with the garden, while Samuel worked to rebuild the house after the fire. We've tried to restore the house to his standards in memory of this man who provided so much employment and was very good to the people of the area back in the 1950s when things were very bad economically in Ireland.'

The interview was going along fine, with lots of chat about the house and the magnificent gardens, and Conor was feeling confident; it seemed to be going OK.

'So, Conor, as a local man here in the West Clare area, you must have heard the stories that the house is haunted? Have you seen or heard anything unusual in the months while the work has been going on?' Moira's green eyes danced with merriment, and a mischievous smile played on her lips; she was delighted to have put him on the spot.

Corlene must have blabbed about the noises they heard. He could murder her. He was uncomfortable, but he had to talk his way out of it. 'Well, Moira, you know what we Irish are like for stories – they're the lifeblood of the country – and an old rambling castle like this one, left idle for years, is bound to capture the imagination.' He chuckled and went on. 'This place certainly has a lot of charm and history and stories attached to it, and for guests, we can guarantee an experience like no other.'

'So is it haunted? I've heard about strange sounds?' She wasn't letting it go.

Conor thought of the feeling he got when he and Ana were in the playroom. If there was something, it seemed wrong to capitalise on it for commercial gain. He knew Corlene loved the idea of the place being haunted, thought it was a brilliant marketing ploy, but the image of a little boy burning to death in a fire affected Conor and he just couldn't do it.

'No, not to my knowledge. The truth of the story is that a little boy died in this house, Grenville King was his name, and he was only four years old when the house was deliberately set on fire in 1921. Whatever grievance there was between English landlords and the local people – and God knows there were plenty of reasons for the tenants to be angry – he was an innocent child and his death was a tragedy. People will always tell stories, but that's the reality of what happened. I, for one, think we should let the little lad and all the King family rest in peace. It's a new era. Very exciting things are going to happen here, and we can guarantee that people who come here will have the time of their lives. How could you not?' He smiled and gestured out the window to the majestic vista, his demeanour giving away nothing of the fury he was feeling.

Moira wound up the interview, and the crew started packing away the gear. Conor was going to have this out with Corlene the minute they were gone. He'd expressly told her his feelings on the matter, and she deliberately went behind his back. She was not getting away with this. He wasn't going to dance like a little puppet to her every mad notion. She was an astute businesswoman, and a successful one, no doubt about it, but he had his integrity and wasn't giving it up for Corlene or anyone else.

'So, Conor, where would a lady go to have lunch and maybe a glass of wine around here?' Moira placed her hand on his arm and smiled seductively.

'Well, unfortunately we're not up and running as a kitchen fully yet, but there's loads of nice places along the coast. The Wild Atlantic Tavern do lovely seafood. It's only about three miles north of here. My wife and I go there often.' His smile was broad, but the message was clear.

Moira nodded slowly, getting the hint. 'Fair enough. I'll check it out.' She offered her hand, which he took. 'The best of luck with it all. It is amazing.'

'Thanks.'

Conor walked her to her car and heaved a sigh of relief when the crew all retreated down the avenue.

Corlene was on the phone in his office when he came back in. She beckoned him in and indicated she'd only be a moment.

'What are you talking about? This is ridiculous! We need to have heating that works properly throughout the building. Now are you a plumbing company or a travelling circus? Just sort it, and I don't want to hear any more excuses. You're being paid to do a job!'

She listened intently.

'Look, I don't give a damn about flow and return or whatever it is you're blathering on about. Just make the damned heating work, OK? Let me know when it's done.' She hung up; phone manners clearly were too much to ask for at this late stage.

She turned to Conor. 'So how'd it go?' she asked. 'You look so hot today, by the way. I love that shirt. You should always wear blues and greens – brings out your eyes.'

Conor chose to ignore her remarks; it was easier. 'Corlene, you know perfectly well that I won't capitalise on the death of a child, no matter who he was or how long ago it happened. You told Moira Delaney about the train noise you think we heard after I specifically asked you not to. I dismissed it, but if you do that again, I'm going to have to seriously consider if we can work together. We have to be able to trust each other, Corlene, otherwise this is not going to work.' Conor knew the best way to deal with her was head-on.

At least she did look a little shamefaced as she said, 'OK, OK. Easy, tiger. That's fine. Whatever you think. I just thought it was a cute angle, but if you don't think so, well, you're better at stuff like that than me. I'm sorry, OK?'

'Fine. But we need to be clear.' Conor was not going to be fobbed off; she had to understand.

'I said OK. Look, is there something else bothering you? You've been in really bad form lately.'

'What? Nothing. I'm fine. I just don't want to be part of that paddywhackery nonsense of ghosts and leprechauns and all that. I hate it all, always have. We have a smashing country here, with traditions and history and music and food and so much great stuff, and making up plastic paddy crap covered in shamrocks and shillelaghs just does my head in.'

Corlene sat and observed him for a long minute. 'Conor, I've known you for eight years, and I think I know a bit about human nature. Something is not right with you. It hasn't been for weeks. You're doing a great job here, so this isn't a work concern – it's as a friend. You were there for me when I needed a friend, so if you need to talk, well…'

He considered her offer. It would be good to talk to someone, and especially a woman, who might give him some perspective on what was happening with him and Ana, but he decided against it. If Ana ever thought he discussed the private details of their marriage with anyone, she'd be so hurt, and if that person was Corlene, well, that would be too much altogether. Still, Corlene wasn't going to be fobbed off with nothing.

'Thanks, Corlene. I'm fine. I suppose it's just a bit of a strain having my parents-in-law in the house, everyone speaking Ukrainian, even the boys. They are great people and I really like them, but Ana has so much to do taking care of them and the twins…'

'That she has no time for you?' Corlene was sharp, you had to give her that. 'Foolish girl.'

'Well, that's not really it.' Conor bristled. He wasn't going to let Corlene say anything bad about Ana. 'I just wish we had a bit more time… But with the boys off school for the holidays…' He shrugged. 'Nothing major. We'll be fine.'

'Why don't you take some time off? Get away for a while? You've got a place in Spain, don't you?'

'Yeah, we do, but she can't really leave her folks at the moment. Maybe later in the summer, if I can be spared here. We'll see. As I said, it's not a big deal.'

'Nico the gardener and Ana seem to get along well,' Corlene said casually. A bit too casually.

Conor felt himself getting defensive. 'Well, they speak the same language, so yeah, it's nice for her – and for him, I assume – to chat in their mother tongue. We invited him over for a barbecue a few weeks back. It was good, and he's called a few times since.'

'Oh, OK. I just wondered. I saw them having coffee in town the other day, and he was telling some of the others about a place he went to out in the Burren for a walk with Ana last week…'

Conor felt himself get even more defensive. 'Just wondered what, Corlene?' His voice was cold. 'What did you just wonder? What are you trying to say?'

He didn't want to admit even to himself that there may be something in what Corlene was driving at. First Artur and now Corlene – did everyone think there was something going on between Ana and Nico? He didn't often let what people said get under his skin, but the idea that people were talking about Ana behind his back made him so angry.

'Nothing! Relax, I'm on your side. Look, it's nothing, I'm sure. I just... Well, I didn't know if you knew...'

'Side? There is no "my side". Ana and I are fine. And you didn't know if I knew what, Corlene?' His voice was raised now. 'Knew that my wife was having coffee with a friend, or that she went for a walk? For God's sake, Corlene, she's entitled to a life, you know. She can have friends who are men. I'm not that insecure.'

Corlene crossed to where he was standing. 'Look, Conor, I'm not trying to upset you.' She put her hand on his back.

'How dare you?' He was furious now. 'My wife is a wonderful person who is honest and loyal, and she would not do that to me any more than I would do it to her, no matter how much someone tried to convince me otherwise.' He wanted to hurt her, to lash out at her for questioning Ana's integrity. 'It's an alien concept to you, Corlene, but we actually love and respect each other. I can't believe that you'd say such crap about Ana, I really can't. You go through life wreaking havoc and expect everyone to just put up with you, but I'm not having this. No way. People are not toys for your distraction, Corlene. Dylan wasn't a doll you could pick up and put down when it suited you, but you treated him like one. And now here you are saying things about my wife, who has never been anything but welcoming to you despite the fact that you constantly flirt with me in front of her. Y'know, I'm starting to think this whole thing was not such a good idea after all.' He couldn't stay there a second longer, so he turned and left, slamming the door behind him.

He didn't care that everyone stared as he rammed his car into gear and sprayed the gravel as he drove off at speed away from Castle Dysert. The blood pounded in his veins as he drove the narrow coast road. The sun glistened on the azure Atlantic, and the emerald-green hills tumbled towards the rocky shore. Normally, the wild landscape of his home soothed his spirit, but not today. He was so angry. How dare Corlene suggest Ana was being unfaithful, because that's what she was saying. Ana would never do that to him, any more than he'd ever do it to her; it was just Corlene stirring things up. She loved creating mischief, and drama followed her around.

A nagging voice kept talking in the back of his head, though, no matter how hard he tried to ignore it. Nico was much younger, closer to Ana's age. He was a handsome man, he spoke her language, and Conor had seen them deep in animated chat several times when Nico was at their house. They discussed Russian literature, or music or poetry – things he had no idea whatsoever about. Danika loved Nico, and the boys were impressed with his soccer skills; everyone except Artur seemed smitten.

Conor had dismissed it on the day of the barbeque and put it to the back of his mind. Of course he didn't think that there was anything going on between them, but why then did Ana not say she had met him for coffee or gone for a walk with him? If what Corlene said was true, why all the secrecy?

Conor turned up the radio to full volume, trying to drown out his own thoughts.

CHAPTER 16

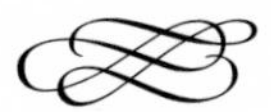

Conor and Corlene sat together at the top of the room where all the various tradesmen, engineers, gardeners and administrative staff were gathered to hear what they had to say. The two had not really spoken in person since the argument three weeks earlier, communicating instead through short, curt emails. The hotel was within a few weeks of opening and the work was on time and on budget, so everyone was happy. John Gerrity had submitted his final report, and everything looked good.

Conor stood up. 'Right, everyone, I want to thank each and every one of you. This was a gigantic project, one that some people said we were crazy to take on, but I had faith in the people here to make sure everything was done on time and to the correct standard.' Conor's voice carried over the full-to-capacity room.

He glanced in Nico's direction. He'd never said anything to Ana about what Corlene had alluded to. Ana did mention Nico's name a lot, but Conor thought maybe he was just overly sensitive. He tried to put it all out of his head, dismissing it as ridiculous gossip. He had been so busy, meeting tour operators and agents from overseas, getting the word out among his contacts and designing itineraries, as well as attending lots of press events, so he'd hardly had time to think.

Artur was standing at the back, smiling encouragingly. The decision to bring him to Ireland had turned out to be an inspired one since he could turn his hand to anything, knew where everything was and was unfailingly pleasant in the execution of every job. What had started out as almost an act of charity on Conor's part had turned into a truly terrific appointment.

Conor went on. 'I'm really happy to be able to tell you that the building has passed its final inspection and we are ready to roll. That couldn't have happened without the dedication and hard work for the last six months of everyone here. Now you have all received a bonus, as per the agreed terms of your individual contracts, for playing your part in getting Castle Dysert open, but as an extra thank you, we have arranged a wrap party – that's what they call it in the movie business, right?'

A chuckle rippled through the room.

'The Wild Atlantic Tavern is ours for the evening, the bar is free, the food is free, and we are going to be entertained by some very special musicians as well, so it should be a great night. Call your other halves, your kids too if you want to, but please remember to leave the car. We'll have a minibus service operating all evening to ferry you all home. Just leave the names of those you want to attend with security. We'll all knock off for the day now. I know there are still some loose ends to tie up, but we'll get to them in the coming days. For now, let's relax and congratulate ourselves on a great job.'

As the crowd filed out, delighted at the prospect of finishing work and heading to the pub.

Artur shuffled up beside him. 'Anastasia come here later with Joe and Artie?' he asked.

'I hope so, Artur. I'll call her and see if she would like to, but she may be busy.' Conor was so impressed at how Artur had mastered the rudiments of the English language in so short a time.

'It good she come. Big day for you. She come, stand beside you. You do this. Make many job, help many peoples.' Artur was so sincere. Conor felt a rush of affection for the man.

As the crowds of workers passed them by, Nico stopped and spoke in Russian to Artur. Did Conor imagine it or did Artur seem a bit off with him? He didn't give Nico the usual big beam for which Artur was famous.

'English, only now English. I must getting better. Ana coming to be with Conor today. Big day for him, important for family, for Joe, for Artie, yes?'

Nico hesitated for a moment before speaking. 'Of course. It's a great achievement. Congratulations, Conor.'

'We all did it, but thanks.' Conor wasn't rude exactly, but he couldn't help resenting the younger man, probably for no reason. For the first time since he'd met Ana, Conor felt their age difference.

As Nico walked off, Artur patted Conor on the back. 'Russians no good. Always take what not for them. You good man, good for Anastasia, good for family. Now I check...' He struggled to think of the word, then pulled a small notebook out of his overalls pocket and rifled through the well-thumbed pages. Conor noticed Joe's writing. 'Boiler!' Artur said triumphantly. 'Still heating not work in top floor. I don't know what is problem, but I get something from company many pages in Ukrainian, so I try fix now.'

'Artur? Can I see?' Conor gestured to the notebook, which the other man handed over happily.

'Joe write me English words are difficult. See – spanner, wrench, hammer. And there' – he pointed at the page again – 'Ukrainian. Better than dictionary. Only word I need and word I forget, not all.'

Conor could have hugged him. Joe's writing was neater than he'd ever seen it, and the spelling was almost perfect.

'I cannot do English without Joe. He so...' – Artur pointed to his temple with his index finger – 'and he do...' – Artur searched the pages again for the word – 'calibrations! Yes, he can. Very, very...' He gestured to his temple again.

It was too difficult to explain that Joe struggled at school, but it was just the best news that his little boy had found a way to express his talents. And that he and his grandfather had done this almost without them knowing was really wonderful. Conor felt a rush of guilt. He'd been so busy and, if he was honest, so upset about the way things were between him and Ana over the last few months, he'd not spent as much time at home as he would normally have done. When he drove tours, he was away a lot, but when he came home, he was all theirs. He realised the last time he'd had a kickaround with his sons was nearly two months ago.

Hopefully he could convince Ana to bring the lads out to the Wild Atlantic Tavern for the evening; it would save her cooking, and lots of the lads from the boys' class would be there since many of their parents were working on the project in some capacity, so they'd have kids to play with. He decided to ring her. Why did he feel nervous as he pressed 'call'? He used to talk to her several times a day, but now they just sent texts, usually to do with dropping or collecting the boys or some other domestic instructions.

'Hi, love,' he said immediately as she answered.

'Oh, hi, Conor. Everything OK?'

'Yeah, sure, fine. Listen, there's a bit of a celebration going on here...well, up the road in the bar. The final building checks are done, and the hotel is ready to go. We're laying on food and music and all of that. Dylan and Laoise are coming to play as well actually. Will you come with the lads?' He prayed he wouldn't have to try to convince her. The silence while he waited for her answer seemed like an hour.

'Ah, well, can Mama come? *Tato* is there already, so I don't want to leave her alone...'

Conor sighed with relief. 'Of course Danika can come. Why don't I pop in and collect you – that way you can have a drink. We might even leave the car and come back for it tomorrow. What do you think?'

He thought he heard enthusiasm in her voice. 'Great, that sound like fun. Give me a bit of time for getting showered and dressed, and Artie is covered in the flour – he and Mama are baking a cake...'

Conor chuckled. It was just like old times. 'No problem, darling. I'll be there in about an hour, OK?'

'OK, see you later.'

She was just about to hang up when he blurted, 'Ana, I love you so much. You know that, don't you?'

'I do. See you in an hour.'

THE BEER GARDEN was full of plumbers, plasterers and tradesmen of all kinds, as well as housekeeping, kitchen and gardening staff. The volume was high as they drank pints of cider and beer in the afternoon sun. The owners were slaving over an enormous barbeque, and sausages and burgers were being eaten as fast as they could produce them. The atmosphere was one of satisfaction at a job well done. Everyone was in great form, and the chatter was punctuated by bursts of laughter. The beer garden was decorated in a Wild West theme, for a reason Conor had yet to determine. The woman of the house was mad for line dancing and American country music, so any chance she got, she churned out the Americana.

Conor sat on a hay bale watching Joe and Artie and loads of other kids daring each other to jump off the bales piled high to provide seating. He was enjoying the feeling of the sun on his face as he sipped a bottle of beer. Ana and her mother were deep in chat with Valentina. She had been at their home with Ana when he went to collect everyone, so she tagged along as well. Whereas Valentina was all jewellery and make-up, Ana was the opposite, one of the many things he loved about her. She was wearing a silvery-grey dress she'd made herself, and with her short blonde hair and no make-up, Conor thought she looked like an angel.

A shadow crossed him, and he looked up to see Laoise standing there with a replacement bottle of beer for him and one for herself.

'Mind if I join you?' she asked. Her hair was now pink with purple streaks, and she had added more tattoos to her ever-increasing collection of body art. Her nose was pierced, as were her navel and her ears, several times.

'Sure, sit down. I see you've been colouring yourself in again?' Conor smiled and accepted the new beer.

She clinked her bottle to his and sat beside him. 'Deadly, isn't it? 'Twas so sore, though. See this here?' She drew his attention to the inside of her forearm. 'That's the full sheet music for Turlough O'Carolan's concerto for harp. Not just the melody either, all the ornamentation as well. My dad says it's just lazy – would I not just learn the tune rather than writing it on myself – but he's ancient and hasn't a clue. And anyway, I've been able to play that from memory for years.'

'And what about when you're seventy and wrinkly and you look mad?' Conor teased her.

'I won't look mad! I'll look like someone who lived an interesting life, not some boring auld wan in a nursing home wittering on about the cats or whatever. Anyway, I'm young now, and that's all that matters. Dylan was going to get one for my birthday, but he bottled it, big baby. I gave him an awful time over it.' She winked.

'I can well imagine. The poor lad doesn't stand a chance up against you.'

Laoise was unusually silent for a moment, and Conor enjoyed the tranquillity. He was very fond of her, but he wasn't really in the mood for banter. He'd love it if Ana came over and sat with him, but he didn't want to ask her to.

Eventually Laoise spoke. 'Conor?'

'Yeah?' He rested his head on the bale behind him and closed his eyes.

'I know it's not my business or anything, but Corlene is really upset that you two fell out – I mean really upset. She told me what happened the other night. She was trying to look out for you, like be a friend, y'know?' Laoise was no longer the super-confident character she usually was; she was treading very carefully.

'You're right. It's not your business,' Conor said. Bad enough that Corlene had made those accusations about Ana, but now she was talking to others about the situation. The last thing he needed or wanted was to have everyone they knew sticking their tuppence worth into his relationship.

'Come on, Conor. Stop being like this. We love you and Ana and the boys, and we hate seeing you like this.'

Conor sat up and glared at Laoise. 'Like what? Seeing me like what, Laoise? I'm fine, Ana is fine, and we'd be grand if everyone could keep their big noses and gobs out of our lives.'

A loud burst of laughter and screams drew their attention to the other side of the garden, where several young boys, including the twins, squirted the crowd with water pistols. One of the victims was Ana, and Conor felt his gut wrench as he saw Nico beside her, offering her some paper napkins to dry herself. He used one to wipe her face, and the way she looked at him as he did so made Conor feel physically sick.

Laoise saw it too and turned to him. 'Sure, Conor, everything is fine. You can keep telling yourself that, but we both know it isn't. He's sniffing around Ana, and you need to step in, do something. All this glowering and eating the head off anyone who tries to get you to see what's going on in front of your face is only making the situation worse. She is stuck at home all the time, looking after her parents, looking after you and the boys. She is a smart woman, she needs more, and he's offering her that. I called the other day, and he was there, in your kitchen, the two of them chatting so intently when I came in that I just wanted to hit him a box into his stupid smug face. He knows I hate him, by the way. He's trying to seduce Ana and charm Artur and Danika and even the boys. Ana is feeling lonely and bored and not important, and along comes this eejit with all his flowers and his talk about Russian ballet or whatever, and she's alive again, Conor, and she's having her head turned. And what are you doing? Nothing. Working all the hours up in that hotel, and getting into fights with your friends who care about you and want to help.'

Conor got up and walked away, out to his car, but Laoise followed him to the car park.

'Just leave me alone, will you? Please. I need to be on my own.' He was gutted. Maybe Laoise was right and he was losing her.

She caught his arm and spun him around to face her. 'No, I won't. You don't need to be on your own. You need to go in there and be with your wife. Come on, Conor, you need to fight for her.'

Conor ran his hands through his hair in frustration. 'What are you on about, fight for her? This isn't the Wild West, Laoise, despite the mad decorations in there. I'm not some kind of meathead that goes and drags my woman away, thumping anyone who gets in my way – you know me better than that. And Ana isn't the kind of woman who'd appreciate it either. She's her own person, and she can choose her own friends. I'm not the kind of man to go in there making demands. I trust her, and I love her, and I…' He couldn't go on.

'Keys,' Laoise demanded with her hand out.

Conor just looked at her.

'Give me your car keys. You're right – you do need to get away, just to calm down. But you've had a few drinks and I've only had a few sips, so I'll drive. Now get in.'

Sighing in resignation, he gave her the keys and sat in the passenger seat.

They drove to the beach and parked facing the sea. Families were packing up toys and picnics as the sun sank over the Atlantic. They just sat in silence. Conor was distraught.

'I don't think anything has happened, like physically. Not yet anyway.' Laoise spoke quietly, but every word was piercing.

'How do you know?' His voice sounded strange, husky, even to his own ears.

'Well, I don't, not for sure. We had a chat the other day, and while she certainly has mentioned things like Nico thinks this or Nico said that – you know the way at the start of something you just keep bringing the person into conversation – I don't think anything has happened.'

Conor knew that Laoise, whatever else she might be, was totally honest. 'Did she mention me?' Each word was painful to say, embarrassing and humiliating.

'Just that you were at work all the time.'

'I'm there all the time to get this thing up and running so I don't have to be away on tour, away from her. That and the fact that everyone in my house now speaks Ukrainian except for me. Danika and Artur are nice people and they try not to leave me out of things, but Ana gets so exhausted from translating that it's just easier on her if I stay out of it.' Conor tried to make Laoise understand.

'Yeah, but in the process of getting it so right, you're losing her. Come on, let's walk on the beach. I want a cigarette, and you'll have a stroke if I smoke in your lovely new car.' She got out and waited for him, lighting up as she did.

'Maybe I have already.' Conor fell into step beside her.

'Lost her? I don't know, but I do know this – you need to *do* something. She told me she was genuinely upset when she saw you with Corlene that night. Not talking behind your back, but I was babysitting the lads when she went to join you after the meeting. She came home in an awful state.'

'But she couldn't seriously think that I had anything going on with Corlene, for God's sake. Like as if I'd ever cheat on her with anyone, but with Corlene?'

'Well, it's what she saw. What I don't get is why you and she aren't hammering this out. It's like you've stopped communicating or something. You two were so tight, so united. Now... Well, now it's not good.'

Conor thought for a while. Laoise was right – he and Ana weren't talking like they used to. He wanted her to be the one to reach out this time, he supposed. He felt like he'd made all the effort over the past few months, and she just remained passive or something, which wasn't like her at all. Maybe he didn't initiate a real conversation because he was afraid of what she might say: that she was leaving him, that they'd have to fight over the boys, that their life together was over. The longer it went on, the harder it got.

'Hey, I've an idea. Me and Dylan are playing next month in Dublin – we're in Vicar Street for four nights – but after that, we're free for a week. Why don't you two leave the boys with us and go off to Spain? Just the two of you?'

'Thanks, but she wouldn't come. I was surprised she even agreed to come to this today, but of course I now realise she only said yes because he was going to be there too.' Conor hated the bitterness in his voice.

'You don't know that. You haven't asked her,' Laoise said bluntly.

'I know.' Conor sighed, finally accepting what was going on in his life.

CHAPTER 17

'Hello?' Conor answered his mobile for what seemed like the fiftieth time that day. The agency had sent an army of potential serving, kitchen and grounds staff to be interviewed, and there were also deliveries needing to be signed for every five minutes. He was totally swamped and there was no sign of Corlene.

On top of that, Corlene had appointed a hotel manager without consulting him. He was furious, but when he'd emailed her about why he wasn't included in the hiring of such a vital role, she said she'd sent an email asking if he wanted to sit in on the interviews and got no reply. When he checked his inbox, he found it was true; he'd just never seen the email.

And if that weren't bad enough, she'd offered the job to none other than Carlos Manner, a jumped-up South African who Conor and Ana knew from the Dunshane and who was a total eejit. Apparently, it was all done. She'd offered him the job, and he accepted, signed a contract and worked out his notice. There was no going back.

Conor had tried to spend more time at home since his conversation with Laoise and made efforts to connect with Ana, but it was hard. They'd made love last night, something that hadn't happened for ages, but even that was different, not like the way they were together usually. Afterwards, they lay there, she sleeping facing away from him – or at least pretending to be asleep, he wasn't sure – and him on his back. He'd felt so alone. He'd tried asking her if she was OK, suggesting they go out, even go away to a hotel for a night, but nothing was working. He knew if he mentioned he was worried about her and Nico, she'd either lose her temper or get upset; neither was a good outcome.

'Conor, it's Dylan. How's everything goin' over there?'

'Ah...grand. Well, busy, y'know. Very busy actually.' Conor didn't want to sound impatient, but he had so much to do and really didn't have time for a chat.

'Sure, sure. Is Corlene there?'

'No. She was due to be down yesterday, I thought – she was in Dublin. But she's not here yet.' He tried not to sound like he was complaining but probably failed.

'That's so weird. She normally calls me every day, twice most days, but I haven't heard from her all week. Her phone is going to voicemail. Have you tried calling?' Dylan's tone was light, but Conor was sure Dylan knew how things were between him and Corlene.

'Er...no. I've been so busy –' Conor began.

'Yeah, you said. But maybe you wouldn't be so flat out if Corlene was there to help, right? Don't you think tracking her down is a good idea?'

'Yeah. Look, Dylan, I've people waiting here for me, so can I call you later when things calm down?' Conor didn't want to have this conversation, but also there were three very irate-looking delivery guys waiting to get in to see him, and meanwhile the candidates for various positions kept on coming.

'Sure, Conor. Look, I don't know what's going on, but something is wrong with Corlene and I'm worried about her. But I'm also worried about you. Can you just track her down and sort this out? I'm tied up here with gigs and stuff for another day or two, and then I swear I'm coming over to help. I don't know what I can do exactly, but I could answer phones or wash pots or something.'

'OK, Dylan, I'll do that. Look, it's fine. I'll recruit some extra help from the people here, get them interviewing waitresses and stuff like that. I'm hoping to recruit a new receptionist. She and I have been friends for years, and she'll be a great help. So honestly, don't be worrying.'

'Sure, sure, whatever you think. But you will try to track down Corlene, OK?'

'I will. Talk later.'

Calling Katherine was the first thing he'd do. She'd apparently just left the Dunshane after thirty years working there because she couldn't deal with what the French chain that bought the property wanted her to do, such as wear a yellow polo shirt for starters. Katherine was old school, very proper and all of that, but she had a heart of gold and she and Conor had become good friends over the years. He'd heard what had happened from a driver he met in town last night. The new management must be the reason Carlos Manner left as well. There and then he resolved to get Katherine on board at Castle Dysert. He should have cleared it with Corlene technically, but he just couldn't be bothered.

If Katherine could start right away, then she could take over the interviews, and that would be a huge weight off his shoulders. He scrolled through his phone for her number.

'Hi, Katherine. It's Conor.'

'Hello, Conor. Your name came up on the screen, so I knew who I was speaking to before you introduced yourself.'

He smiled. She was seen as prickly, but she wasn't really. She'd had his back on more than one occasion over the years, and he really liked her.

'Listen, do you want to come and work with me at this new place, Castle Dysert?'

She didn't speak for a moment. 'Work with you doing what? I had heard it mentioned that you weren't driving tours any more and that the castle had been bought by an American, but I don't understand really what –'

'Yeah, that's true. Corlene Holbrooke is the main shareholder. She actually was on a tour with me – you might remember her when you see her. But I've bought in as well to the hotel – well, a soon-to-be hotel – and we need a head receptionist. I think you'd be perfect. It's a five-star resort, beautiful place and grounds. What do you say?'

'Well...I...I'm flattered that you thought of me, Conor, but...'

'But what? You want a job, don't you? You're not looking to retire yet?' He paused, allowing the question to sink in. He could tell she was considering it. He thought for a moment; she would need the job to be a promotion, not just be hired as a receptionist, and now that he was talking to her, he knew he needed her to agree.

He went on. 'This is really a gorgeous place, and you'd have a managerial role if you'd like – administration manager, running the reservations and the front desk, whatever you wanted really. The money is excellent, better than the Dunshane, and besides, I need you. Nobody could do this job like you could. Come on, Katherine...' Conor knew if she were standing in front of him, he could gauge it better, but he hoped his charm offensive was working.

'Well, I... This is all a bit sudden, but all right. I suppose I could give it a try.'

'Brilliant! Can you start today?' Conor was beginning to see a light at the end of his tunnel of work.

'Today? No, of course I can't start today! I don't have anything ready!' Katherine was unusually flustered.

'Katherine, a recruitment agency has sent me over what seems like a hundred people for positions in housekeeping, kitchen, maintenance, groundskeeping, and they are building up outside. I can't interview them all, and anyway, I haven't a clue what to even ask them. You know this stuff better than anyone – didn't you run the Dunshane for decades? Please, Katherine, I'm begging. Throw on a suit, get in your car, and you could be ploughing through them by two o'clock. You'd be doing me the most fantastic favour, and you'd also establish yourself with the new staff as the boss. Will you do it? Please? For me?' He hoped her resolve was weakening.

'Fine. Though what kind of a disorganised place I am entering into, I can't imagine. I'll come and see, but if it's not suitable, I won't be staying. I'll get there as soon as I can. This had better be a good position you're offering me, Conor O'Shea, or I promise you, you will regret messing me about.'

Conor could hear the hint of relief and gratitude in her voice, despite the sharp words. To be unemployed in your mid-fifties and also unmarried, was, for a woman like her, a depressing prospect. She was old school and was never going to buy into what she would see as modern corporate nonsense. But Castle Dysert needed Katherine, and Katherine needed it.

'Fantastic! You're a star. I always said it!' Conor chuckled.

'You always said a lot of things, Conor O'Shea, and I believed about a quarter of them. See you later.' She hung up.

Conor almost punched the air in delight. Katherine would be brilliant. Now, Corlene was the next thing. Dylan was right; it was weird not to have heard from her.

He signed for the deliveries and immediately radioed for Artur. Artur was in the maintenance yard but replied instantly, and Conor asked him to come up to the house.

When he arrived, Conor brought him into the office. 'Artur, there are a lot of deliveries of things coming for the next week – furniture, appliances, all of that stuff. Can you be responsible for checking each one to make sure it is what we ordered?' Conor spoke slowly and clearly, and his father-in-law understood.

'You want I do it? You are sure? Is important job… I don't want to make it mess…'

Artur was so conscientious. Conor put his arm around the older man's shoulder. 'You won't. You are very careful with everything you do, so this will be the same. Each delivery will have an order number, which is listed here.' He opened up a file on the computer. 'You check the number against the one on the sheet the driver will have, then you check the goods as they are unloaded to make sure they are what they are supposed to be, the right number and all of that. Is that OK?'

Artur was focused diligently on the file Conor had opened.

'I'll do the first one or two with you, and then you'll see.' Conor was convinced Artur could do it; he just needed confidence. It was truly astonishing the speed with which Artur had learned English, all apparently down to Joe's intervention.

The rest of the afternoon passed more easily, and both Artur and Katherine worked brilliantly in their new roles. Katherine was happily installed in the drawing room, interviewing, and Artur was efficiently taking deliveries and delegating labourers to move things to where they should go.

By five o'clock, Conor had time to catch his breath. He called Corlene, but like Dylan, he just got her voicemail.

He called Dylan back, thinking maybe he'd heard something.

'Hey, Conor.' Dylan sounded upset.

'Any word?'

'No, nothing. I'm really worried, Conor. I actually came up on the bus to Ennis. I'm at the Old Ground and she isn't here. She said she'd be staying here until the castle was ready. I thought they might know something, but they haven't seen her since Sunday. She has a room here and lots of her stuff is in it – the manager went up to check – but she's missing.'

'Stay there. I'm coming in. Is Laoise with you?'

Something was definitely wrong. Corlene never switched her phone off, and she certainly would never abandon Dylan like that.

'No, she's gone to London to see her brother. He's recording an album and needs her to play harp and fiddle on it. She's back on Saturday.' Dylan sounded miserable.

'OK, come out to the roundabout. I'll pick you up in twenty minutes.'

'Thanks, Conor. I don't want to be in your way – you're so busy with the hotel and everything…'

'No, it's grand. We can have a cup of coffee and a chat, and sure you can give me a hand if you've nothing else to do.'

'Sure. I've a few gigs, but apart from those, I'm free. You don't think anything bad has happened to her, do you?'

Conor hated to hear the worry in Dylan's voice. He was twenty-five now but a young twenty-five, and the insecurities of his youth were not far beneath the surface.

'No, no, of course not. She's probably just gone to schmooze someone, as she says. Don't worry, we'll track her down.' Conor tried to sound confident, but he was really worried about her now as well.

He stuck his head around the drawing room door where Katherine was looking fiercely at a young girl who was attempting to fold towels for inspection. His friend looked just like she used to at the Dunshane, tall and thin with a black skirt and jacket, blouse buttoned up to the neck, her dark hair pulled back into a severe bun and not a hint of make-up. She was a woman who meant business, and woe betide anyone who got in her way.

'Excuse me, I'm sorry to interrupt, but could I have a quick word?'

Katherine looked over at him, and the girl seemed to breathe a sigh of relief at the interruption.

'Certainly,' Katherine said, then followed him out into the corridor. 'Honestly, some of those people the agency sent are simply halfwits or bone idle. At least half of them won't do at all. I am going to ring the recruitment consultant myself and explain what calibre of people we are after. I mean, we are paying far above the average hourly rate in the sector, so you would think they could find better.'

Conor smiled inside at how proprietorial Katherine was already about the place. She was so loyal and regarded her work not just as a job but as something much more personal.

'That's exactly what you should do. As I said, I haven't a clue, so you know best. Ring the one in the agency up and roast the ears off her. No better woman.' Conor grinned to show he was only teasing. 'Now, I need to go out. I shouldn't be long, but can you hold the fort? Artur, Ana's dad, is taking deliveries. He's got a team of young lads moving furniture and stuff, so he's fine, but his English isn't perfect. So if he has trouble, can I tell him to come to you?'

'Of course. How is Anastasia? I could really do with someone like her here. She was a wonderful member of staff at the Dunshane, even if she did take her eye off her job in the end to admire a certain bus driver.'

Katherine didn't often joke, so Conor laughed, though he wished he could turn the clock back to those days when he was sure of Ana's feelings for him.

'She's fine, doing well, up to her eyes with the boys and her parents. She'd love to see you, I'm sure. We'll have time for a proper chat and a cup of coffee once this all is up and running.'

'That's fine, Conor. Go off now. I have your mobile number in the event of a catastrophe. I'm in no rush this evening, so I'll be here.'

He could have hugged her, but she would have probably collapsed at his forwardness. So he simply said, 'You're one in a million, and we're so lucky to have you.'

'Go on now with all that old nonsense. You'll pay me well and I'll do the job, simple as that.' But the pink tinge that came to her cheeks told him she was glad to be needed again.

CHAPTER 18

Conor had never seen Dylan in such a state, dishevelled and fighting back tears.

He'd picked him up at the appointed spot, and when they got to a wide bit of road, Conor pulled over so they could talk.

'Dylan, I know you're worried, but she'll be OK.' He wanted to reassure the distraught young man.

Dylan took a deep breath to steady his ragged breathing. 'I'm sorry. It's not just that. It's… He just called me again, that's why I'm upset. I just don't know what to do… And now Corlene has gone missing…'

'What to do about what?' Conor kept his voice low and gentle.

'My father. Corlene told me that she didn't know who he was, that it could be any number of people, but then this guy got in touch with my grandma and said he was my dad and that he wanted to contact me. Grandma told Corlene, but she…I don't know…didn't want me to meet him, so she just told Grandma to keep him away. He knew my name was Dylan Holbrooke, though, and he googled me. Then I got a Facebook message from him, this Larry Costello, and he says he's my dad, and that what's more is his grandpa and grandma came from here.'

'So what did you do?'

'I confronted Corlene, obviously, asked her straight if she'd been lying to me all these years. Y'know, Conor, when I was a kid, I'd daydream all the time about my dad, especially when she'd hooked up with some other jerk and I had to move schools or houses or whatever. I'd imagine that he didn't know I existed, that he'd got married and had two nice kids, that he and his wife would find out about me and adopt me, and I'd have a brother and a sister and a real home and everything. Stupid, I know, but that was all I wanted.'

'That's not a stupid thing to want at all. So what did Corlene say?'

'Well, she denied it all at first, more lies like before. I thought she'd changed, y'know, that things were finally better. But no. I thought, "Here we go again. She's just the same, a selfish liar."' He wiped a tear from the corner of his eye with the back of his hand, frustrated at his own emotions betraying him. 'In the end, she had to admit she'd been lying to me and that this Larry Costello was my father. She tried to say he was bad news and that I was better off without him and all that stuff. We had a huge fight – not just about him but about everything, all the crap she put me through growing up – and I told her she was a terrible mother and that I wished she'd had an abortion because it would have saved me from being her kid. I said really awful things, called her horrible names, and she just drove off.'

Conor sat back and tried to think what the best thing to do was. The story of Corlene and Larry Costello wasn't his to tell, and he could see both sides. He wished he'd made more of an effort to patch things up with her before this. She had only been looking out for him, but he just didn't want to see it. If anything had happened to her, neither he nor Dylan could forgive themselves.

'OK, Dylan, here's what we're going to do – we're going to find her. Your mother is a smart lady – she just needs a bit of time to process all of this. But in the meantime, we'll look for her everywhere we can think of.'

'But, Conor, this isn't your problem and you've got enough to do with the hotel opening soon and everything.'

'Well, I'm partly to blame for her taking off, I think. She and I had an argument a few weeks ago. Did she mention it?'

'She never said anything to me, but she had a few drinks and told Laoise, who kinda told me. For what it's worth, Conor, I don't think Ana would ever cheat on you.' Dylan was anxious to reassure him.

It touched Conor that in the middle of his own problems, Dylan was thinking about him and Ana. He smiled. 'I don't think so either, Dylan, but one problem at a time. I lost my temper with your mother when she suggested it, and things haven't been right between us since. I'm just a bit preoccupied with everything, you see, but I should have put things right. I suppose the fight with you also made her feel very isolated, so she just took off. But don't worry – we'll find her.'

They sat in silence for a while, both thinking the same thing, neither comfortable saying it.

Eventually, Dylan spoke. 'She wouldn't do anything like…like… drive off a cliff, would she?' He seemed much younger than his years.

'No way, absolutely not. She's a survivor, your mother. Look how often in her life she was really back to the wall, but she always finds a way. She'd never do that.'

They went to the local Garda station to report her missing, and the sergeant arrived just as they were giving her description to the young policeman at the desk.

'Conor, how are you? We haven't seen you at the golf club for a while. Everything all right?'

'Ah, Bernard, great to see you. Yerra, yeah, I'm grand. Just up to my eyes with this new resort we're doing out at Castle Dysert, no time for golf. Actually, we're here to report a missing person.'

'Right, sure. Come into my office there and we'll get the details. Thanks, Eoin, I'll take it from here.' Bernard Keane dismissed the young guard, who looked like it was his first day on the job.

He closed the door and Dylan and Conor sat down.

'So, who's missing?'

Conor and Dylan told him the whole story, about the arguments and everything, and Bernard just sat and listened.

'Have you tried friends, family, anywhere she might go?'

'I have. I called my girlfriend's parents. Corlene is good friends with Siobhan, my girlfriend's mom, but they haven't heard anything. The woman who does the day-to-day running of Corlene's other business didn't know either. I called other friends and my grandma back in the States, but nobody's seen or heard from her.'

'OK, son, the first thing is not to panic. We see hundreds of missing person cases every year, and nearly always the person is found safe and well, so we won't get unduly concerned just yet. Now she drove off, you say? So we'll need the reg and the make and model of her car, and we'll have all the patrol cars look out for that. We can check hotels and so on, as well as hospitals just in case there was an accident. So leave it with us, and I'll give you a call tomorrow, Conor. Will you two be together?'

Dylan looked so alone and frightened that Conor answered for him. 'We will, Bernard. Dylan will be with me until Corlene turns up. And she will turn up, Dylan, I just know she will. She's a bit cross with the pair of us, and she has good reason to be. But we'll find her, and we'll patch things up, and everything will be grand, OK? Thanks, Bernard. I'll talk to you soon.' Conor shook hands with the sergeant and he and Dylan left.

In the car, Dylan showed Conor the messages from Larry Costello. Conor took the phone to read them.

Hi Dylan,

I don't know if you are who I think you are, but if your mother is Corlene Holbrooke, then I think I'm your dad. I'm sorry to just blurt it out like that, but I didn't know how else to contact you. Your Grandma Holbrooke wouldn't give me your contact details. I saw your photo on your website, the one of your album cover with pictures of you and the girl you play with, and you remind me so much of my brother Danny at that age. I can't believe you play Irish music. I saw some videos on YouTube, and man, you are awesome! I'm a journalist, and I play a little guitar – not as well as you play those pipes, though. How'd you learn to do that? Your grandparents on my side are Irish, so I guess that's where you get it from.

Look, Dylan, I don't think your mom is going to be too pleased to have me back in your life, but you're an adult now so you can decide for yourself. I'd love to meet you. I could even come visit you in Ireland. I've always wanted to visit where my family came from. I'm sorry I wasn't there for you growing up. I didn't know you existed until I saw something on the internet about Corlene's business, and then I saw you. I'm blown away to have a son, so if you want to meet me, I sure think we'd have a lot to talk about.'

Love from Larry (Dad)

Conor knew he'd have to tread very carefully. From Dylan's perspective, the note seemed genuine, so why wouldn't he want to meet his dad? But he thought back to his conversation with Corlene that night, when she told him about what happened... Dylan did not need this guy in his life.

'And he's calling you now as well?' Conor asked.

'Yeah. Well, the number on our website for people to contact us about gigs or whatever, he called that. He left a message. I don't know what to do. I'm so mad at Corlene, but I know from the way she talked about him that she didn't want me to see him. She wouldn't say why, just that he was no good for me. Like, she hasn't seen him in years! She doesn't know what he's like. She's judging him based on what she knew of him twenty-four years ago. People change, right?'

Conor knew Dylan wanted him to reassure him, to tell him he should call his father back, but he couldn't do that. 'Actually, in my experience, Dylan, they don't. People can change on the surface, how they look, what they say, but really deep down, people don't change much at all. At least that's what I think. Why don't you send him a message saying you need some time to think? And that you'll get back to him once you've done that, but in the meantime to give you some space? What do you think of that as an idea? That way you haven't really made any decision. We can concentrate on finding Corlene first, and you and she can sit down and have a rational conversation about all of this. Maybe she has a very good reason for not wanting him in your life, or maybe not, but she is your mother and she deserves at least a chance to explain.'

'But I did give her a chance and she just took off –'

'Yeah, after you called her horrible names and told her she was a terrible mother. So that hardly counts, does it?'

'I guess.' Dylan was despondent.

'Dylan, I don't really talk about this, it's something from my past, but my father left my brother and my mam and me when I was eight. He went to work in England and never came back. It affected each of the three of us differently, and none of it in a good way, but we were as well off without him. Being a father is more than just the biology, y'know? Now, I'm not claiming to know anything about this guy, or about what happened with your mam, but he says he didn't know you existed. But didn't you spend the first few years of your life with your granny in a little town in Alabama? And I'm guessing it's not a huge place. I think your mother told me about 8,000 people. She got pregnant as a young girl, stayed at home and had you, and he's saying he never knew? That seems a bit far-fetched to me, if you don't mind me saying so. Your mother stayed on at school to get her diploma, the same school he went to. I don't know. It's tempting to imagine a fairy-tale ending, of course it is. I used to make all kinds of excuses for my auld fella when I was young, but he chose to leave us. Simple as that. He was useless and didn't care about us. So maybe I'm bringing my own baggage to this thing with you and this Larry fella. But it seems to me if he was rocking up into my life after all these years, I'd want to know all the facts and I'd want answers to some questions.'

Dylan was silent, but Conor thought he'd managed at least to plant some seeds of doubt in his head.

'Maybe. I don't know. Grandma doesn't like him either, and I trust her more. I asked her why, and she said I should talk to my mom. It's like she knows something but doesn't want to say. Look, let's just find Corlene first, and in the meantime, I'll do what you suggested, just message him back and ask him to give me some space. Thanks, Conor. It's like you kinda always know what to do.'

Conor sighed. 'Oh, yes, Dylan, I'm grand at solving other people's problems. My own, however, well, that's another story.'

CHAPTER 19

Conor reread the text one last time. It was the first break he'd had all evening. Everyone had gone home and he was alone in the castle. He thought he'd seen Dylan leave earlier with one of the guys from the site. Dylan had mentioned he was going to go through Corlene's stuff at the Old Ground Hotel to check for clues. Conor had been trying to call Corlene all day, but her phone was still switched off. If she was just trying to get away, maybe she would read a text. It was worth a shot.

Corlene, please let us know where you are. We're all really worried about you. I'm sorry for the row we had. I know you were only looking out for me, but I just didn't want to hear it – a case of shoot the messenger. Dylan is really devastated and feels like it's his fault you left. The reality is we probably both drove you to it. Anyway, we want you to come back, or at least please let us know you're OK. Conor xxx

He pressed send and hoped for the best. Corlene had an iPhone too so the messages were sent as iMessages, and within seconds, the little blue balloon was marked 'delivered' – would it do that if the phone were dead? He didn't think so. It was too late to check with the tech people, but he'd ask them in the morning.

He sent Ana a text next.

Hi, pet. Really sorry I'm so late. Things so busy and still no sign of Corlene. I'll be home in 20 minutes if you're still awake? Love you. xxx

He was trying to be extra considerate and loving towards her rather than taking the surly approach that had failed so miserably. He sent her flowers and ran her baths when he came home, taking care of the twins while Danika cooked.

He had reviewed the contract Corlene signed with Nico, and the groundskeeper was under contract for at least another six months. Conor had hoped that if Nico thought he was moving on, then Conor's chances of getting everything back to normal would be better.

He was still really worried about Corlene despite the text, though he couldn't let on to Dylan. What on earth could have taken her away at such a crucial time? Castle Dysert was her pride and joy and was due to open in ten days' time, the first groups were booked in from the US, and there were many events scheduled before that.

There was a familiarisation event being held the next day, where tour operators and travel agents were being treated to lunch and a tour, with the hope that they would use Castle Dysert on their itineraries. Many of them were old contacts of Conor's, but it was Corlene who had made it all happen.

Conor checked the computer and confirmed that all the deliveries for the day had been received. He needn't have bothered; Artur was doing a fantastic job, much to the annoyance of several truck and van drivers who had to wait until every last thing was counted and checked. Artur and Katherine were a formidable team; nothing got past either of them. Katherine had approved the menu with Chef for the lunch tomorrow, and the staff all knew what to do and where to be. He didn't know how she'd done it in such a short timeframe, but she had.

Conor's phone beeped in his pocket.

I'm OK. Sorry for bailing out. I have something I need to do. It's important. But I'll be back as soon as I can. Tell Dylan I love him. C x

He tried calling her number immediately, but again it went to voicemail. Whatever she was doing, she did not want to talk to anyone. At least she was OK.

He gathered his keys and jacket and left the office.

The hallways seemed so peaceful now, and everything shone and was either refurbished or replaced. There wasn't a speck of dust or anything out of place. The tour operators couldn't be anything but impressed. The lawns, with their blooming autumnal flowerbeds and ornamental trees leading to the shore, were illuminated strategically as well – a lighting designer had been brought in from Sweden – and the effect was magical. There were many times over the past months when Conor had wondered if he'd made a terrible mistake, if he should stick with what he knew, but now that it was finished, and more importantly that Corlene was OK, he felt good about the decision to be involved with Castle Dysert.

He checked his phone again. Nothing from Ana. She was probably asleep, he told himself.

As he turned to go out the front door, he stopped. There it was again, the faint sound of a toy train set. He stood stock-still, hardly daring to breathe. He had to strain to hear it, but it was there, the puffing sound of a steam engine, followed by a whistle. But it couldn't be. He'd told Daniel to pack up the whole lot and ship it out. He was sure Daniel had said it was done, albeit with bad grace, and the movers were coming soon to take it away for auction; Daniel had coincided the collection of the playroom contents with the return of several more pieces that had been repaired.

The hair on the back of Conor's neck stood up, and he felt clammy and cold. He wasn't imagining it. He knew he wasn't. The sound was coming from upstairs, and something propelled him upwards. He went into his office and took out the huge brass key from the drawer. He climbed the sweeping staircase with its scarlet deep-pile carpet. Sage-green drapes hung at the windows, held back by moss-green and red silk ropes. Conor gripped the oak banister as he climbed the stairs. The bedrooms, each with a botanical theme as a tribute to Beatrice King, were ready to go. When he reached the third floor, he walked along the corridor to the door that led into the attic. It was so cold up there. So many experts had looked at the plumbing system, and even the internal walls were insulated in case that was the problem, but nothing seemed to work.

He unlocked the door and walked into the room, his heart thumping loudly in his chest. Everything was just as it had been the day Ana and he had gone in there, months ago now. Nothing seemed to have been touched. Why would Daniel not have done as he asked? He was sure the architect had said it was done, but clearly it wasn't. Maybe he still hoped to convince Conor to keep it all.

He shivered. It was absolutely freezing, and the air was still inside the room. The china dolls with their creepy faces lined one wall; the glassy-eyed teddy bears still sat on the couch. Then he saw them, the packing boxes, all thrown in a corner, discarded. They had been used but now were empty.

Conor decided to take matters into his own hands and began throwing toys randomly into the boxes. He didn't even care if they broke; he just wanted the whole bloody lot gone. As he filled box after box with dolls and books and colouring pencils, he tried to ignore the loud beating of his heart. When he went to pick up the track with the little toy train, the small red and green engine began to move. It made the exact sound Conor had heard before, the click-clack of the wheels on the tracks and then the little steam whistle. He stood frozen to the spot.

Nothing could make him stay in that room. There was someone in there. He didn't know if it was Grenville or Samuel or Sarah, but one of the Kings was in that room, he was sure of it.

He bounded down the stairs and out the front door, just stopping in time to turn on the alarm. He could barely get the key in the ignition, his hands were shaking so badly. Eventually, he got the car started and drove home.

CHAPTER 20

'Dad! Dad! Will you take us swimming? Mammy says she can't, and I want to try the new diving board. They've put in an even higher one and everyone in my class is scared of it, even Artie is scared. But I want to do it, so will you bring us?'

Conor woke to his sons pummelling him to wake up. Beside him, Ana groaned. 'What time is it?' she muttered groggily.

Conor checked his phone on the bedside table. 'Ah, lads, it's five o'clock in the morning! Go back to bed, and I'll see if I can get away sometime today to take you, OK?' He was exhausted. It had taken him ages to fall asleep, as the events of the previous night went round and round in his head. He'd wanted so badly to wake Ana and tell her, but he didn't.

'But you said that yesterday, and you never came home until after we were asleep! Please, Dad...please?' Artie's little face was pleading, and Conor felt a surge of guilt at how little time he'd spent with them of late.

He sat up and pulled the boys into his arms. 'You are right – I've been a rubbish dad for the last few weeks. But I swear to you, and I really mean this now, it's only temporary. The hotel will be opened in ten days' time, and the new manager is coming on Friday, so he'll be doing all the stupid jobs that I'm doing at the moment. So if you can be patient with your ancient knackered old daddy, then I swear we'll all go to Tayto Park for a long weekend just as soon as I can get away I promise. Is that a deal?'

'OK, brilliant!' they chorused. It always made Conor and Ana smile when they said the same thing at exactly the same time.

'Are Mammy and *Didus* and *Babusya* and Nico coming too?' Joe asked innocently, but it was like someone punched Conor in the stomach.

He forced his voice to sound normal. 'Well, definitely Mammy. We can't go anywhere without her because I'd be crying too much as I'd be so lonely.' Conor was determined to hide his hurt that they saw Nico as part of the family.

They giggled at the idea.

'But I don't think *Didus* and *Babusya* would really be into roller coasters and scary things like that, and they'll probably stay at home so it will just be us four. But nothing will happen if you two don't get back into bed this second and don't come near us again for at least two hours – do you hear me?'

'OK.' Joe grinned and gave Conor a kiss on the cheek.

'What about Nico, though? He'd like roller coasters?' Artie hugged his dad as he spoke.

Conor knew Ana was awake beside him so chose his words carefully. 'Well, I'm sure he does, but he's not in our family and this is a family holiday, so Nico will have to stay here too. I want to have Mammy and you two all to myself because I miss you and I love you all so much.'

The twins seemed content with that explanation and wandered happily back to their own beds. Conor lay back down, figuring he'd probably never get back to sleep now. He lay there on his back, debating if he should just get up and go to work; if he did that, he might get away a bit early and could take the boys swimming. Just as he was about to throw back the duvet, Ana turned and put her head on his chest, throwing her arm across him. Conor could hardly believe it; nothing like that had happened in weeks. She nuzzled into his neck, kissing him. He wanted so much to react. He knew if he turned to her now, they would make love, but he didn't want to relive the impersonal experience of last time. She ran her hand over his bare chest, and before he knew it, she was on top of him. It was all at her initiative, and as they made love passionately, reaching climax together, he tried not to cry with relief but failed.

'Conor, what is wrong?' Ana wiped his tears with her fingers. She'd never seen her husband cry before.

'Nothing. I'm fine. I'm grand, honestly…' Conor was mortified. He hadn't cried in years, and not in front of anyone since he was a kid.

'You are not fine. Please, Conor, tell me. I…I don't know why we are so – I don't know the word – apart from each other. I… Something is wrong, I know it, but…' Now she was crying too.

Conor drew her into his arms, holding her as tightly as he dared, almost afraid to let her go, to lose the intimacy again. Long seconds passed as he deliberated. Maybe he shouldn't say anything. Maybe things were OK again and bringing it up was only going to spoil this moment. He thought of Laoise's words – they needed to hammer this out.

'Ana, can I ask you something? And please don't go mad at me or go silent – just answer me.'

'Of course. Anything.' She leaned up on one elbow, looking down into his face.

'Do you love me, like the way you used to, or has something changed?' He knew he wasn't asking her what he really wanted to know, but fear of the answer was stopping him.

'I love you, always, everything, the same. But I…I think I am losing you. That night I see you with Corlene…'

'But, Ana, darling, I explained that. I know what it looked like, but it wasn't anything like that.'

'I know that, I do, but always she says things and looks at you like you are hers. Anyway, I think I don't make you excited any more, like I am fatter than I was, and I have droopy breasts and a saggy belly and these marks from when the twins were there.' She pointed ruefully at her abdomen. 'And I don't have interesting things to say because all the day I am here just in the house. I don't blame you if you go... You are so handsome and all women look at you. Even Miss Carney, she looks like this at you, and that woman who interview you for the television, she the same. You don't see it but I do, and I just feel invisible really.'

He wanted to reassure her, to make everything OK again, but he had to ask her first. 'And Nico, did he make you feel not invisible? I know you and he have been spending time together.' Each word hurt to say, and he knew the next few seconds would forever change his life.

Ana looked so very sad, and long seconds passed before she spoke. 'Always we are honest, so I tell you. Nico is... He is a friend, and with him sometimes I feel better than I do with you because we talk about things like when I studied at university and things like that, like about my life before here. And yes, I did go to restaurant for to have lunch with him, and one other time we went for a walk to the dolmen in the Burren and I did not tell you. I was going to, but you seemed so cross. I was afraid you might say it was over or something. Also I would not be happy if you were going to walk in the Burren with another woman, so I was wrong.'

Conor tried to digest what she was saying. He needed to know more, no matter how much hearing it hurt. 'Do you have feelings for him?' He knew he sounded gruff, but he couldn't help it.

'I have feelings like friend. I like to talk with him, like I say. But not feeling like wanting him, like I do you, you know? I promise, nothing like that. I just felt like me when I was with him. He remind me of my friends when I was student, long ago. I don't have to try all the time with another language, so it was easy. But no, I don't want him like a man, no. Definitely no. If Nico was a girl, it would be so much easier. Sometimes I wish he was because then it would be OK to have friend. I know that Valentina is a good friend, but – is mean for me to say this, I know – but she don't go in university, she don't read books or go to ballet. And for you Irish, I know you thinking all Russia, Siberia, Ukraine is same, but is not. Nico is like me, same kind of life, same kind of family. We know same music, same films. We clicked, like you say.' She was adamant, and the vice grip panic had on his chest loosened a little.

'And what about him? Does he feel something for you?' It was now or never, and he wanted to get it all over with.

Ana sighed and Conor sat up. He wanted so badly to hold her again, but they needed to have this conversation first.

'I don't know. He don't say that, but my father speak to me after the party in the pub, and he was angry. Never was he so mad with me in my life. He say that I was not behaving right, like that I was making Nico think something is happening, and that you are such a good man and so kind and that I don't deserve you. He says I should not be such friend with Nico and how you was so angry. And then after that, I don't see you so much and I think he is right, so maybe if I just let you alone, you will come back to me.'

Conor remembered how Artur seemed quite sharp with Nico that day at Castle Dysert. His father-in-law didn't speak perfect English, but he also didn't miss a trick. It felt good to know Artur was on his side, even though Conor wasn't from their part of the world like Nico was.

'So I had nothing to worry about?' Conor asked his wife, whom he realised now he adored even more than the day he married her.

'Of course not. Never, never, Conor. You're my love. I'm sorry if I made you sad, or if you think something going on with me and Nico. Never do I think about him like that. I just liked having someone to talk to. But I will tell him today – no more. Nothing. When I hear that Artie ask you can we bring Nico, I feel so ashamed. When I kiss you before, I was so scared you would say no. I was so...' She swallowed as if trying to find the right words was excruciating.

Conor realised, maybe for the first time, how hard it was for her, always speaking to him in a foreign language. No wonder she gravitated to someone who understood her better than he did. 'I was so scared too, Ana. I thought I was losing you. Corlene and I had a huge argument. She told me about the lunch and the walk you and Nico had, and I just didn't want to hear it. She was looking out for me, but I went mad and shouted at her and stormed out. I'm crap at this kind of thing, pet, I really am. I'm great at solving other people's issues – that's no bother at all – but when it comes to my own emotional state, I'm a total eejit. That day in the beer garden, when the kids sprayed you with water and Nico wiped your face, I was watching and I couldn't move. I swear, it was like there was a weight on my chest and I just couldn't bear it. Laoise took me off for a spin, tried to talk some sense into me, told me I should batter him actually. And y'know, if he was in front of me in that moment, I just might have.'

'I think you would win.' She smiled, but then a shadow crossed her beautiful face again. 'But, Conor, there is something else. Why you don't tell me about the ghost noise in the hotel? I watch the programme on TV, and she say it and you say is nothing, but is it?'

He sighed and the whole story came out, everything, including last night's terrifying events.

Ana shuddered. 'There is a ghost there. I feel this cold when we go in that room, and *Tato* was saying that they cannot heat the top of the castle no matter what they do. What will we do? So much money, so much time, but it cannot work if is… What is word…'

'Haunted. Yes, I know.' Conor pulled her down onto his chest and held her tightly. At least she was asking what *they* were going to do, not what *he* was going to do. Though undoubtedly a ghost in Castle Dysert was a huge problem, his Ana loved him and not bloody Nico, so that was spectacularly good news. 'I honestly don't know what to do, but we'll think of something, I'm sure. Maybe if we just get all the stuff out, then the ghost or whatever is making this stuff happen will get out too.'

'So apart from ghosts, are we OK?' She cuddled up to him, kissing his chest.

'If you say we are, then we are. Ana, I've never looked at another woman since I met you, and I swear on our kids' lives that I never will. I love you, your gorgeous body, your saggy tummy and your stretch marks.' He rolled over and kissed her belly as she stifled a scream of laughter. 'They're there because you gave me my beautiful sons, so those marks are like medals of honour. And I think you're fascinating – you've never once bored me in all these years. I think you are so smart and funny and interesting. And you know what? I'm going to learn bloody Ukrainian. I am, seriously. If your father can learn English, then I can learn that mad language. So at least some of the time, you won't have to speak a foreign language to talk to me.'

They made love again and held each other afterwards, silent and content. Life was great again.

CHAPTER 21

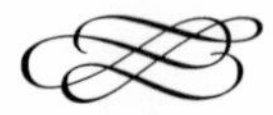

Conor walked into the castle to find Katherine standing in the dining room. He was on top of the world. Things were fantastic again with him and Ana, Corlene was OK wherever she was, and the hotel was on schedule and on budget. Even the ghostly happenings upstairs could not put a dent in his good mood.

He was actually looking forward to the lunch that day; he was really proud of how the castle had turned out and wanted to show it off. Many of his former colleagues were coming. He knew they thought he was mad to give up the road, where the money was good and the freedom was better. At least that's how many of them saw it, mostly those who had wives and kids at home but also those who managed quite a few extracurricular activities with ladies who were on their holidays and who were seduced by the charm of not just the drivers but of the whole Irish experience.

Conor had never heard of a romance that started on a tour between a driver and a visitor that didn't end in tears. He had no interest in that; he never had, even before Ana. Any women he went out with in the past were nothing to do with his job, and he had the respect of many people in the business because of it.

He spotted Daniel and called him into his office. 'That playroom in the attic – I thought you'd boxed everything up?'

Daniel looked confused. 'I did. Well, I got two of the lads to help me, but I wanted to make sure everything was packed properly. The stuff is worth a fortune, but you are determined to get rid of it, so…'

Conor didn't say anything about his discovery. 'So where is all the stuff now?'

'In the corner ready for the movers today. They're delivering some bedroom furniture I sourced at an auction in Dublin last week and taking that stuff back with them to the same auction house.'

'Right, thanks. I'll let you get on. Busy day today. Oh, what's the story with the heating up there? Any progress?'

'No, nothing. The radiators have all been replaced, and Artur took the whole boiler apart and put it back together again. The whole thing works perfectly on the ground floor, the first and second floors, but the third and the attic – nothing.'

'Right.' Conor nodded. 'Thanks. Keep them on it, will you? I've to meet all the new staff ahead of the big lunch today.'

He left Daniel and walked towards the dining room. As he did, Katherine approached him.

'A word. Now.' She walked past him back in the direction of his office, so he followed.

'What's up?' he asked as she closed the door firmly behind them.

'There's been talk among the staff that the castle is haunted. They say that's why the heating won't work on the top floor, that it's because of the deaths in the house, and some of them are claiming to have heard noises. Unless we nip this in the bud, it's going to get out of hand.' Clearly, Katherine didn't believe any of it.

Conor thought quickly. 'Right. Give me five minutes, and I'll be down and speak to them.'

As soon as Katherine left, he went to the App Store on his phone and downloaded a ringtone. It would have to do in the short term.

'Good morning, folks, are we all set?' he asked as he approached the large gathering. The entire household staff, including kitchen staff, waited for him in the dining room.

Conor stood at the top of the room and addressed them. 'I believe some of you have expressed concern about the heating situation in the castle, and some people seem to be under the impression that there is something other than a logical explanation for this. Well, let me tell you that the issue is with the strength of the pump. We are having to source a pump from somewhere in Germany to be strong enough to pump the water to the top floor. So there is a perfectly logical explanation. Now also some people seem to be worried about noises. Is this the one that's causing all the panic?' He took out his phone and played the toy train ringtone he'd just downloaded.

Several of the staff looked at each other.

'That's the sound my phone makes when I get a text. As you know, I'm around every bit of this place all the time, so if you heard that sound, that's what it was. OK, now that we've solved all the mysteries, I would be delighted if everyone could go about their business. It's in everyone's interest that this launch is a success, and stupid old stories about pookies and things that go bump in the night are serving nobody well.'

An older woman who'd been taken on as head of housekeeping raised her hand. Conor recognised her as Sheila Dillon from the village; she had a son who was about to finish secondary school, and her teenage daughter was pregnant. There was no sign of a man in the household, so this job would mean a lot to her.

'Conor, can I just say – and I do think I speak for everyone when I say this – we want this place to be a success as much as you, more even, because it's a living for us. So I think we should all just get on with our jobs and get this place up and running smoothly.'

Nods and murmurs of agreement abounded from the gathered crowd of uniformed workers. Clearly, the ghostbusting section was small.

Everyone looked so smart in their black uniforms trimmed with red and dark green. Katherine had been meticulous with recruitment, taking only those who passed her rigorous inspection. These were dedicated people, determined to make this work. It was such a boost to the economy of the area, and they needed it. He had to make this place a success, as much for them as for him and Corlene.

'I'm very happy to hear that, Sheila, and I agree completely. Right. Let's put this behind us and get this place in order. I know you'll all do your very best today. I've used all my contacts and considerable charm to get everyone who matters in terms of bringing business to us here today, so let's give them a real Castle Dysert–style welcome, OK?'

The crowd chuckled. Crisis averted, at least in the short term.

Despite a less-than-auspicious start, the day went wonderfully. Nico took groups on garden tours, while Conor entertained, wined and dined them inside. The staff were courteous without being stuffy, and even though the resort was at the uppermost end of the price scale, the tour people were made to feel anyone they sent to Castle Dysert would be made welcome.

Conor had bussed them all from wherever they came from to enjoy the hospitality, so the day really went with a swing. As he took groups around, showing them bedrooms and the spa, as well as the library and the drawing room, one lady in a group asked about the children's facilities. There was a kids' pool with slides in the leisure centre as well as an all-weather play area outside that Conor pointed out, but she persisted. 'It says in the brochure about an indoor playroom?'

'That's something we're working on this week.' He smoothed over it and went on. 'As well as the facilities, we'll be offering a babysitting service by fully vetted and qualified childcare professionals, so it's really an ideal family holiday resort as much as for couples and groups. Going forward, we'll be getting some horses as well. At the moment, the stables are the kind of nerve centre of the maintenance teams, but once everything is totally finished, we'll be adding a few horses, so that will be an option for guests as well.'

He was busy for the rest of the afternoon, talking to old friends and colleagues and meeting new people, and he was exhausted by the time the last bus pulled away down the driveway. He couldn't wait to get home to Ana. It felt like this morning might not have been real, and he wanted to make sure everything was still all right. She'd texted him a few times during the day, just photos of the boys or a smiley face and a kiss, but each one was like winning the lotto. He took his phone out once he was back in the office.

Hopefully getting out of here soon. Can't wait to see you. xxx

Katherine came into the office. 'Conor, you handled that nonsense well this morning. Now, I've been thinking. You've been run off your feet these past few weeks – how about you take a few days off until we are ready to open properly? I don't know when you'll be able to take holidays again, so it's a good time. Everything is more or less set to go, and Artur and I can manage anything else that comes up. There is nothing really more for you to do. Daniel is overseeing the finishing touches, Chef has the kitchen running like clockwork, housekeeping is all set to go, and everything is in shipshape. What do you say? I can hold the fort until Corlene gets back. And the new manager should surely be arriving soon.'

Conor had yet to break the news to Katherine who the new manager was. Because he'd had so many other issues to deal with, he'd more or less forgotten about the dreadful Carlos.

'Katherine, I should have told you before now, and I didn't because I was afraid that you wouldn't come and work here if I did, but the new manager is Carlos Manner. I didn't hire him, obviously, Corlene did, and due to a mix-up with emails, I didn't go to the interviews. He has a year-long contract, so we're just going to have to put up with him.'

He saw the look of horror on her face. 'But what I will do is explain to him that both he and you answer to me, not you to him. He won't be in any position of authority over you whatsoever. I'd rather he had nothing to do with the place, obviously, but that's the only solution I can come up with. What do you think?'

Katherine was inscrutable once the initial shock wore off. 'I worked alongside Mr Manner at the Dunshane, as you know, and I can manage him fine. Don't worry about it, Conor.'

He was relieved. If it was a choice between Carlos and Katherine, he'd take the imperious Miss O'Brien every day of the week, but this was better.

'So will you go, take Ana and the boys away before all the madness starts in earnest?'

Katherine must have had some inkling as to what was going on. There was no other reason she would suggest he take leave the week before the hotel opened.

He was about to refuse and then thought better of it. He could take Ana and the boys away tomorrow, and they could spend some time together, just taking it easy. It would be heaven.

'If you're sure, I think I will. Ana and I have had a rough few months, to be totally honest with you, but I think – I hope – it's all sorted out now. Some family time would be just what we need. And as you say, once the guests start arriving, there will be so much to do. We'll probably have hiccups, so I'll need to be here.'

'I'm glad things are better. You two are good together and your children need you both. She is a lovely girl, Anastasia, always was.'

Conor grinned. 'I'm a lucky man all right. Right so, I'll take off with the family for a few days, but I'll give you a call tomorrow or the next day.'

'No need, but I'm sure you will. I know you're heavily invested here, emotionally as much as financially, but try not to focus on this place or the people in it too much. Your family needs you too.'

Conor nodded. 'Thanks, Katherine. You're absolutely right. It was a bit tricky there for a while.'

Katherine noticed everything; it was why she was so invaluable all those years at the Dunshane. And what she said next confirmed what Conor already knew.

'Also, speaking of financially, I was just going through the wages bill with the accountant. We've so many new staff to get set up, and I noticed the cost of specialist gardening. Undoubtedly, it was necessary at the beginning when the place was such a wilderness, but now it's just maintenance surely. So perhaps we could employ someone local, maybe even keep one of the better local labourers? That would significantly reduce costs.'

Nothing in her demeanour suggested anything personal to Nico, but Conor knew better.

'Yes, we'll look at that when I get back.' He smiled his thanks, and their eyes held each other's for a moment.

CHAPTER 22

Dylan checked his phone for messages the moment he woke. There was one from Laoise, sent at 4:12 a.m. She was having a great time in London obviously, and he wished he'd gone with her. Everything here was just so crazy and confusing.

He had done as Conor suggested and contacted his dad, or the guy claiming to be his dad, and said he needed some time to think. The man messaged back right away, and Dylan read the message again, for the millionth time it seemed.

I totally understand, Dylan. This must be such a crazy thing to happen. I'll back off, of course, but I will ask you one thing – just give me a hearing, just one. I know your mom and your grandma want what's best for you, but they hate me. I had a bit of a reputation when I was young, and I'm not saying some of it wasn't deserved, but you know how small towns are. People make decisions about you and that's it. Anyway, because of that, they'll never get behind you and me meeting, and I want just one chance to give you my side of the story. But whenever you're ready, Son. It's totally up to you. Love, Dad

Dylan was staying at Castle Dysert until Laoise got back. Conor had suggested it, and he had nothing better to do anyway.

He could go home, back to his and Laoise's apartment attached to her parents' place, but he wanted to stay around in case Corlene showed up.

He called Diarmuid and Siobhan just to let them know where he was. He loved living near them, and it was nice that they worried. The best of it was Diarmuid was just next door, so if Dylan was having trouble with a tune or his reeds weren't singing out properly, he could just call in and help was there. Once or twice they thought about moving further away – Laoise sometimes thought it was a bit lame to be living so close to her parents at her age – but they always immediately dismissed the idea; they loved it where they were. They had all the freedom and independence they wanted but with the backup of home comforts. Especially because he'd never really had a stable home, he would be happy to stay with Diarmuid and Siobhan forever.

Still nothing from Corlene. She'd texted Conor but not her own son. That was so typical of her, he fumed. Just when things were on a better footing with them, she did this. His entire childhood and teenage years were a time of cringing shame as she got them into the most awful situations. He'd lost count of the number of times they were evicted, him having to stuff what he could of his belongings into trash bags under the beady eye of some landlord that hadn't been paid for months, or marched out of a store in front of everyone for shoplifting because Corlene made him do it. He was always the new kid, the one with no lunch money or proper books. He was put into emergency foster care every time Corlene was questioned by the cops, never for big things but usually petty fraud, stuff like that. She always got him back, even when sometimes he wished she wouldn't. Then every few months, they'd find themselves staying with some guy. Some of them were OK, but mostly they weren't. They'd take what they could get from Corlene and then they'd kick them out again. Same old story every time and still she never learned. He'd wished so hard she could just get a job, get an apartment, cook a meal like a normal mother. But it never happened. She was always on the brink of the next big thing, promising him repeatedly that their worries were over, that from now on it would be perfect. But it never was.

When he was sixteen, she announced they were going on a bus

tour of Ireland, and he remembered the horror he felt. First, they couldn't make rent, so how the hell were they going to pay for that? And anyway, she wasn't going there for a vacation; she was hunting again. The last guy gave her some money to go quietly, so she used that to pay for the trip.

She was convinced she would meet someone, a new husband who was loaded and old and about to die, and she'd charm him and they'd be in clover forevermore. Dylan was a goth in those days; it was easier when you went to a new school if you looked like a total weirdo rather than just poor. He had one pair of jeans, ripped to shreds, and he'd bought a pair of oxblood sixteen-hole Doc Martens boots from a thrift store with money his grandma had given him for his birthday. He read that you could use egg white to make your hair spike up, so he shaved one side and made huge spikes on the other, and he wore white make-up and black eyeliner to complete the look. He wanted to exude 'leave me alone', and it mostly worked.

He would never forget the feeling as he followed Conor and a bunch of really ancient people out to the bus that first day in Ireland. One of them was Bert, who ended up being the one who saved Corlene – and him. That whole tour was just insane, with a big Irish American cop falling for a woman who looked like a scarecrow until Corlene got her hands on her and turned her into a normal-looking old lady. That's where Corlene got the idea for the business. The lady, Cynthia, couldn't get it together to get with this guy, a big fat cop who at the time Dylan thought was about a hundred, so Corlene fixed her up but also showed her how to get him or something. Dylan was still a bit hazy on the details, and he was happy that way. The idea that Corlene was making a ton of money now as a kind of life coach was a joke, but she was doing it.

But he had to thank her, because if she hadn't come to Ireland, he would never have heard Diarmuid play the pipes in that church, never met Laoise, never have the dream life he did.

His phone rang. Laoise.

'Hey, did I wake you? I got your text saying Corlene had been in touch, and I was so relieved. Otherwise I would have come home – you know that, right?'

'Of course I do. It seems like she's fine, though she still won't actually talk to me. But how come you're up? You texted at like four a.m.'

'Yeah, it was so class. Cathal got a call yesterday from this, like, massive promoter to say that some band had pulled out of a really brilliant festival last minute and so could Unprecedented Incompetence fill in. The fiddle player that broke his hand, Jamie – I'm filling in for him – is gutted even more now because I got this gig too. Cathal was totally, like, well, I'll have to check and get back to you, and we were all squealing with excitement. Anyway, we got paid a wad of cash and we played to, like, I dunno, 80,000 or something. It was amazing. So we went for a few drinks after and a kebab that was so yummy when I was eating it but I feel a bit sick now, but maybe that was the cider and tequila shots... I dunno. I was going to get my belly button pierced again later. I saw this cool thing – it looks like a huge sharp tooth going in one side and out the other. But now I'm feelin' kinda rough, I mightn't. Anyway, how are you?'

Laoise always spoke in a stream-of-consciousness way, and when Dylan first met her, it was all he could do to keep up. Being from Cork, she spoke faster than other Irish people anyway, and the way she just said whatever came into her head, and changed subjects without even a breath, took him ages to get used to.

Dylan wished with all his heart he was there with her. She sounded so buzzed.

'So where is she? I didn't ask straight out 'cause, like, I didn't want to be bringing it up. You're probably sick of talking about it.'

'Yeah. I can't believe it, though – she texted Conor and not me. And my father has been on again.'

'Did you tell Conor?' Laoise was suddenly very serious. 'About this guy claiming to be your dad?'

'Yeah.'

'And did he tell you what to do?'

'Not really. You know Conor – he kinda lets people make their own minds up. But even he's against me meeting him. He's totally, like, he's such bad news. And it's so annoying since he doesn't even know the guy. I was really surprised at Conor. He's not judgey at all usually, but Corlene probably told him a pack of lies to make herself look less of a disaster, and he believes her. I just need her to come home so she can explain it. Like, why did she tell me she didn't know who he was?'

'I dunno, babe, I really don't. But however crazy she was, she is so much better now, and she totally loves you. So, like, I don't think she'd keep your dad from you if he was OK, y'know? Like, is there something she's not telling you? Or that Conor knows? 'Cause he's pretty straight up and if there was something that she told him, well, maybe there's more to it than what we can see. But y'know what? We don't have a clue, and we'll just have to wait for Corlene to come back, I suppose. When will that be, do you think?'

'No idea. She didn't even call me, just texted Conor, who she was barely speaking to before she left, so that says a lot. I'm so mad at her I'd probably just yell at her if she called now anyway.'

'This is crap. I wish I was there now. Will I come back? I can get an earlier flight?'

'No, no, I'm fine. I'm here in the castle. It's really amazing now. I'm helping because Conor is going on vacation for a few days with Ana and the kids…'

'Oh, good! Is everything OK with them, do you think? Is that plonker Nico still sniffing around?'

Dylan smiled. For all her crazy, Laoise was as loyal as a dog. 'I haven't seen him, but Conor seemed in better form anyway, so I guess not. Conor suggested I just message my dad and put off meeting him until I speak to Corlene, so I did. My dad messaged back, saying he wants me to meet him just once to hear his side of the story, that Corlene and my grandma just have it in for him because he was a bit wild as a kid. Y'know, Laoise, I think I'm gonna do it. Like, if I wait until Corlene is here and Conor is back, they'll try to stop me, and I have a right to meet him and make up my own mind, right? I'm twenty-five, not five. It's not up to them.'

'I suppose so…' She didn't sound convinced. 'Look, why don't you just wait. You haven't seen this guy your whole life, so why not wait for another couple of weeks? Like, Corlene might have something she needs you to know. I don't know...'

'Well, if she did, she's had twenty-five years to tell me. No, Laoise, I'm going to tell him to come over here. If he wants to meet me that badly, he can come here.'

'OK...if you're sure. But once you open this can of worms, it might be hard to close it again, y'know?'

He loved hearing the concern for him in her voice. 'I love you, Paddy,' he said quietly.

'Me too, Yank.'

He chuckled. It was their code.

'Hey, I got a gorgeous new tune. I got it from a French fella who is doing sound for Cathal's band.'

Dylan felt his heart lurch. He trusted Laoise, but she was so gorgeous and talented and funny that any French fella with eyes would fall for her, and they were great at all the chatting-women-up kind of talk.

'He's an awful clown altogether, thinking he's God's gift to women when in fact he's short and skinny with a receding hairline. I told him I'd a boyfriend, and he still had a crack at me, the big eejit. Anyway, the tune is class. It's a kind of Breton march thing, but the turn is a slow air – it's going to sound brilliant. I can't wait to get home to play it for you. We can vamp it up with some electric fiddle behind the pipes for the march and then the harp for the air, maybe a bit of whistle. It's so cool.'

'I can't wait either. See you Saturday, but I'll give you a call later, OK?'

'Sure, babe. Talk later.'

Dylan stared at his phone. Larry had given him his cell in the first message; all he had to do was press 'call' and his life would be changed forever. Maybe Laoise was right, maybe he should wait, but he didn't want to hear all the opinions. It was his life, his choice. He found the message and pressed the number. He could hear his heart thumping as he waited for the call to connect.

'Hello?' a woman answered.

Maybe he had the wrong number. He didn't know what to say.

'Hello? This is Larry's phone. Is anyone there?' The accent was an Alabama one for sure.

'Er, yeah, can I speak to Larry, please?' His voice sounded odd to him.

'Larry,' she screeched, 'someone looking for ya.'

'Who is it?' a man's voice shouted from the distance.

'I dunno.' She sighed. 'Who's lookin' for him?'

'Um...Dylan Holbrooke.'

'Hang on,' she said to him, and then yelled again. 'It's some guy named Dylan...something.'

He heard the phone being moved and soon the man came on the line.

'Dylan, is that you?'

'Yeah, it's me.' He wished he had something else to say. Silence crackled on the line.

'Sorry about that. That was my...my friend there. I was just... Anyway, it's great to hear your voice.'

'Well, you said I should call, so I... Well, if you wanted to meet me, then I'm in Ireland. I live here now. But you know that...' Dylan wished he didn't sound so flustered.

'You want me to come over there?' Larry asked.

'Well, if you wanted to. You don't have to...' Dylan began. This was a terrible idea. He wished he'd never called.

'Sure, sure, I want to. Let me work it out, and I'll call you when it's done, OK? Listen, Dylan, does Corlene know you're in touch with me?'

'No, no...she doesn't.' He wasn't going to go into why.

'OK, cool. That's good...well, better, until we meet. Where should I fly into?'

'Shannon or Dublin, but I'm in Clare, near Shannon, and most of the US flights land there.'

'Cool. Shannon it is then. I'll let you know the details. I'll book it right now. Thanks for calling me, Dylan. I wasn't expecting you to.'

'Why not?' Dylan wanted to know.

'Um...I don't know. I guess I thought your mom would have said some stuff, and since she brought you up... I don't know... Anyway, I'm glad you called. So I hear she's doing OK these days? And you... Like I said in my text, you're really hitting the big time with that girl – Louise is it? I can't say her name...'

'L-A-O-I-S-E. It's pronounced "Lee-sha". It's an Irish name. She's my girlfriend.'

'Lucky you. She's gorgeous in a kind of punky way. I saw you guys are touring and making albums and all of that – wow, that's really something. I can't wait to hear all about it.'

Dylan felt a surge of pride. He had made something of himself despite his upbringing, and his dad was proud of him. 'I'll bring you a couple of CDs if you like. We usually just have our stuff for download, but we put some down on CDs as well for people not into –'

'Hey, you sayin' your old man is a bit of an old-timer? I can download. In fact, I have both of your albums on my phone already – I listen to them in the car. But I'd love some CDs for my mom, your grandma. She'd love to hear you play.'

It had never occurred to Dylan that not only would he gain a father if this all worked out but that he'd have other family too. The thought was exciting.

'OK, well, you let me know what flight you're on and I'll come to meet you.' He tried not to sound too enthusiastic.

'Sure will. Talk soon, Dylan. And thanks again for calling. It means a lot.'

He sounded so sincere and like such a nice guy. Dylan was sure his mother's reticence was just based on bitterness and she had poisoned Conor.

'Bye.' He hung up.

The idea that he might have a father of his own was beginning to sink in. The first part of his life, the bit before he came to Ireland, was a disaster, no doubt about that, but since coming to Ireland he'd had two father figures: Conor and Diarmuid. He looked up to both of them, and while he knew Conor was against him meeting his dad, he hadn't asked Diarmuid.

He thought about it, and he admitted to himself that the reason he didn't ask Laoise's dad for his opinion was he feared it would be the same as Conor's. Diarmuid would back Corlene. Even though they were totally opposite personalities, they liked each other immensely.

Well, it was done now, whichever way it would work out.

He got up and dressed. His pipes case sat beside his bed where he kept it. They were a set made by the Taylor brothers in Philadelphia around 1880. They had been Diarmuid's, but Diarmuid gave them to Dylan about two years ago. Up to then, he had been using a practice set, which were great and had really good sound out of them, but they were nothing like these – ebony chanter and drones, with brightly polished pewter keys, burnished leather bellows, worn shiny from years of playing, and the bag trimmed in dark green velvet with a gold braid. Sometimes he just gazed at them, hardly able to process that they were his. He would never forget the day Diarmuid brought him into his shed, where he had loads of bits of sets of pipes, pieces of leather cut to make bags and a lathe for turning wood. It was like a treasure trove for musicians. Laoise was banned completely because of what her father called her sticky-fingered approach; she'd take whistles and spare strings or anything she could lay her hands on. Diarmuid pretended to get cross with her, but she was a chip off the old block and he could never stay mad at her. Diarmuid had opened a pipes case – he had many sets – and showed him the Taylor set. Dylan had watched Diarmuid play them of course, but he'd never seen them up close.

'Can I take them out?' he'd asked.

'Go ahead.' Diarmuid had nodded.

Dylan recalled that moment of lifting the pipes out of the case. They were heavy, the pewter making them heavier than usual, and the workmanship was incredible.

'Try them.'

Dylan didn't need to be asked twice. As he sat down and tied the strap around his waist and the bellows to his arm, Diarmuid made tea.

He'd installed a wood-burning stove in his shed and also kept a secret stash of *stroopwafels,* Dutch biscuits he was addicted to but that Siobhan had banned because of his health. Every tune Dylan ever learned was while sitting in that shed, drinking tea and eating *stroopwafels.*

He'd placed the drones lovingly across his lap and held the chanter upright as he squeezed the bag to drive air through the pipes. They were perfectly in tune, which was unusual for pipes, but maybe Diarmuid had just been playing them. He started playing 'O'Donovan's March' as Diarmuid just watched and listened. He went straight from that into a set of reels and then to a polka. He felt like he was flying, like nothing on earth could hurt or touch him as his soul sang along with the music. For Dylan, Irish music was like air or food now; he needed it. And when he heard it, or better still played it himself, he could feel his inner reserves being replenished. This was what he was born to do; he was sure of it.

'That's good! You're after getting that polka right. 'Twas a while coming, but that's sounding good now.'

'I think it's the Taylor set making me sound better,' Dylan joked as he went to take them off and put them back.

'Well, you'd better have them so if that's the case.' Diarmuid smiled and sipped his tea.

'What?' Dylan was sure he'd misheard.

'They're yours. If you want them.' Diarmuid was on his third delicious biscuit; if Siobhan caught him, she'd strangle him, but he loved them.

'But I can't afford them…' Dylan was confused.

'I know you can't – nobody can actually, they are priceless – but you don't need to. They're a present. From me to you. Who else am I going to leave them to? The pup Laoise would only sell them and buy an electric harp or something equally ridiculous, Cathal isn't ever going to be a piper, and Eadaoin is a singer, so it's going to be you.'

'But…but they're your kids. I'm just…' Dylan felt his mouth go dry.

'You're my protégé. You may not be my son, and God knows my Laoise and you may not end up together at all as she'd drive you cracked, but I'd like to think of you as more than some "randomer" as my daughter is fond of saying. So I want you to have the Taylor set.'

Apart from the fact that they were worth more money than Dylan could ever dream of paying for a set of pipes, they were of huge sentimental value to Diarmuid. He had got them from his brother, who had got them from another piper and so on, so they went back through generations of fantastic pipers. To say they were his meant he was now part of that chain, and he'd played every single day to improve and develop his skills.

Dylan lifted the pipes out of their case, tied the strap around his waist and blew up the bellows to start playing. Nothing eased his troubled soul like piping. He just got lost in the music and was carried away into another place where nothing bothered him. The chanter sang out and the drones provided a lovely soothing anchor for the tune as it soared. He played all his favourites to warm up and then got stuck into a new tune. He played for an hour, trying to get to grips with the turn on a hornpipe that had been bothering him.

CHAPTER 23

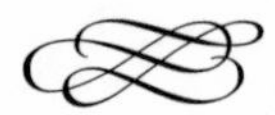

Conor sat across the table from Ana, just looking at her.

'What? Do I have something on my face?' She dabbed her chin with a napkin. They'd just shared a delicious chocolate brownie.

'No. I'm just thinking how lovely you are and how close we came to being in serious trouble just because we didn't talk to each other.'

They were travelling on the route called Ireland's Ancient East and loving it. He never took holidays in Ireland down through the years, mainly because he loved the sun and it only made a very occasional appearance in the Emerald Isle, but now that he had Ana and the boys to show the country to, it was different.

He loved seeing the twins' eyes light up at stories of kings and warriors, mighty battles and magical creatures. The old ruins of the monastic settlements, hives of education and science in the sixth and seventh centuries, sparked their imaginations, and the prehistorical sites, some over 6,000 years old and where the mysterious Stone Age people buried their dead using technology that was far beyond what should have been their capabilities, just left them asking more and more questions. They were at the age where they thought Conor knew everything and his opinion was gospel truth.

'Enjoy it. Soon they will be teenagers and nothing we can say will be clever, just stupid and embarrassing.' Ana grinned as they walked hand in hand over the Hill of Tara.

The boys tormented him for more information about how the Stone Age men got the glittery quartzite boulders from over a hundred miles away without a truck.

'Like, they're the size of a truck, the stones, so they couldn't lift them.' Artie was puzzled.

'Well, I bet Dad could, or if you had loads of fellas as strong as Dad, they could.' Joe was constantly impressed with his father's strength.

'I don't think so, Joe. Even Dad or loads of big men couldn't do it. They'd be too heavy.'

After letting them puzzle it out all afternoon, over dinner Conor finally interjected. 'Will I tell you how the fierce smart fellas above in the university think they did it?'

'How?' they both asked together.

'Well, they think they put down logs, and that they rolled the boulders along the logs, constantly taking logs from the back to the front, and moved them that way.' He watched their little faces as they processed what they'd just heard.

'Wow, they must all have been really clever to think of that.' Artie was fascinated.

'Well, you only needed one smart fella but loads of strong ones – they only need one to think of the idea,' said Joe, then he tucked into an ice cream sundae.

They stayed at a little hotel where they could have an adjoining room with the twins and had eaten out the previous night. The boys were great craic and the chatter was endless. When it was bedtime, Conor read them a story in English and Ana told them one out of her head in Ukrainian, and they drifted off to sleep.

Conor and Ana were alone then. It was like another honeymoon, chatting, laughing, eating and drinking and making love, though quietly this time in case they woke the boys. He never wanted it to end.

As they checked out on the second morning, he rang Katherine. He left Ana to settle the bill and walked outside where the boys were kicking a football on the lawn.

'Hi, Katherine. Everything OK?'

'Hello, Conor. How's the holiday going?'

'Great altogether. We're having a lovely time. I'll probably strike for home tomorrow, though. I'll be in either late tomorrow afternoon or Friday morning. Is Corlene back yet?'

'Yes, she's back in Ireland, but she's had some crisis with one of the vendors, so she's in Dublin dealing with that.'

'I suppose between yourself and Carlos, you have the place running like a mouse's heart?'

Katherine replied, 'I do, and Artur is invaluable, but Carlos Manner isn't here yet. But don't worry – Dylan is also a great help and we are all managing fine without you, no matter what you might think.'

'What? That plonker was supposed to have turned up by now. This is the start of it. I really wish I'd been there – I would not have hired him in a blue fit. Look, I'll leave now and –'

Katherine interrupted his rant. 'We are managing fine. Everything is perfectly well under control, and there is no need for you to go driving like a madman across the country thinking we can't survive. We are in perfect order, better in fact than when you're here because there aren't endless cups of coffee left everywhere.'

'There's no fear of me getting a swelled head with you around anyway, Miss O'Brien, and here was me thinking the whole place was falling asunder in my absence. Look, if you're sure. But do call if you need me – I'm only three hours away. I might just take the lads to Tayto Park – I have been promising them – and then we'll be back, OK?'

'Fine. Enjoy what's left of your break, Conor.'

'Right so, see you tomorrow.'

Conor wondered what could have happened. Carlos had never contacted him to say he wouldn't start on the appointed date, which annoyed him, but then Corlene had been the one to employ him. The idea of Conor being Carlos's boss probably didn't sit too well with the prissy little man. Conor wasn't looking forward to dealing with him, but he'd put him in his box soon enough if it was necessary. If he'd known Katherine would have had to manage alone, he would never have left her. At least she had Artur, and he was so reliable, but still.

'Everything OK?' Ana asked, slipping her arm around his waist.

He'd missed those little gestures so much when things were bad, and he swore he'd never get complacent about his relationship ever again. He lifted her chin and kissed her. 'Fine. But Katherine just told me Carlos Manner was a no-show, so I suppose we'd better think about getting back.' He shrugged.

'Oh, well, maybe we can do this again before the boys go back in school? Will we go back today?'

'No way. We're going to Tayto Park today. I promised them, so we're going. And I want to see you on a roller coaster,' he teased, knowing she hated heights.

'Not a chance. I will watch you, but nothing will make me go up to the sky like that, and falling...urgh! I don't understand why it is so good. But we also go to the Tayto Factory, so I will learn the secret of this famous Irish chip.'

'Crisps. In Ireland we call potato chips "crisps", and French fries are called "chips".'

Despite years of living in Ireland, some aspects of Hiberno-English still confused Ana.

'OK, let's start. What are they called in Ukrainian?' Conor asked as they gathered the twins and got in the car.

'*Kartoplyani chipsy*,' chorused his bilingual children.

He was determined to learn the language. He'd even got a notebook just like Artur's and was writing things down as he went along. Joe was the notebook expert, taking total credit for his grandfather's mastery of English, and was equally determined to work his magic in reverse on Conor.

'Say it after me, *kartoplyani chipsy*.' Joe spoke slowly and Conor repeated.

'See, Dad? It's easy.' Joe was delighted with himself. He turned to his mother and jabbered away in Ukrainian, obviously explaining how he'd have Conor fluent in no time.

'Absolutely simple, Joe. I can't believe it's taken me this long.' Conor's sarcasm was lost on his son.

They had a fabulous day riding the roller coaster and seeing all the animals. Every single thing that they saw, the boys made Conor say the word in Ukrainian and write it in his book. They were so zealous that Ana had to stop them in the end, and Conor shot her a grateful look. They were a team again and it felt great.

* * *

'I'll go and pick her up,' Conor announced as soon as Corlene called the front desk to say she was at the train station. They were a week from opening and he was amazed at how efficiently Katherine and Artur had everything running. The heating still wasn't working, but other than that it was all systems go. Daniel was supervising the hanging of the final sets of drapes in the suites, and the gardeners were hard at work, making sure not one weed showed itself. The castle was like something from a fairy tale.

Corlene still hadn't told him where she'd been, but he guessed she went back to Alabama. She'd visited Bert in Texas and Ellen in Boston sometimes, but she hadn't been a regular visitor back to the States over the years. She'd flown her mother over every summer and really showed her a great time, but they were the only three people she needed to see.

He grabbed his keys and called to Katherine that he was off. Carlos's delay had been explained in a curt email citing some crisis at the Dunshane; he'd had to postpone his arrival for another few days.

As he passed, he saw Katherine holding a tutorial on etiquette for the two young receptionists. She called him back and gestured he should speak to her at the other end of the long desk, away from their ears.

'There was a burst gas main at the Dunshane,' she said quietly. 'Two guests are hospitalised, and the entire place was evacuated.'

'Lord, that's awful! How did that happen?' Conor was shocked.

'They got rid of Jimmy Callaghan and the rest of the maintenance team and employed a company that are not on site but do an inspection once every month and fix anything they see broken. Believe me, they don't see much, which means the work is not thorough nor is it timely.'

'Old Tim McCarthy would never have allowed that, God be good to him. And poor old Jimmy, sure he was there forever. I can't imagine the Dunshane without him.'

'Yes, let go like the rest of us. Just like that. Apparently, guests had complained several times to reception about a smell of gas and it was either never investigated or it was and found to be not a problem. Either way, they're in serious trouble.'

Conor thought he detected a slight hint of triumph in her voice. She was probably allowed that, he thought, with the way she was treated. 'No wonder Carlos is delayed. He's probably got some hard questions to answer now,' he said.

'Indeed. Cutting corners does no good in the long run, but this French crowd, all they care about is bodies in the beds and the bottom line. Customer service, attention to detail, pride in the establishment are all alien concepts.' She paused, and he wondered what she wanted to say.

'Conor, I want to say thank you for thinking of me for this position. I'm really happy here, and I know if it wasn't for you, I probably wouldn't even have got an interview.'

Conor felt a wave of affection for her. When he lived full time on the tour circuit, she kept his post and got his shirts laundered and pressed, and despite her frosty exterior, he knew she regarded him as a friend.

'You were the only one who could do it, Katherine. 'Tis I should be thanking you. If it wasn't for you, I'd probably have cracked up by now. Corlene has been missing on and off for weeks, and without you and Artur, I couldn't have managed at all. And I would never have managed to go away with Ana and the boys. You're such an asset to this place. Now, I need to go to collect Corlene, but Ana and I were wondering if you'd like to come to our house for a bite of supper on Friday after work? You could meet our boys and we could have a proper chat about the old days.'

Conor watched her face melt a little. She used to take care of her elderly mother, but she'd died last year, so he imagined Katherine lived a fairly lonely life.

'That would be lovely, thank you.'

'Great stuff. Sure you can come home with me – we'll both knock off together.'

'I'll really look forward to that.'

And Conor knew she would.

CHAPTER 24

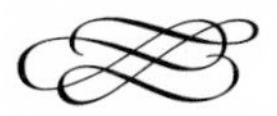

Conor honked his horn and Corlene waved, teetering down the footpath with a gigantic suitcase and wearing totally unsuitable boots with a platform heel that made her about six inches taller than she actually was.

He got out and put her bag in the boot. Neither of them knew what to do next. They normally greeted with a hug and a kiss, but since the last time they met, they'd not had a normal conversation.

'Hi. Nice of you to come back,' he joked, his default position.

'I had more important things to do.' She got into the car.

Nothing more was said, and the silence was deafening. He drove out of town but pulled into a picnic area overlooking a huge meadow.

'Corlene, I'm sorry for the way I behaved, what I said to you that day. I was totally out of line and I apologise. You were just looking out for me – I know that. And I was wrong to lash out at you.' He stayed looking ahead, not sure how she was taking his apology but too apprehensive to look.

'Forget it, Conor. It doesn't matter. I should have minded my own business. I had no right –'

'Of course you had the right. You were, and I hope you still are, my friend, and you were trying to get me to see what I needed to see.

That's what friends do. Things were bad between Ana and me, and as I said in the text, I was shooting the messenger. You were right. Ana and Nico were spending a lot of time together and she didn't tell me about it, so there was something going on. For her, it was just a friendship, but he wanted more, I think. We've talked it out, and everything is OK again. But I shouldn't have taken my frustration at the problems in my marriage out on you. It was wrong and I'm sorry. And saying what I did about Dylan, that was wrong too. Your past is not my business, and anyway, you and he are close now. I was just lashing out.'

'Apology accepted. And as for Dylan, well, he's really mad at me. I've tried to talk to him, but he says he only wants to talk about his father and I just… I can't. I know he's built him up in his head to be this great guy, but he isn't, Conor. He really isn't.' Her voice broke.

'Dylan needs to hear the truth, Corlene. And he has to hear it from you.' Conor spoke quietly.

'I don't know if I can…'

'They've made contact. I tried to get Dylan to wait, to hold off on anything until he spoke to you, but he was determined. You have to talk to him before he allows this man into his – and your – life again.'

Corlene digested this devastating bit of news. 'Where is he?' Her voice sounded strangled.

'At the hotel. Will we just go there? I'll stay with you when you tell him if you want me to, or I can leave you two alone?'

'I need you there.' Her voice was filled with dread. 'We both do.'

Conor drove to the castle, parked the car and led Corlene to his office without bumping into anyone. He picked up the phone on his desk and called through to Katherine. 'Can you get someone to find Dylan for me, please, Katherine, and tell him I need to see him in my office right away.'

'Of course.'

Conor made Corlene some coffee, and they sat in silence. After what seemed like an eternity, but was in fact only a few minutes, Dylan arrived.

'Corlene. You decided to show up. Great.' He was wary. The

resentment and anger at her refusal to tell him the truth, as well as her disappearing act, had done nothing to soften his attitude towards her.

She turned, and he appeared shocked to see her face, so drawn and serious.

'What? Is Grandma OK?' Panic crossed his face, and Conor thought he looked so young, so vulnerable.

'She's fine,' Corlene managed.

'So what? What's happened?' Dylan was worried now.

'Dylan, I need to talk to you, tell you something, and it's really hard. I need you just to listen, OK? When I'm finished, I promise I'll answer any questions you have as truthfully as I can.'

Conor was standing by the window and Dylan caught his eye. Conor gave him a little nod, and Dylan took a seat opposite his mother.

'I'm sorry I took off without a word, but I had to go back to Alabama because I needed proof, something to show you what kind of man your father is.'

Conor heard the tremor in Corlene's voice and wished there was some way he could help her, but this had to come from Corlene to Dylan.

'I told you all along I didn't know who he was, but that was a lie. I know exactly who he is and what he is. My sweet boy, I love you so much, and I've been such a terrible mother to you. I'm so sorry.' She took a breath and composed herself.

'Larry Costello is your father, and he is also a rapist. The night you were conceived, we were all at a party. He came on to me and I rejected him fairly publicly. He was mad – nobody spoke to him like that. He had a huge ego. Anyway, I had to go pee, so I left the party. It was an outdoor thing, so I just went to go in the bushes. He followed me and raped me.'

Conor hated to see the raw pain on Corlene's face and the shock and horror on her son's. Dylan couldn't speak, so Corlene went on.

'Afterwards, he just left me there on the ground, my clothes all torn and everything, so I couldn't go back to the party. My friend came looking for me, and I got up and went home. My mama said I had to go to the police that night, so they'd have evidence, so I did, but it was a waste of time. The Costellos are all well connected, not just in our little town, but in Mobile and Montgomery too. They've got cops and big business people in the family, and I was just a white-trash girl from a trailer park off the interstate. They didn't want to take a statement or anything from me that night. My mama borrowed a neighbour's car to take me there, but they turned us away. We were about to go when a woman police officer walked in and called us back. She took the statement and told us that she would pass it on and he'd be questioned. But he never was, and the statement disappeared.'

Tears were now coursing down Dylan's cheeks, and his mother leaned over and wiped them.

'Mom, I...' Dylan hardly ever called Corlene 'Mom'; he was used to calling her Corlene. When he was a kid, she didn't want people to know she was a mother.

'It's OK, sweetheart. I'm OK and you're OK and we've survived. We've survived so much, you and me. But Larry Costello is a rapist, and mine is not the only statement to go missing. I've been researching, talking to people, others who heard about similar stories. But he's untouchable. The Costellos are wealthy and powerful, and it seems that if you are rich enough or well-connected enough, you can get away with anything. My friend Clarisse lived near me – she was with me the night it happened, and she was the one who brought me home, bleeding and whatnot. I needed to see her and to find that woman cop. Not for court evidence, but for you – I needed you to believe me.' Corlene sat there, staring right ahead, not crying, showing no emotion.

'Of course I believe you! You'd never make something like that up. You didn't have to go over there to get evidence...' Dylan was distraught.

'Thank you.' Corlene was sincere. 'But I do have it. Hard proof that he did this to me and at least two others, probably more. Two of his other victims actually spoke to me, and they said there are more. The local chief of police is his brother-in-law, and his daughter is married to the son of the county registrar.

'He is a monster. He's all charm and stuff on the surface, but underneath, he has a black heart. I don't want him in your life, and I don't want him near Laoise or Ana or any of us. He's really dangerous, Dylan.'

Dylan stood and went over to his mother. He pulled her to her feet and put his arms around her. Together, they stood there, clinging to each other, and Conor slipped quietly out of the room.

* * *

DYLAN CHECKED the flight number online about ten times. He was finally going to meet his father. Neither Corlene nor Conor knew, but Dylan needed to look at the man's face once in his life. He needed to tell him face-to-face that he knew what he was. Even if Larry Costello never faced prosecution for what he'd done, he would die knowing what the look of hatred on his son's face was like.

Every time Dylan thought about his mother, images of her as a teenager kept springing to his mind. His grandma had photos of her when she was fifteen and sixteen. It always struck him that she looked geeky if anything. He assumed the transition to trampy was later, but now when he remembered those photos, he saw her as an innocent girl just trying to live her life.

The past few days, he and Corlene had talked a lot – about Costello, her life, their lives together, all sorts of things – and he felt like he was actually getting to know her for the first time.

He spoke to his grandma on the phone, who was relieved that Corlene had finally told him the truth; afterwards, he'd cried in Laoise's arms. It used to frustrate him that his grandmother never condemned her daughter's behaviour when she should have, but now he knew why.

Whenever he managed to stay at a school for any length of time, his grandma would remind him how Corlene always helped him with his homework. In her house, she kept medals Corlene won for spelling bees and stuff like that when she was a kid, but none of that used to fit with the image of her he'd held all his life. Learning what he did, and remembering what she did to keep him, moved him in a way he couldn't express. She could have easily had an abortion – most other girls in her position wouldn't have hesitated – but she kept him. And even though his life was chaotic and downright bad a lot of the time, he never doubted that she loved him. Even when he'd go into care, she would move mountains to get him back. She should hate him every time she looked at him – he'd seen photos on Facebook and knew he looked like his father – but she didn't. He knew she didn't and that she never would.

The flight landed on time, and the people started to filter out, all laden down with luggage. Frustratingly, big family reunions were happening in front of him in the arrivals area and his view of the doors was obscured. He went to the side barrier and waited.

Eventually, a man walked through, carrying only a duffel bag. He was medium height and build, with dark hair and blue eyes. He wore a cream Ralph Lauren polo shirt and blue jeans and looked like the most average person imaginable. Dylan wondered if it was him.

Dylan moved around to the access area and stood there, now that the loud family had shuffled off to the car park.

'Dylan?' The man stood in front of him, looking nervous.

'Yeah, you must be Larry.' Dylan felt more confident than he had on the phone, something to do with this man being on Irish soil, like he was in Dylan's patch or something.

Laoise hadn't come to the airport – Dylan wanted to meet his father on his own – but he'd promised to call as soon as he could. She knew what he was going to do and backed him a hundred percent. He knew she'd be worried, and he loved her for it.

'How was the flight?' Dylan asked, keeping the conversation light as they headed towards the exit.

'Great. Man, it really is green, and how cute is this airport? Through security, immigration, everything, in ten minutes. It's so hot in Alabama, everything is movin' slow as molasses right now. It's sure nice to feel the fresh air.'

Dylan led Costello to his and Laoise's van. They'd bought it last year with gig money, and it meant they could carry their own sound system, which they'd also bought. He loved it.

'Nobody here drive a pickup?' Costello asked as he gazed around the car park.

'Nope, not really. You'd see an odd one, but not much. It rains too much. Everything would get wet.' Dylan smiled.

'Y'all soundin' a bit Irish there, boy,' Costello joked. 'Ain't nothing left of Alabama in you, that's for sure.'

'I suppose I am. I've lived here since I was sixteen, and my girlfriend's Irish, and all her family obviously, so everyone I mix with except for Corlene is Irish.'

'And how is Corlene doing?' Costello seemed nonchalant.

'Great, she's just great. She's got a lot of good people around her, looking out for her, y'know?' Dylan smiled again, taking any double meaning out of his words.

'Good. I'm glad to hear things worked out for her. So tell me about you, Dylan. I want to know everything.'

'Well, I'm really happy. Life is good.' He was non-committal and amazed himself at the confidence he felt.

He put the van in gear and drove out of the airport. Within moments, they were in open countryside. Dylan glanced sideways, sizing his father up again. It was going to be fine.

Costello prattled on about the countryside and himself, how successful he was, how wealthy, and Dylan let it wash over him. The guy was a total jerk without ever being a criminal.

As they drove down a lonely country road, Dylan pulled into a clearing where the forestry commission accessed the hundreds of acres of farmed forest. The ground was rutted from the heavy tyres of tractors and trucks, but being a bank holiday, there was nobody about.

'I want to show you something.' Dylan jumped out of the van and noted the look of confusion pass his father's face.

Still, he got out and followed Dylan into the woods a little way. Without warning, Dylan swung and cracked Costello on the jaw, sending him flying backwards onto the ground. His face was actually comical, so shocked was he to find himself on his ass in the mud. Dylan was very strong from playing the pipes for so long – they were such a physically demanding instrument – and from the kick-boxing he did to stay fit. He knew his own strength and knew Costello wasn't going to beat him.

'What the…?' The other man tried to get up, but Dylan kicked him in the kidneys as he did so, sending him sprawling on his front.

By now, he was filthy and fuming. 'You little shi –' He managed to stumble to his feet.

Dylan waited, then punched him again, this time in the stomach, and as he bent double, Dylan landed another punch to the man's face. Costello fell backwards and banged his head on the concrete kerb but was still conscious.

Dylan bent down beside him as he groaned and tried to get up, and spoke quietly. 'I've never hit anyone in my life. I was brought up better than that. But you deserve it. I know what you are, and I know what you did to my mother, and if I ever see your miserable face again, I will make sure that I am the last person you ever see. Is that clear? So get the hell out of our country. You have no business here. There's nothing here for you. Stay away from me and from my mother. I never, ever want to hear from you again. You are dead to me. Go back to Alabama and get the hell away from me.'

Dylan left him there. He figured Costello would stagger out onto the road eventually and someone would pick him up. He drove off, sure he'd never set eyes on his father again.

CHAPTER 25

'That talking to you gave the staff was a short-lived thing, I'm afraid, Conor.' Katherine entered his office, having knocked first. 'Apparently, they're still hearing noises, and the top floor is freezing. I went up there myself to see what all the fuss was about, and I have to tell you, they're not imagining it. We've had several plumbers, the engineers, and even Artur take the whole system apart and put it back together again, but there is nothing wrong – well, nothing they can see anyway. I don't know what's going to happen. We have guests arriving for the weekend for those suites, and at the moment they are like the north face of the Eiger. What are we going to do?'

For a split second, Conor considered telling her about his experiences in the attic, but he thought better of it. She'd probably think he was off his head for one thing, and secondly, he just had a feeling that he needed to solve this himself, though how was a total mystery. He was a person who kept his own counsel all his life, only revealing what he wanted to, and in this case, Katherine could not help so it was best kept to himself.

'I've no idea. Artur explained the whole thing to me last night, with Joe's help, and it seems there is nothing to be done. The flipping radiators just won't come on. I don't know. Look, can we rearrange the people we have booked in and confine them to the first two floors? I know they booked suites, but it's just not going to be possible, and if word gets out that we are totally booked, then that's good, isn't it?'

'And I suppose I get the job of contacting all these people and telling them that the suite they wanted is no longer available and they'll have to settle for a plain old room instead?' She gave him a wry smile.

'You suppose right. However, Carlos is coming today, so you could leave it to him if you wanted?' Conor knew she'd never allow Carlos to usurp her like that.

'No, of course not. I'll take care of it right away. I'll say that it's an unforeseen hitch with the conservation people, that something needs to be restored. At least that way they won't think the place is a death trap. God alone knows what Carlos Manner would say. He'd no doubt make a bad situation worse.'

Conor sighed as she left. There was definitely going to be a power struggle between Carlos and Katherine, one that Conor would be expected to adjudicate. Well, he made no bones about it – his money was on Katherine every time. But Corlene had had such a rough time that he didn't want to add to her problems. And if Carlos Manner wasn't being treated as he would deem appropriate to someone of his elevated status, he would become a very big problem for Corlene. After all, it was she who had hired him.

Wearily, Conor removed the huge key from his desk drawer. He'd have to go back up there. Daniel was supposed to have had everything shipped out of there two days ago, and Conor wanted to check.

He went upstairs, greeting many of the new faces who'd recently been hired. The place looked spectacular, to be fair to Daniel. Conor had stayed in hotels for most of his adult life and knew there was not one in Ireland to rival Castle Dysert. His feet sank into the sumptuous carpet as he walked down the corridors. The bedroom doors were open; Katherine was going on an inspection tour later, and woe betide the housekeeping staff if everything didn't pass muster with her. The Atlantic Ocean glittered in the distance, and the antique glass that

Daniel had insisted on gave the view from the top floor almost a dreamlike quality. The cold was obvious, nobody was imagining it, and it was not due to lack of heating. It was an unusually warm autumn, the heating wasn't even on, and the other parts of the castle were a perfect temperature.

He put the old-fashioned key into the lock and the door opened easily. He dipped his head to get in through the small door, and once he entered, he just stood, dumbfounded. The whole playroom was exactly as it was the first day he and Ana went in there.

Whatever about Daniel – he knew that he'd boxed everything up himself. The empty boxes had been piled against the wall and he'd filled them. He was certain of it. And yet here was everything back where it was originally, the glassy-eyed teddies on the couch, the colouring pencils out on the table, the books on the shelf.

The hair on the back of Conor's neck stood up. He just wanted to leave, to get out of the building and never return. As he turned, the little train came around the track again, making the same click-clack sound and then blowing the little steam whistle.

He stood transfixed as the train went round and round on the track. Did he imagine it or had the room suddenly got even colder? Conor's heart thumped in his chest and his mouth felt dry. He closed the door and forced himself to speak quietly, his voice shaky. 'Grenville, is that you? Have you been making your train go around the track? You shouldn't be here, Grenville. Your mammy and daddy aren't here any more, and neither are Samuel or the others. This place is going to have lots of people here very soon, and you need to go and be with your family. I have two little boys at home, one called Joe and the other is Artie, and they are just a little bit older than you. They would be very scared if they got left somewhere on their own, so this must be very frightening for you. But your parents and your brother and sisters aren't coming back here, so if you stay here, you'll be all on your own.'

He felt ridiculous, and if anyone heard him, they'd cart him off to a psychiatrist. But there was something happening in that room, and if he was in any doubt before, he wasn't now.

He had nothing more to say and the train had stopped on the little track, so Conor turned and opened the door. He sighed with relief when it opened – the idea that it might be locked had crossed his mind. He went down the steps into the third-floor corridor once more. He wasn't sure what to do, but he knew he had to do something.

Several people tried to grab his attention as he walked quickly through the castle, everyone with a pressing query or something to say, but he managed to sidestep them. He passed Dylan as he went down the front steps.

'Hi, Conor, is Corlene here? I really need to talk to her –' Dylan began.

'Yep, she's in the dining room I think,' he called back over his shoulder as he jogged to the car.

He thought Eddie might have some idea.

Father Eddie Shanahan was the parish priest in Ennis, and while Conor wasn't a practising Catholic and was fairly ambivalent about the whole church thing in general, he liked Eddie on a personal level and he'd often played a round of golf or had an odd pint with him.

Eddie had even married him and Ana, as she was a devout Catholic. He'd made the ceremony really nice and personal, and it had meant a lot to both of them. Eddie even went to the trouble of finding a priest in Dublin who spoke Ukrainian and who came to Ennis and concelebrated so that Ana's parents and her sister could understand.

Conor pulled up outside the parochial house just as Eddie was coming home after a funeral. Conor knew this was a good time to catch him. He'd never changed in all the years Conor had known him. He was a small man with a round belly and a shock of white hair. He wore his black garb with the priest's collar, but over it today he had a ragged old grey cardigan. The children of the parish called him Father Santie, as when he called to the primary schools, he always brought sweets. Joe and Artie loved it when he called to their classroom, and he always knew what matches they'd won or what they were learning about. Joe especially loved it because occasionally Eddie would pretend to cajole the teacher into giving the children a break from homework.

Eddie stopped at the gate as Conor got out of his car. 'Ah, Conor, how are you? Come here to me now. Aren't you doing great things above in Castle Dysert, I hear, and you've the whole place working there...fair play to you. There's plenty of families out there now that are glad of the job.' Eddie led Conor up the short path to the front door and put his key in the lock. 'But what are you doing here? I thought you'd be up to your elbows. Sure 'tis tomorrow the big opening, isn't it?'

'It is, but I've a problem and I thought you might be able to help me or point me in the direction of someone who can.'

Eddie hung up his sweater and glanced at Conor. 'Is it a coffee problem or will it need something stronger?'

'Definitely a cup-of-coffee question. I even brought scones.' Conor held the paper bag from the bakery aloft.

'Well, that does sweeten the deal all right.' Eddie was delighted. 'Though don't let Doctor O'Reilly see them! I'm on a tablet for cholesterol, and he says, "Now, Eddie, this is not a licence for you to do wreck with the diet, do you hear me?"

'Righto, says I, but sure, since I'm taking the auld tablet, my cholesterol is 4.3 and I'm eating all round me. They leave us very few bodily pleasures in the priesthood, so we're all the last word when it comes to the sweets and cakes and the like.'

Conor followed him down the hall and into the kitchen of the large square stone house, once shared by three priests in the parish and a housekeeper, but now Eddie was there alone. He was trying to manage the huge parish by himself as the priests just weren't there any more, or at least not in the numbers they were when Eddie and his classmates were ordained in the seventies. It was a lonely life, Conor always thought.

If he were in any job other than the priesthood, he'd be retired, but if anything, he was having to work harder. Conor judged him to be in his early seventies, but he was fit and sprightly despite his diet.

Eddie busied himself with the coffee and finding milk and mugs while Conor stood, gazing out the window.

'How's Ana and the lads?' Eddie asked.

He probably assumed it was marital problems Conor had, and a week or two ago, he'd have been right, but this was much more peculiar.

'Flying it. They're all enjoying being back at school, Ana is getting a bit of peace and quiet for a change.'

'And I see Mr and Mrs Petrenko are here too. They are really swelling the numbers at the early Mass,' Eddie joked.

Artur and Danika rose every single morning from the day they arrived and drove into town for seven o'clock Mass. They remarked to Conor how shocked they were at the almost empty church each day. He'd explained, through Ana, how Ireland had changed a lot and how there was a lot of controversy surrounding the Catholic Church, so fewer people were practising in the way that they had in years gone by.

'They never miss it. Artur is coming on great with the English, so he tells me he can understand most of the Mass now. Danika is still struggling, but our Joe is determined. He taught his *didus* – that's Ukrainian for granda – all by himself, so he's delighted with himself. Danika is his next victim. Not to mention me – he has me learning Ukrainian. He's like a terrier, that boy, once he gets an idea into his head. He has my heart broken but won't let up.' Conor chuckled.

'It's been great, though, because before the holidays he was struggling a bit in school. Artie, the other fella, is bright as a button, which makes it even harder for poor old Joe. Artie takes after his mother, brains to burn, but I think Joe is more like me. He's able to do it fine, but he just can't see the point in fractions or the planets or whatever.'

Conor put milk in his coffee, while Eddie split the freshly baked scones and then slathered them with butter and jam.

'Ah, sure now, Conor, you're no clown either. Maybe you weren't excited by the books, but there's few men I know could do what you do with such ease. Dealing with all those people and all their many issues, and yet you seem to solve it all effortlessly while entertaining them and educating them all at the same time. Sure, Declan was only saying the other day, how do you market what you have as a skill set? That's what they call it now, a skill set.'

Conor recalled Father Declan Sullivan, an Irish American who had come on a tour with him a few years ago. At the time he was a priest, but he left the religious life for a woman he loved and never looked back. Declan and Eddie had formed a close bond.

'I don't know about that, Eddie. Some days I feel I'm way out of my depth. But don't let on, will you?' Conor grinned and took a sip of his coffee. 'How is Declan anyway, and Lucia?' He remembered them so well. After Declan had left the priesthood and they'd moved to Italy to be with Lucia's mother.

'Doing great. Baby number two on the way now, so little Eduardo will have a brother or sister. He's a little dote. I was out there to visit them last month. He's just talking, and he tells everyone he's named after me.' Eddie sounded like a doting granddad, and Conor was so happy for him.

'Is he working?' Conor asked, then sipped his coffee.

'He is – in a vineyard, would you believe? Lucia's family are fairly well-to-do and they own a huge vineyard, so he's learning how to be a winemaker and he's loving it. His Italian is almost fluent – I suppose all that Latin he learned in the seminary came in useful – and they live in a little house on the estate. Lucia is due in about two months, I'd say, and she is blooming. You'd hardly recognise her. She's put on weight and looks just radiant.'

'I'm delighted for them. Give them our love when you're talking to them. He sent an email a while back asking us to come and visit, and sure we just might if we can get this hotel up and running smoothly.' Conor took a bite of the scone, which was melt-in-the-mouth delicious. He didn't usually go for sweet things – he saw too many of his driver colleagues become obese from all the free food on the tour circuit, so he was fairly disciplined – but Pat Mac's scones were legendary in Clare, so he couldn't resist.

'So what can I help you with?' Eddie was gentle but knew people often skirted around an issue rather than just coming out with it.

'Right. Well, this is going to sound mad right, but... First off, do you know the story of Castle Dysert? What happened there back in the 20s?' Conor needed Eddie to see where he was going with this.

'Well, I know it was burned, like most of the big houses, and that one of the children died in the fire, but that's about all.'

'Right. Well, the child that died was called Grenville King, and he was only four. Apparently, the father, Grenville senior, was warned but he ignored it, and the IRA set the place alight anyway. They got everyone out except this little boy who was a poor sleeper and often went into the playroom at night when he couldn't sleep.' Conor went on to explain what Martin O'Donoghue had told him about how Samuel King, Grenville's twin, came back and refurbished the whole place and then committed suicide.

'God, those were desperate times all right, and that poor man. Now that you say it, I think I did hear something. But yerra, old pishogues about ghosts and the like, I don't be listening to it much.'

'Well' – Conor exhaled – 'the place is haunted.'

One look at Conor's face told Eddie he wasn't winding him up. 'You're not serious, are you? What makes you think that?'

Conor explained about the different things that had happened since the first day he broke into the house, and when he was finished, both men sat in silence.

Eventually, Eddie spoke. 'You do know that if this was anyone else in Ennis telling me this, I'd tell him to go away and get his head read, don't you?' There was no hint of a joke in his voice. 'I know we in the Church are big on spiritual happenings and miracles and all the rest of it, but... I don't know what to say to you, Conor. I mean, if you say it's happening, I believe you. You're one of the most level-headed men I know. But God above, this is hard to make sense of.'

'You're telling me?' Conor shook his head. It felt good to get it off his chest anyway, even if he did sound like he was a few sandwiches short of a picnic.

'Right,' Eddie said. 'I'm going to ask you something, and don't think I'm not believing you, but do you think that if you had never met Martin and you never heard the story of the Kings that you'd be hearing these things now? I'm only asking because, well, Martin is a clever man and a well-travelled one and all of that, but he's been listening to his mother all his life and she's as cracked as the crows. I mean, she's a witch or something, allegedly, and according to her, she and I are on different sides of a war despite me never putting in or out on the woman. I mean, every time I go to visit St Enda's – you know, to visit the old folks, and that's a laugh in itself as 'tis I should be in there with them, 'cause half of them are better than I am, but how and ever – she roars and screams that I'm the devil and all sorts. And they tell me she doesn't have dementia or Alzheimer's or anything – apparently, she's totally sane! Well, I beg to differ.'

Conor was stunned. He'd assumed Martin's mother was dead. 'I know what you must be thinking, but I'm telling you, Eddie, I'm not imagining it.' He was sure.

'So where does that leave us? I know some people, long ago especially, if they thought there was something going on in a building, they'd have a Mass said in the room. And I will if you want me to, but…' Eddie looked doubtful.

'Did you ever hear of that working?' Conor was interested in general terms; he had no intention of having a Mass said in the playroom.

'Well, there was a farmer out near Kilrush with a bad hip, and he was in agony from driving his cattle about two miles longer than he needed to morning and evening. There was an old broken-down bit of a cottage on his land, and the cows would not pass it. No matter what enticement he offered nor what flaking and beating he gave them with a stick from behind, nothing would get the herd past the house. Now they say that someone was murdered there or something, donkey's years ago, I don't know. But he asked me to come out and say a few prayers in the house, so to keep him happy, I did it. And I said the prayers of the last rites, and sure enough, the next day the herd trotted past, not a bother on them. But sure I don't know.'

'I know, but who's to say? I heard all that stuff myself over the years, and while I wouldn't say there was nothing to it, I took most of it with a pinch of salt. Listen, Eddie, we'll keep the prayers in the room as a reserve. I'll try anything. But I think I'm going to visit Mrs O'Donoghue first. She's the only one who knew the Kings – not Grenville and that generation, but Samuel and his wife. It's worth a shot, isn't it?' Conor knew he was probably grasping at straws.

Eddie sighed and nodded. 'Well, tread carefully, my friend, and whatever you do, don't say you know me or she'll batter you with this auld gnarly whitethorn stick she keeps under the covers. Good luck with it anyway.'

CHAPTER 26

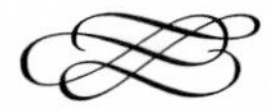

Conor arrived back to the hotel to find reception deserted. He walked towards the ballroom and realised the entire staff were assembled there, being addressed by a voice he recognised. As he entered through the large double doors at the back, he was treated to the sight of none other than Carlos Manner. He hadn't changed a bit: the immaculate suit, sparkling-white shirt, thin-featured face with the long nose and thinning brown hair oiled and combed straight back from his head. He was standing on the band platform, a lectern in front of him.

Daniel had picked the lectern up at an auction and Conor thought he was mad, but he rightly pointed out the castle would host conferences and that people liked to have something to stand behind when they spoke. How Carlos found it and pressed it into commission so quickly was a testament to how important he thought he was.

He was explaining to everyone in his clipped South African accent what he expected of them and was so superior and condescending in the way he spoke to them that Conor wanted to go up and catch him by the ear and throw him out. He was a supercilious twit who specialised in making his staff miserable. Conor kicked himself mentally; if he'd not been so stubborn and pig-headed with Corlene and actually gone to Dublin to interview the candidates, he could have vetoed Manner right away. But the hotel was opening tomorrow and they needed a manager badly.

Corlene wasn't there but Katherine was, and Conor knew by her face she was none too pleased with this new approach. Conor made his way quietly up the side of the room towards the area where Manner was holding court. Katherine saw him and rolled her eyes.

Conor needed to make his presence felt. The staff had seen him come in, and they were looking to him to determine if this eejit was now calling the shots. He walked right onto the band platform, interrupting the new manager mid-flow.

'Ah, thanks, Carlos, for that. I see you've introduced yourself to everyone. They've all been playing a blinder these last few weeks, so I'm sure they'll all be happy to show you the ropes. You'll be part of the team here at Castle Dysert in no time.'

Carlos gazed at Conor with barely concealed contempt. The man had never forgiven Conor for going above his head at the Dunshane and getting his own way regarding the holidays Ana was due.

Conor extended his hand. After a split-second delay, Carlos took it.

'I think, given my role, it would be more appropriate for you and the rest of the staff to address me as Mr Manner.' He spoke quietly.

'Oh, we don't stand on ceremony here at Castle Dysert, Carlos. It's all first names here. Now, we'll let everyone get back to their business, I think, and you and I will have a chat in my office.'

Conor turned to the hundred or so staff, all looking very smart in their uniforms, who were watching the exchange between Conor and Carlos avidly. 'Now, folks, I think we'd all better get back to work. We've got a very busy day tomorrow. Lots of guests and the who's who of Ireland, as well as all the press, here tomorrow night for the big party. There's a lot to organise, but I just know you'll do it beautifully. I have every faith in Team Castle Dysert.' He winked to lighten the heavy threats that had been issued by Manner.

The crowd dispersed but Conor asked Carlos and Katherine to wait. Once the room was cleared, Carlos spoke. 'I really think –'

'We'll get to what you really think in a few minutes.' Conor's smile never reached his eyes. 'But first, I know you and Miss O'Brien here are old acquaintances. Katherine is working here now in a managerial capacity, the same as yourself, so I hope you will get along. As you know from the Dunshane, she is the most efficient front-of-house person in the business, so between her skills and yours, I see no reason this hotel wouldn't run like clockwork. Now, let's all go and have a coffee in my office, and we can go over the plan for tomorrow.'

Katherine and Carlos followed him down the tiled corridor to his office. They were barely inside when Carlos started, as Conor knew he would. Katherine sat serenely like the cat who got the cream.

'Very well, Conor. I was under the impression that the position was that of hotel manager? That is certainly the conversation I had with Miss Holbrooke.' Carlos was getting hot under the collar at the prospect of sharing power with Katherine.

'*Corlene*' – Conor made a point of emphasising her first name – 'appointed you as a manager, and that is what you are. I'm not seeing the problem, Carlos.'

'Well, the problem is, I did not anticipate being in conjunction with…' – he checked himself – 'with anyone else.'

'Well, Carlos, we all work for someone, right? And we are all part of the team. You know better than most what it takes to run a hotel – a lot of people pulling in the same direction. We all have to work with others, take other people's opinions into consideration. So we are all here as a team working together to make this place a success. Katherine is a vital part of this team, and I hope you will be too.' Conor deliberately kept his tone light but hoped Carlos knew he was deadly serious. He needed to get this man in check at the beginning.

Carlos stood there seething.

'Is working for me a problem for you?' Conor asked eventually.

'No…Conor. No, of course not.' Carlos was getting flustered now; this was not how he envisaged his first day, Conor felt sure. Normally, Conor would go to someone's rescue who was that uncomfortable, but he remembered the way this jumped-up twerp had treated Ana so just sat back and watched him squirm.

'So Katherine is the problem?' Conor was like a vulture circling his prey, and he knew Carlos could feel his plum job slipping between his fingers.

'No, no. It's no problem at all for me to work with Miss O'Brien. We've known each other for many years now, so no. Everything will be satisfactory…' Carlos's normally pale complexion was turning puce under Conor's searching stare.

Conor never broke eye contact. 'Great.' There was no enthusiasm in his voice. 'Let's get to work. Miss O'Brien will brief you on what needs to be done. She's the only one in this whole place who knows what's going on in every single department.'

Katherine stood and spoke for the first time. 'Mr Manner, I have admired some aspects of your managerial skills in the past, so I hope we can work together to make this a resounding success. This is a wonderful opportunity for both of us, and there is security and real job satisfaction on offer here if we can work amicably together. So I suggest we make every effort, both of us, to embrace this new venture with enthusiasm and positivity.'

Carlos knew when he was beaten. 'Yes, I hope so too, Miss O'Brien. Now let's get to work, shall we?'

They were only gone a moment when Corlene appeared.

'Well, if it isn't the Scarlet Pimpernel. Back here to do a bit of work, I hope?' Conor gave her a hug to show he wasn't serious.

'Absolutely. And I'm sorry for checking out. You did an amazing job of keeping everything on track. I really appreciate it.' Corlene was different these days, less brash.

'No bother. Did you and Dylan sort everything out?'

'Yes. He spoke to Costello and told him not to come, that he knew everything and to leave him and me alone, so hopefully that will have done it. Now, enough about him. How is our new manager settling in?' She poured herself a coffee and sat down.

Conor sat opposite her. 'I didn't go into the details because we weren't on the best of terms at the time, but I would not have hired him, as you know. He and I go back a long way, and he was horrible to Ana when she worked at the Dunshane. He and I had a few run-ins.

Long story short, he is not my biggest fan, and frankly, I can't stand him either. I know I just said I wasn't happy with the appointment, and either way, there's nothing we can do about it at this stage, but we'll have to see how it works out. He hates Katherine too, by the way, just for good measure.'

Corlene smiled. 'OK, now I'm intrigued. Someone who doesn't love Conor O'Shea? This I gotta hear.'

Conor told her the stories of how he had dealt with Carlos in the past, culminating in the stand-off about Ana.

'Do you think he was sweet on her himself?' she asked.

'No, I don't think so. I'm not sure women are his thing. Though that said, I don't think men are either. Who knows? Look, he'll do for now anyway. There's so much to be done, and believe me, he'll get it done. He had the Dunshane running like clockwork. They all hated him, mind you, but he gets the job done.' Conor shrugged. It was a pain undoubtedly, but in the grand scheme of things, he had bigger problems.

He picked up the phone on his desk. 'Hi, Jane. Can you hold all my calls and don't let anyone in while I have a meeting with Corlene?' He paused while the new junior receptionist answered politely. 'Great, thanks.' He hung up.

'This looks serious. What's up?' Corlene asked.

'It kind of is. So remember the first time we came here, the sound we heard?'

'Yeah, sure, the one you refused to use as a marketing ploy?'

'Yes. Well, I've heard it several times since. In fact, I've seen it.' Conor's eyes never left Corlene's face.

'Seen what?' Corlene asked. 'Conor, if you've got something to say, just spit it out.'

'The castle is haunted. I'm sure of it now. It's why they can't get the heating to work on the third floor.' There. He'd said it. He went on to explain about his visits to the room, the packing and unpacking of the toys, the train set.

Corlene looked intently at him. After all they'd been through together, Conor knew she trusted him.

'I...I don't know, Conor... In the cold light of day, it all seems so crazy, but then I did hear that sound and there is no logical reason the heating won't work. Supposing it's true – just let's go with that for a moment – we can't operate a haunted hotel. What are we going to do?'

'Well, I spoke to a friend of mine – who happens to be a priest actually, but that's got nothing to do with it – and he told me Martin's mother is still alive, the woman who was friendly with Beatrice King all those years ago. He said something about how she tried to remove the spirit or whatever she did. Remember he told us about her?'

Corlene nodded but appeared dubious.

'Well, I think I should go and see her, see what she thinks we should do. Neither of us is equipped to deal with this. I haven't a clue, and neither do you, so it's worth talking to her, isn't it? At least she won't be calling the men in the white coats for the pair of us!'

'I guess so. But I don't think some old lady who calls herself a witch is gonna be able to come in here and solve this...' Corlene was sceptical.

'But think about it, Corlene. We might have a ghost, a supernatural force, in the hotel, so what do you fight supernatural with?'

'I dunno. Ghostbusters?' Corlene started to laugh.

'Well, yes, in a way. Other supernatural things, like the mechanisms of this world, are not creating this thing that's going on, so we need to get the right people on the job. This is your specialty, finding the right people and getting them to do what we need them to do – outsourcing. So this is something else we need to outsource.'

'OK, do it, whatever it takes. Go talk to the old lady witch, and if anyone can get her to fix this, it's you.'

He nodded and got up to go.

'Oh, and Conor, Nico handed in his notice this morning. He called me personally since I was the one who hired him in the first place. He just said he got an offer of a new garden that he had always wanted to work on, somewhere in Asia – I forget where he said it was – but anyway, he's taking it. I said I was sorry to hear it but I understood.'

'Right.' He hadn't expected that. Nico gone from their lives was a good thing. He just hoped Ana would see it like that. 'When is he going?'

'Today,' Corlene answered but said nothing more.

'Right. Thanks for letting me know.'

* * *

CONOR WALKED into the old stables where Nico had his office. There were two local lads there moving topsoil when he arrived.

'Morning, lads. Is Nico around?' Conor thought he caught a glance between them but then figured he'd probably imagined it.

'Er…he was, but…er… Let me just check there, Conor.' The older lad ran inside one of the stables that had been converted into a makeshift office, while the other looked awkward as he stood waiting outside.

'Don't let me stop you. I'm sure you've a lot to be getting on with,' Conor said pointedly. If this fella thought he was going to witness some kind of a showdown, he was very much mistaken.

Nico came out of the office and spoke to his two young assistants. 'Would you please go up to the wisteria garden and check for any of my tools? There may be a pouch with secateurs and a few other things.' He dismissed them, and then he and Conor were alone.

'Hi, Nico. Could we have a chat, do you think?' Conor kept his voice neutral.

'Sure. Come into the office. It's a bit of a mess, but…' Nico looked and sounded dejected.

The office smelled of peat moss and linseed oil and all manner of potions Nico had made to restore the gardens to their former glory. Nico offered him a seat but he stayed standing.

'You've done a great job. I don't know, but if there's a next life, Beatrice King must be looking down happy.'

'I hope so. It was a wonderful project. Like uncovering something magical, you know? But Corlene has told you I'm moving on? Another very wealthy American has bought a property in Bali that needs my magic touch.' Nico smiled sadly.

As Nico made coffee, his phone buzzed on the desk and lit up. The photo on the home screen was of him and Ana. Conor tried to stay calm.

Nico had the grace to look embarrassed. 'I'm sorry, Conor. I should not… Well, you know…' Nico grabbed the phone and furiously pressed buttons to make the photo disappear.

Conor took a deep breath. This young attractive Russian had tried his level best to come between him and Ana, so by right he should want to pulverise him. But Conor wasn't that kind of man. And anyway, Conor was the winner here. Ana had chosen him, not Nico. He could afford to be magnanimous, so he simply nodded.

'OK… I… Well, I don't really know what to say, so I'll just say goodbye.' Nico held out his hand.

Conor didn't respond, forcing Nico to withdraw.

'You are a very lucky man, Conor. I envy you.'

'Yes, I know I am.' He thought for a moment. 'Are you going to say goodbye to Ana before you go?' The thought of a tearful parting between his wife and Nico sent a sharp pain through his chest.

Nico looked Conor directly in the eye. 'Ana has already said goodbye to me, Conor.'

Conor's eyes never left his. There was more to that sentence than the words conveyed and they both knew it.

Nico went outside and returned with a large bucket, from which were growing several tall stalks. 'These are for Joe and Artie. The national flower of Ukraine is the sunflower, and they wanted to grow some for Ana as a surprise. They planted them, and I have been taking care of them here. Maybe you could bring them home? Tell the boys to plant them against a sunny wall.'

'Of course. Thanks. We'll do it this weekend.' Conor took the bucket and nodded. 'See you, Nico.'

'You won't. I promise.' Nico held up his hand in a wave and then turned to gather his things.

CHAPTER 27

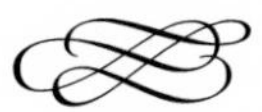

'I just wanted to say thanks for the opportunity, but I'm not going to stay on here.' Sheila Dillon stood in front of his desk, apparently resigning.

'But why, Sheila? I thought you liked it here?' Conor knew she needed the job, so he was puzzled as to the reason for the sudden change of heart.

She sighed, and Conor could tell she was close to tears. 'I do, or I did anyway. I need this job, but your man, that new fella – honestly, Conor, I can't work for him. He's a total pain in the arse with all the airs and graces on him. He's been on my case all morning because I don't bow and scrape the way he wants me to. He made another big speech this morning about appropriate levels of familiarity with guests and saying Irish people were bad with boundaries and he just wanted to make sure we all knew our places. He stared me down the whole time. I might be skint, but I don't need to put up with that kind of rubbish.'

Sheila was really good at her job; she was older than a lot of the staff and had a certain authority because of it. Managing and rotating laundry on the scale that they envisaged when the hotel was fully operational was no mean feat, and Sheila was shaping up to be excellent at it. There was no way he was allowing this.

'Sheila, can you do me one favour? Just wait here. Have a coffee.' He nodded at the espresso machine Corlene had installed in the office for him with a Post-It saying, 'We're going to need a lot of this.' 'But don't go anywhere. I'm going to sort this out, OK?'

Conor strode down the corridor to the right of the main entrance where all the offices were and walked straight into Carlos's office without knocking. Carlos looked up from his computer screen, incredulous that anyone would have the audacity to barge in unannounced.

Conor had no time to pussyfoot around him. It was time for some straight-talking. 'Look, let's dispense with the façade now that it's just us. I didn't know Corlene had hired you. I wouldn't have, to be honest. I never got along with you and I know how you feel about me, but we need to pull together. I won't pull rank on you for no reason, Carlos, and insofar as is practical, you can have your head, but stuff like accusing a perfectly innocent woman, and a great worker by the way, of being overly familiar with the guests is just not happening. We want the exact opposite of that reverential claptrap here. It's a five-star resort for sure, and people will be treated well by friendly and helpful staff, but none of this Downton Abbey stuff, right? I know exactly how you ran the Dunshane. I saw it with my own eyes, and I heard more than enough from Ana. Let me be crystal clear – that approach will not work here. You will be courteous and treat all the staff here with respect. I will not have you bully or threaten or accuse anyone. Am I making myself clear, Carlos?' Conor stared straight at him.

Carlos returned the glare with no effort to conceal his animosity. 'Well, Conor, since we are being so candid, I would not have taken this position had I known the situation. I may still choose to return to the Dunshane, as I am frankly horrified at the way this shambles is being run, but then, with all due respect, you are a bus driver.'

Carlos was testing his authority. Conor knew that the way Carlos saw it, Corlene was the real boss.

'Suit yourself. Go on back there. We've managed this long without you, and we'll be fine. But hold on – didn't I hear that you left under a cloud, that the discount chain of hotels that now owns the Dunshane more or less told you to go or be pushed? Katherine O'Brien is doing a grand job, despite what you think, and between us we'll be fine. So if you think going back to the Dunshane is the best thing for you, then be my guest.'

Conor knew Carlos would love nothing better than to tell him where to shove his job, but he wouldn't dare. The hotel business in Ireland was a small one, and a person was only as good as their reputation.

And Carlos Manner had a reputation. He was efficient and timely, and he did work hard, but the downside was he was insufferable. Ana had been dead right when she said every business felt they needed a Carlos, someone to do the dirty work. Maybe Conor was naive, but he disagreed with that approach. He was of the philosophy that if you paid people properly and treated them with respect, then they reciprocated. Having said that, he had never run a hotel before, so maybe he was too optimistic. Still, he'd like to give it a go.

Carlos was weighing up his options. Conor could almost hear the cogs whirring in the other man's mind.

'I will stay. But there will have to be parameters so that you and I are not constantly trying to do the same job. Perhaps a schedule of areas of responsibility? I have my areas, you have yours, and we stay out of each other's way insofar as is possible?'

In any other circumstance, dealing with anyone else, Conor would have been happy to compromise, but what the man was suggesting was a partnership, and what he needed was for Carlos to understand that Conor was the boss. Being the boss didn't sit naturally with him. He'd always worked autonomously. He'd been employed by tour companies, but they let him at it, as he knew what he was doing. He'd never had anyone work for him before. But Carlos would see any chink in the armour as a victory.

'Well, Carlos, that isn't really feasible. Certainly, I will allocate certain areas of the day-to-day running of the hotel to you, but ultimately everything will be overseen by me. You may not make any decisions, for example, to do with staffing or changes to the systems we have in place without checking with me first. And as I said this morning you need to work with Katherine very closely. I don't expect to be bothered with every little trivial thing – that's why you two are here.

'Now on that subject, I have Sheila Dillon in my office threatening to leave because you accused her of behaving inappropriately or some other such rubbish. That's exactly the type of thing I'm talking about. If you have a genuine concern about someone in our employ, then you need to bring it to me and I'll decide what's to be done. You can't go off on solo runs. Sheila is a wonderful worker and really committed to making this place a success, so under no circumstances am I going to let her just walk out the door. So here's what's going to happen. You are going to come down with me now to the office, and you will apologise to Sheila, sincerely, and tell her it was your first day and you are a bit nervous so you made a mistake. You will ask her to reconsider, and as a gesture, you are going to ask me to add three days to her annual leave. I'll agree and hopefully she'll forgive you.'

'Well, that is quite out of the question. I –' Carlos was going pink in the face.

'It's that or the road – for you, not Sheila.' Conor was stern.

'Fine.' Carlos almost spat the word.

Conor realised having a manager in such dire form could only result in more tears from the staff, so he'd soften his approach later, but for now he had to remain tough and fight fire with fire.

The meeting with Sheila went better than he'd hoped. Carlos seemed genuinely contrite, though Conor knew he wasn't, and Sheila relented and went back to work. Just as Carlos was about to leave, Conor called him back.

'Look, Carlos, let's not go making more work for ourselves here. I do need you – you know more about this business than I do – but we have a great team here and need to keep them happy. This is not the Dunshane. I don't want you bawling them out over stupid stuff. Maybe Tim wanted that but I don't. The way I see this, you have two options. The first is that you accept that I'm running this place and that if you pull stunts like that, I will overrule you. We saved face this time, but in the future I won't spare your blushes. Or, second option, you can refuse to accept that and you might as well pack your bags now. I'm not going anywhere, so it's me or nothing. That said, I'm not in the business of being a tyrant. I just want us all to pull together in the same direction. What do you say?'

Carlos stood in the centre of the office, looking around at the lavish surroundings, and Conor wondered if he was even going to respond to the bit of olive branch he'd offered. The silence went on so long, Conor was about to speak again, but then Carlos looked him directly in the eye and said, 'You're right. I do know more about running a hotel than you do. There are some things that are happening here that are just not sustainable in the long term. For example, do you know that the wine cellar is unlocked? Wine is being delivered here and then left in the cellar at the back of the kitchens, and several of the younger labouring staff have become wise to that fact. That is not me being a big bad wolf – that is me saving this business money. Additionally, people are clocking others in and out. It's only a few minutes here and there, but in my considerable experience in the hospitality industry, that will only escalate if it goes unchecked. The nature of this industry means you need a lot of casual or seasonal staff, and they are not here to build up the business or protect our reputation. They are here for the money and to get as much of that as possible for as little work as they can get away with. Not all staff certainly, but a sizeable proportion. I do happen to recall a very diligent Ukrainian waitress that was whipped from under our noses, so there are many good people.'

Conor thought he detected the shadow of a smile. 'OK, fair enough. What else?' Conor gestured that Carlos should sit and offered him a coffee.

'No, thank you,' the other man replied primly, sitting down as if he were teetering on the edge of a cliff. 'The dispensers you have for soap are releasing too much. This will cost you money over the years, and it also increases scum on the bathroom sinks. The tumble driers are venting into the room beside the cellar, which could raise the temperature and affect the wine. The fabric conditioner being used currently is too fragranced and will cause allergic reactions in those with sensitive skin, the very old or the very young. There is animosity in the scullery between the kitchen porters because of a romance gone wrong with somebody's sister. More energy is being expended in insulting each other than actually doing the job they are paid to do – efficiency suffers when personalities take over. You will need to place stair grips on the carpets on the front stairs, as at several places they bulge slightly and someone could trip. These are just preliminary observations, but enough to be getting on with.'

'Agreed. Can you address all of these issues without reducing anyone to tears or causing them to storm out, and let me know how it goes? I never doubted your ability or your attention to detail. The Dunshane was the success it was because of you, but I just need you to take a better approach to the human resources end of things.'

Carlos stood, bowed his head curtly and left, leaving Conor's door open behind him.

Conor sat back and sipped the coffee he'd made. It could have gone worse, he supposed. Manner was an odd fish, there was no doubt about it, but he knew his stuff. If he could be controlled in terms of his attitude, it might just work out fine.

Now, on to the more pressing problem. He shut the door and lifted the phone on his desk, dialled St Enda's and waited.

'Hello, St Enda's Hospital.'

'Hi, my name is Conor O' Shea, and I was wondering if I could come to visit a patient, Molly O'Donoghue?'

The receptionist seemed confused by the question. 'Are you a relative?'

'No, I've never met her, but I know her son, Martin. I work at the new hotel in Castle Dysert, and I'm doing a bit of research about it. Martin thought his mother might know about it?'

'Hold on, I'll go and ask her – she's just across the corridor. You aren't Joe and Artie's dad, are you?' she asked.

'I am. Sorry, who am I talking to?' Conor should have known;

everyone in Ennis knew everyone else.

'Oh, my name is Pauline Forde. I've never met you but I know Ana. My boy Colm plays hurling with your lads. Ana mentioned you were up in the castle now, and when I heard O'Shea, I put two and two together.'

'Nice to meet you, Pauline. Just shows me how I should be making more time to bring the lads to training. Things have been so crazy here, I've been leaving poor Ana to do everything.'

Knowing the connection, Pauline dropped her voice slightly. 'Look, I don't want to be talking, but Molly is a bit… Well, she can be a bit difficult to manage sometimes. If you're expecting a sweet little old lady and a trip down memory lane, then I'd have to warn you, she's not likely to comply.'

Conor laughed. 'Don't worry, Pauline. I'm a friend of Eddie Shanahan's and he's filled me in.'

'Oh, poor Father Shanahan! She screams at him – honest to God, she's like a banshee. It's a wonder he comes back. Well, sure, I'd say it might be better just to turn up. She'll either take to you or she won't, but you can take your chances.'

'OK. What time would be best? And thanks for the heads up by the way.'

'Well, the rest of the patients go to Mass at eleven every day, but she's not into that, to say the very least, so maybe around then? At least if she roars the head off you, you won't have it witnessed by the whole hospital.'

'That's great. I'll pop up in the morning. Thanks, Pauline. I'm kind of terrified but I'll have a go.'

'Yerra, her bark is worse than her bite. She's all right really, just a bit daft…and vocal. See you tomorrow.'

Conor hung up.

He wondered what he'd do if Molly had no ideas. The cold, the noises – these weren't things he could keep under wraps for very long. No, this would have to be sorted out. He just wished that the whole multi-million-euro investment's success wasn't hinging on some mad old woman in a hospital bed.

CHAPTER 28

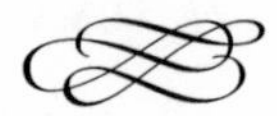

Molly O'Donoghue was dozing in her bed when he arrived. The three other beds in the sunny ward had been vacated; presumably the occupants were gone to Mass. Asleep, she looked like a normal old woman except for her long silver hair, brushed carefully and held back by a piece of string. She wore a purple bedjacket, and her face in repose looked wrinkled but carefree. Conor thought Martin was about sixty, which put her at eighty at the youngest, though she was probably much older.

He sat down on the seat beside the bed, waiting for her to wake. He wasn't going to risk waking her. The blue veins stood out on her thin hands, and her fingernails were very long and manicured into points. There was one book beside her bed, *The Spiral Dance: A Rebirth of the Ancient Religion of the Great Goddess* by an author called Starhawk. Conor picked it up and flipped it over.

'And what makes you think you can come in here and take another person's possessions?' A deep smoky voice from the bed interrupted his reading.

'Oh...sorry... I was just...' She'd startled him.

'Just reading my book. Put it back.'

He did as she asked and wondered if there was a way to salvage the conversation. 'Of course, I'm sorry. I just had never seen it before...'

'Of course you haven't. Why would you? Anyway, what do you want? Are you a doctor?'

'No...no, Mrs O'Donoghue, I'm –'

'I'm not a missus, never was. My name is O'Donoghue, Molly O'Donoghue. I have the same man's name I was born with. I've never understood all of that changing your name rubbish. What is any woman doing only exchanging one man's name for another?'

'Oh, right, Miss O'Donoghue. I know Martin.' Conor hoped that would help.

'So what? So do I. Is that what you came to tell me?' She sounded bored now and gazed out the window beside the bed where a robin had landed, picking at crumbs someone had placed there.

'No. I work at Castle Dysert, and I wanted to talk to you about the Kings.' He decided being direct was the best approach.

She never took her rheumy eyes off the robin, but he could see she had heard him. He said nothing, waiting for her to respond.

'Beatrice King loved robins. She used to put out seeds and grew gooseberries just to attract them.' She snapped her head around to face him, the movement far faster than he would have imagined someone of her age was capable. 'Martin told you, did he? About them?' she said eventually.

'Well, yes, he told me the story. He also said that you believe the spirit of Grenville still lives in the house.' Even knowing all he knew, the words sounded ridiculous.

'And you don't?' She fixed him with a stare.

'No, I do actually. In fact, I'm convinced of it.'

She hooted then, a huge cackle of laughter. 'What's he up to now?' she asked.

'He plays with a toy train set – we can hear it sometimes. And we can't get the heating to work on the top floor. We've had every kind of expert you can imagine, but nobody can explain it. And –'

'The train, he's still at that?' she whispered, grabbing Conor's arm with her long bony fingers.

'Yes, I've heard the train more than once. Look, Miss O'Donoghue, we are trying to get a hotel off the ground. We employ a lot of local people. But we just can't keep going. We haven't had any guests stay yet, but our big opening is this evening, and frankly, I'm terrified about what might happen. There's going to be press there and...' Conor was trying his best.

'I don't care about that. I couldn't care less if the place burned to the ground. No good will come out of there – too much has happened. But that boy, he needs to move on. Beatrice knew it – that's why she spent so much time in the garden, couldn't bear to be in that house – and, well, it drove Samuel mad in the end, the cold, the bloody train. That's why he did it, you know. He thought if he built him a playroom, that if he wouldn't pass over, then at least he'd have something else to play with, but nothing worked. They couldn't stop it with all of their money and power, and you won't be able to either. He's a child. He wants his twin. He isn't evil or trying to hurt your business. He's a little boy who is lonely, and he wants someone to play with. He wants his mother.'

Conor's heart sank. He had convinced himself that she would at least have a suggestion. 'So what do we do now?' he asked her. 'Can you try again? Whatever you did last time? Maybe it would work this time?' He knew he sounded desperate but had to try.

'He doesn't know. He's just a child. He doesn't know he shouldn't be there. For him this is normal.'

'And can you communicate with him, or could anyone else? Tell him to go?' Conor was grasping at straws.

'No. I can't, and I don't know anyone else who could. Now get out of here. I can't help you.' She turned and closed her eyes.

Staying was pointless, so Conor stood and walked away from the bed.

'She must have liked you,' said a woman on reception. She had short dark hair and must have arrived while he was talking to Martin's mother. 'I'm Pauline. You must be Conor.'

'Oh, hi, Pauline. Nice to meet you.' He shook her hand. 'I don't know about that. She just basically told me to rev up and get out, so I don't think I impressed her much.'

'Ah, you did. Usually she throws things and screams.'

All the way back to the castle, Conor pondered what to do. Every conclusion was the same – nothing. He'd tried talking to the little boy, he'd spoken to a witch, he'd talked to a priest... He wondered if maybe he should try a psychic medium – he'd seen ads on the TV for them. But he immediately dismissed the thought, imagining charlatans preying on the bereaved, telling them that they could bring messages from their loved ones.

When he got back, the grounds surrounding the castle were a hive of activity, everybody working to make the gala opening a huge success. That is, everyone except a small boy in the attic.

CHAPTER 29

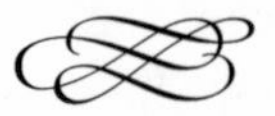

'Well, how did it go?' Corlene met him at the car.

'Badly. She knew all about it and told me that there was nothing she or anyone else could do about it. He doesn't know why he's here, he doesn't know where to go next, and we're stuck with him – that's the main gist of it.'

'We're not imagining this, are we, Conor? Like, are we just victims of an elaborate prank?'

'I wish we were.' Conor sighed and stood, gazing out over what they had created. It was all so perfect. The ocean glittered as the bright sunlight bounced off the gentle waves. The seabirds circled, diving for fish, and the air was fragrant with the perfume of all the shrubs and flowers on the lawn.

Together, they walked up to the imposing façade, its red sandstone walls warm to the touch from the heat of the sun. The grounds looked magnificent; the riots of colour from the flowers, shrubs and trees punctuated the space perfectly. The castle was gleaming inside, warm, welcoming and beautiful.

They went straight to Conor's office, passing Carlos, who was explaining to a maintenance man exactly what needed to be done with the soap dispensers, and Katherine, who was checking all the champagne flutes that were being stacked in a tower around the champagne fountain for the drinks reception.

'What about Martin? Could he help us?' Corlene was flustered now, something Conor had never seen before. She was a doer, who succeeded on the basis of hard work, smart deals and people management. She'd never faced a problem like this and was totally at a loss.

'We can call him, but to be honest, I really doubt it. I rang him to ask if it would be OK to visit his mother, and he said it was fine but didn't venture any further. I even thought we could get one of those psychic mediums, but I don't know… They all seem like cowboys to me. And anyway, the fewer people who know about this, the better.'

'Agreed.' She sighed. 'Look, let's just get this thing over with tonight and hope nothing happens. It's going to be you and me on show for the world to see, and this has to be spectacular, nothing less.'

The rest of the day was spent checking and answering queries from the various departments. There were 200 guests staying that night, and another 200 coming for the opening gala party. Laoise and the band were tuning up in the ballroom, and the kitchens were hopping with activity.

Conor stopped by the reception desk. 'Are we all set?' he asked Katherine.

She looked up and raised one eyebrow. 'Surely you should know? You are the owner. This aspect, the reservations and reception, is all ready, and as far as I know, housekeeping is just putting the finishing touches to the last of the rooms, but as for the kitchen and the grounds staff, I've no idea. Perhaps you should check with Chef? Or Carlos Manner?'

'Right.' Conor had just wanted a friendly word, someone to say it was all going to be OK.

He was heading off in the direction of maintenance when he spotted Carlos in conversation with Artur. He really hoped Carlos wasn't upsetting Ana's dad. Artur was so diligent and committed, Conor would murder Carlos if he spoke out of turn. He was just about to intervene when he saw Artur smile and nod – maybe all was well.

'How're the men?' Conor asked as he approached them.

'Very fine, Conor, very fine. Always I say stairs need fix, but other man, Daniel, he say is not in way of long ago, but…' Artur shrugged.

'But he is no longer here.' Carlos smiled tightly. 'And it is not Mr. Coffey who would be sued if someone tripped. So Artur here has made some ingenious little clips that we can screw to the riser. They hold the carpet in place and can't be seen. Really resourceful. Thank you, Artur.' Carlos was actually smiling. Conor couldn't believe it. And he'd praised Artur's work. Maybe something of their talk had sunk in.

Artur went off about his business, and Conor was about to continue on to the kitchen when Carlos spoke quietly, drawing a man to Conor's attention; he was standing at the ballroom door, watching the band set up.

'Who is that?' Carlos asked.

The man was dressed in jeans and a blue checked shirt and stood out. Everyone else was either in a uniform or a shirt and tie, or they were in workmen's gear.

'No idea. Has he been here long?'

'I don't know. I noticed him about twenty minutes ago. He was engaging the staff in chat, but when I came close, they went back to their duties.'

I bet they did, Conor thought to himself. 'OK, I'll see. Thanks, Carlos.'

Conor approached the man, who was now watching Laoise most intently as she played a tune on the harp for the sound check. Conor stood beside him and listened as she finished the haunting air. 'She's something else, isn't she?' he remarked.

'She sure is.' The man's accent was American, Southern.

'I'm Conor O'Shea. I'm one of the owners of the castle.' Conor introduced himself in the hope that the other guy would do the same.

'Larry, Larry Smith. I'm a freelance journalist, just thinking of doing a piece on this place you've got here. It sure is something.'

'Well, it took a lot of refurbishment, but we're very pleased with the result.'

Conor knew Corlene had invited press of all descriptions to the opening, but he thought she said they were all to come later. Maybe this guy thought he would steal a march on the others by arriving early.

'Well, there's a tour later for all press, so if you want to just head into reception here, the staff will fill you in on all the details.' Conor went to leave, but the man fell in beside him as he walked. He seemed to be very stiff in his movements and limping slightly.

'Afghanistan.' The man smiled. 'I was over there covering the war and was in the wrong place at the wrong time.'

'I'm sorry to hear that. You should be quite safe here, though. Enjoy your visit.'

Just as Conor was about to head in the direction of the kitchens, the man put his hand on his arm. 'Say, a couple of old guys in the bar last night were telling me this place is haunted. Is that true? I'd love to do a piece on it for you if you want, get a bit of extra publicity?'

Conor bristled. He needed an article like that like a hole in the head. 'There's no truth whatsoever in it, just an old bit of gossip, so there's nothing to write about from that point of view. But the history of the castle and the families that lived here over the years is very interesting. As I said, there will be a press tour, and we've put a pack of information and things together, so be sure to get one of those. Now if you'll excuse me, I've a lot to do today as I'm sure you can imagine."

'Sure, sure. In the meantime, you mind if I take a look around?'

Conor felt the guy was smirking at him like he wanted to get one over on the stupid Irishman. 'That won't be possible at the moment, I'm afraid. We are having our official opening tonight and the staff are very busy putting the finishing touches to everything, so it's all off limits to the public for now.' Conor hoped the man heard the steel he deliberately inserted into his voice despite the friendly delivery.

'No problem,' he drawled. 'I hear you.'

The man wandered off, and Conor made a mental note to tell Carlos to keep an eye on him.

'Hey, boss man! How you doing?' Laoise bounded out from the

ballroom towards him. She then sucked some vile-looking green concoction out of a plastic cup with a straw.

'Great, good to see you. I won't even ask what's in the cup. It looks like sludge.' Conor grinned.

'It's a kale and spinach smoothie with a shot of wheatgrass. Actually it's gross, but I need to replenish the old vitamins and stuff, what with my rock-and-roll lifestyle, y'know?'

'Never having had a rock-and-roll lifestyle, I wouldn't know, but I'll take your word for it. So you all set for later? I've got to go to the kitchens. Walk with me – I've no time to stop for chatting.'

'Ah, look how quickly he has turned from humble bus driver to ruthless businessman. Sad to see,' she teased.

'Go way outta that, you pup. I'm flat out I can tell you, though. Anyway, is the music all sorted, sound working and all of that?'

'Grand, grand. Relax, boss man, all is cool. There's some small issue with the electricity supply or something, but the lads in the overalls are all over it.'

He looked down at her and felt a wave of affection. She might look like she'd frighten the dogs, with her blue-black hair now woven into dreadlocks and more tattoos and piercings than he could have thought possible, but she was a fabulously talented musician with a heart of gold.

'Laoise, I never said thanks for the chat that day of the party. I needed to hear it, and when it comes to my personal life, I know I can be a bit, I dunno...'

'Grumpy? Stubborn? Unapproachable?' She grinned.

'Yeah, I suppose so. I just don't let people in – I never have. But anyway, thanks. You're a great friend and I'm lucky to have you.'

'No probs. You two are all loved up again anyway, I hear?' She threw the remains of the horrible-looking green stuff in the bin.

'Yes, all fine again. She and the boys are coming tonight actually. The lads are up to ninety with the excitement.'

'Great! I'm looking forward to seeing them. I promised them we'd have a bonfire on the beach some night next week as well, sausages and football and night swimming – the works.'

'Good luck with getting their mammy to agree to that.' He chuckled.

'I'd mind them, though. Like, you do trust me, don't you?'

For all of Laoise's worldliness, there was a vulnerability to her that made Conor protective. 'Of course we do.' He gave her a quick one-armed squeeze.

'I've got to ring Dylan. He went off this morning like a bear to find my father – him and Mam came up from Cork last night because Dad had a gig in Doolin. Dylan is all up in a hoop because there's something wrong with the reed in his chanter. Anyway, I think they have it sorted now. He needs to come back and do a sound check.'

'OK, I'll leave you to it.'

Chef was bawling someone out in the kitchen and Conor decided it was not a good time to chat with him, so he went to his office and called Katherine, Artur and Carlos in. They were there within minutes.

'OK, lads, I just need a progress report on how everything is going.'

Katherine was happy to say everything on her end was under control. Artur was doing a few last-minute bits of maintenance, and he assured Conor that he and all the workmen would be out of the building within the hour. Carlos said Chef was after a major flare-up, something to do with burned duck, but he'd be grand – normal practice for him it would seem – and the waiting staff were briefed and ready. Porters, barmen, housekeeping – everything was fine.

Conor trusted Katherine and Artur completely but was still unsure of Carlos. He wanted to confide in them, or in someone other than Corlene, about the Grenville King situation, but it was best kept quiet for now. If something happened – and he hoped against hope that it didn't – it would be easier if they knew, as they could try to keep everyone else calm, but he decided against it.

'Lads, you are only fantastic. I can't tell you how much we value the three of you. You really are the key to making all of this work. It's going to be a good night hopefully, and once this is over with, we can get down to proper business. The tour operators are really on board, and we have loads of enquiries already.

'Now, it's probably nothing, but there was a guy lurking around outside. I would like all three of you to keep an eye on him. He's wearing a blue checked shirt and jeans and has dark hair. He wanted to go looking around the place, and I told him it was off limits. He's a journalist of some description, or he says he is anyway, and some locals were filling his head with stories about the place being haunted, so he's sniffing around. The press were told to come later, but he showed up this morning. Anyway, it's probably nothing, but let's just be vigilant.'

The press, tour operators and travel agents arrived at the appointed time, but of Larry Smith there was no sign. Conor took them on the tour, showing the suites on the third floor but ushering people quickly back downstairs so they wouldn't notice the cold. Afterwards, they gathered in the breakfast room, which had been set up for afternoon tea.

The antique silver tea and coffee pots shone, and the china tiered trays that Daniel had bought for some outrageous amount of money did look good. He'd also bought a Royal Doulton tea service for sixty people for a song from a hotel in Eastbourne in England that was closing down; he had been quick to point out the discounted price when Conor exploded at the cost. The room was filled with chatter and enthusiasm as they all tucked into the mouthwatering treats on offer. Once everyone was fed and watered, Corlene addressed them. She said that Conor was really the man behind the whole project and invited him to the podium. He had a speech prepared, but he decided just to wing it.

He recognised many faces from his old life in the tour business and relaxed. Everyone seemed very impressed. He told them all about the work they'd undertaken and the gardens and everything. The vast majority of them wished him well, though there were one or two who were green-eyed monsters, he could tell. Apparently, Mad Mike had been bad-mouthing Conor and Castle Dysert every chance he got, but when Conor heard about it, he just laughed. Josephine from his old office was there and mentioned the complaint about Mike's behaviour from James Deegan, the hotel manager in Killarney, and how they had given him a formal warning. Mike was mortified, apparently, and blamed Conor one hundred percent. Josephine promised to book several tours in, and Conor was glad he had kept on such good terms with his former boss, even though juggling both the castle and his former career for a while there had been exhausting.

He mingled and chatted and actually really enjoyed it. The tourism industry was good that way, supportive of each other, and he was really proud of what they'd achieved. The afternoon ended on a very positive note.

They all filed off to relax, avail themselves of the spa facilities or the library, or just take a stroll. They were to return for the opening dinner that evening. Conor gathered his inner three again in his office for a post-mortem of the afternoon. Carlos wanted to talk about the heating again, but Conor cut him off.

'I know, Carlos. We've the best plumbing minds in the country on it, and we'll figure it out, I'm sure. Now, if everyone is happy enough, I'm off home for a shower and to collect Ana and the boys. I'll be back by six, and dinner is at seven, so we should be OK. Of course, if anything is needed, just give me a bell, and Corlene is around anyway.'

Katherine shooed him out the door.

CHAPTER 30

Conor turned the key in his front door and walked in to find Danika putting the finishing touches to the twins' outfits. They looked absolutely adorable in matching cream linen suits with royal-blue shirts underneath. Danika had made the outfits from scratch; they were perfectly done and fitted both of them to a T.

'Danika, they look absolutely handsome. Guys, I hope you gave *Babusya* a big hug and a kiss for making you these suits. You look fantastic.'

'We made her a card, with a picture of us in all scruffy clothes and then one of us looking sharp in our suits.' Artie grinned.

'I look like James Bond!' Joe giggled. 'Shaken, not stirred...' he imitated.

Danika laughed happily, delighted to see the joy on her adored grandsons' faces. She issued instructions in Ukrainian, and Conor managed to understand at least most of it. He had an app on his phone that he put on when he was driving – if anyone saw him, they'd think he was losing it, talking to himself in the car – and his Ukrainian was picking up. At work, he practised on Artur every chance he got.

'Yes, exactly,' he said, then echoed their grandmother's rules. 'Sit on the sofa, watch TV and do not eat or drink anything. And definitely no outside. We need you to stay clean, OK?'

'Did you understand what *Babusya* said?' Artie was incredulous.

'I'm full of surprises,' said Conor with a wink. 'But not a word to Mammy. I want to surprise her. Now, I'm going to get ready, so sit there and stay clean or dire things will happen!'

They both giggled at his mock-stern voice.

'Where is Mammy actually?'

'She is gone to get something in the shop,' Joe called over his shoulder as he and Artie settled down to watch *Scooby-Doo*.

Danika produced Conor's navy pinstriped suit, freshly pressed, and on a separate hanger, a pale-blue shirt. He felt bad about her always having all the family's clothes laundered, repaired and ironed so perfectly, but Ana explained she loved to feel useful, like she was pulling her weight. She was a seamstress in Kiev and had taught Ana dressmaking skills, with the result that Ana made all her own clothes. Ana had a quirky style, rarely wearing things that clung to her lovely figure, but she had a way of getting fabric to fall so that it accentuated her curves. Wherever they went, people complimented her on her outfits, and she amazed women by saying she made them herself. It was one of the many things he loved about her. She couldn't care less about fashion or designer handbags; she had her own style.

He wondered what she'd wear tonight as he stepped into the shower off their bedroom. He stood under the hot jets of water with his eyes closed, allowing the rhythmic drumming of the water on the top of his head to soothe away the stresses of Grenville King, Molly O'Donoghue, Corlene and Dylan, Nico, Carlos and all the other sources of consternation in his life.

He felt her arms go around him before he knew she was there. 'Your mother and the lads are downstairs,' he murmured into her ear.

'I've locked the door,' she whispered back as she kissed him. 'But we'll have to be quick.' She giggled.

After they'd made love, he'd told her about his last conversation with Nico.

'How do you feel now, about everything?' Conor asked as her head rested on his chest, feeling huge relief that they could talk about it now.

'I just feel sad it had to happen like this. I was stupid to think we could just be friends. To be honest, it was nice to have him admire me, but when he behave like it could be more, then I know for sure, no. He don't say, straight out, nothing like this, but he sometimes look at me, or… Anyway, I don't want him, I only want you, so I hope he is happy. He is nice person, but for me, no. I tell him it is not good for me to see him, so he decide to go to this other garden. It's best, I think.'

'He had your photo on his phone,' Conor said quietly. It hurt him even to say it, but he wanted everything out in the open.

'I… That is not what I want, but it is for me to blame this. I should not have had friendship with a single man. I knew he was…he liked me, and I thought because I didn't like him, like that way, it would be OK, but no. I am sorry, Conor.'

'Don't be. You did nothing wrong, my love. I understand how lonely it must be, and how hard it is never being able to express yourself as you'd like to in your native language.'

'Look, it is now over. And look at the time. Go get dressed.' She shoved him out of bed.

Ten minutes later, Conor appeared in the kitchen, dressed and ready, and Danika clapped with delight when she saw him.

'Very good. Very good,' she said, smoothing the shoulders of his jacket, her eyes examining him for a wrinkle or a pulled thread.

He smiled and gave her his cufflinks to put on. She did, straightened the exquisite gold and navy tie that she had made for him as a gift and stood back to admire her handiwork.

She said something to Joe, which he translated, his eyes never leaving Scooby, Shaggy and Velma as they pulled the mask off some old man, revealing him as the thief.

'*Babusya* said you are the most handsome man in Ireland and everyone will admire you tonight.' Joe giggled once he realised what he'd said, and Artie joined in, both laughing at their grandma giving their dad such a compliment.

'Are we going now?' Joe asked. 'I'm starving.'

'Is there going to be normal food, Dad, not like all fancy grown-up things like raw vegetables and weird sauces on everything?' Artie finished.

'Yes, I've asked Chef specially for lovely normal food. So we are inviting all the posh people of Ireland to our new fancy hotel, and we'll be serving fish fingers and chips, and jelly and ice cream for dessert,' Conor joked.

'Really? Great,' they chorused, seeing nothing whatsoever wrong with that menu.

'No, not really. It's going to be all fancy grown-up food, but there's going to be something you will like for the kids.' Conor ruffled their hair. 'Ana! Are you ready? We need to go,' he called.

She never allowed him to be in the room when she was getting dressed for a night out. She said she needed the time alone to try things out, and she only ever wanted him to see the finished product.

Joe and Artie were deep in discussion about the disgusting things adults might put on pizza, like goat's cheese or asparagus. Conor was about to join in their conversation when Ana walked into the living room. The sight of her took his breath away.

Her short blonde hair was brushed neatly from her face, and long silver earrings hung from her ears. Her sun-kissed skin was accentuated by a hint of make-up, just enough to highlight her features, and she wore the most amazing gold dress, the exact gold of his tie.

She looked like a Greek statue, he thought. The silk draped on one shoulder, leaving the other bare, and then crossed over her breasts. The dress was tight around her tiny waist, from where it hung perfectly to her ankles. Up one arm were several silver bangles. She was stunning.

Here goes, he thought. He'd been practising all week in the car. He hoped he wouldn't make a total eejit of himself.

'Anastasia, *vy vyhlvadaty krasyvo, ya tebe lyublyu. Ya duzhe shchaslyyа lydyna.*'

The entire family stared at him, and then Joe whooped with delight, high-fiving his amazed brother. Danika beamed, and Ana just stood there, her eyes filling with tears.

'Thank you,' she managed, though the emotion was getting the better of her. 'I love you too. And it is I who is the lucky one.'

She moved into his arms, and he kissed her deeply to sounds of pretend disgust from the boys and claps of delight from Danika.

Danika and Artur were going to the event as well, but not until later. Artur was still up at the castle, but Conor knew the moment he landed home, the overalls would be whipped away and Danika would have them both like new pins. Artur was driving himself, and Conor was delighted. Artur had saved his salary for the last few months and had eventually invested in a car of his own. It was great to see him so independent. Only two days ago, he'd asked Conor to help them find a house to rent. They were no trouble as houseguests – in fact, they were a great help – but both of them wanted their own space again. Conor was sure he'd find them something close by once the hotel was up and running. Much as he loved his parents-in-law, it would be nice to have the house back to themselves again.

The avenue from the public road to the castle was decorated in sparkling lights, but it wouldn't really have the full effect until later when it was dark. Conor reached over and took Ana's hand as he drove.

Conor pulled into the staff car park near the stables and went to check on everyone. He left Ana and the boys chatting with Siobhan and Diarmuid and a few of the local people who had been invited. Conor had decided that a venture like this needed the full support of the local community, so he'd issued an invitation to everyone in the nearby village. It only meant a hundred extra, and in the long term, it would be very beneficial to the hotel if the locals were predisposed to the place.

As he walked around the castle, he had to hand it to Carlos – it was a slick operation. Immaculately clad servers moved through the gathered crowds with champagne and canapes, while the string quartet employed for the drinks reception played in the entrance hall. The castle looked magical. Conor said a silent prayer that nothing untoward would happen.

Carlos was behind reception, helping Katherine with checking in as everyone arrived at once. Conor caught his eye as he glanced up and gave him a wink and a nod. He thought Carlos might have smiled but couldn't be sure.

As he watched porters lead guests along the deep-pile carpets to their bedrooms, Conor felt compelled to go upstairs. He greeted a few guests along the way but found himself within moments at the bottom of the three small steps into the playroom. He withdrew his bunch of keys from his pocket, onto which he had placed the huge original front door key, even though it made his keys too bulky. He put the key into the lock, and the door swung into the room.

He stepped inside, once again getting that shiver. The furniture was unchanged, and all the old toys were where he remembered they were from the previous time. He kicked the door closed with his foot and looked down. The train sat still on the track.

He spoke quietly, feeling foolish, but he had to try. 'Grenville, I don't know if you can hear me, but if you can, I want you to know you have nothing to fear from me or anyone else in the castle. Nobody can hurt you. You are quite safe. And if you're trying to tell me something, then I will try to understand and give you what you want. But you must do something for me. Tonight, there are lots of people here in the castle, people you don't know. You must not disturb them. Do you understand?'

Silence followed and the train stayed on the track. Conor felt ridiculous. He left and locked the door behind him.

CHAPTER 31

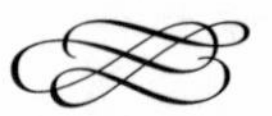

From the upstairs library, Conor looked out the back window to the stables, still used for the moment as garden maintenance headquarters. The courtyard was now a tightly packed car park. The vehicles of the florists, the sound guys and all the people needed to set up the marquee on the lawn where the gala dinner would be held were all parked neatly, and though it was a small space, everything fitted and everyone could get out if need be. Conor knew without checking that it was all Artur's doing.

The drinks reception allowed everyone to see the castle in all its glory, and they decided, given the wear and tear caused by so many people, that having the party in a marquee would be much better.

The strains of music drifted up through the castle as wave after wave of people arrived to see the transformation of Castle Dysert from a creepy old house, choked by weeds, to the most glamorous and luxurious resort in Ireland. The Sunday papers had all promised features, no doubt the result of huge donations from Corlene. He'd told Corlene to keep him out of that kind of skulduggery. She was not as scrupulous as he was, and she regularly teased him that he lacked the killer instinct needed for business. She was probably right, but that suited him fine. One killer shark was all any business needed.

He spotted Ana laughing with her father. He was glad that any bad feelings about the Nico thing that had been between them were over. Artur knew that Ana was not having an affair, but he'd seen through Nico and probably just thought she was being naive. Either way, they were close again, and Conor was pleased.

Joe and Artie had found some lads from their school and were cavorting around the lawn. Conor was about to yell at Artie, who was demonstrating his sliding tackle to his friends at the expense of the knees of his new suit, but it was too late, and anyway, he knew Danika would be able to fix it. Having made sure everything was OK, he made his way back downstairs and then outside.

It took him half an hour to get back to Ana as he was stopped, congratulated and waylaid so often, but eventually he got there. The evening sun was buttery gold as it sank slowly over the Atlantic.

'It is a beautiful backdrop, isn't it?' Ana gestured at the scene.

'You can't beat Mother Nature, that's for sure,' Conor agreed, refusing a glass of champagne. He might have a drink tonight when it was all over, but until then, he needed to be totally clear-headed.

'Artie is sliding on the grass in his suit.' She smiled and shrugged. 'It was too late by the time I did see him to say stop to him. I was going to be cross with him. I wanted you to be proud of us,' she finished quietly.

Conor put his arm around her shoulder, drawing her in close. He kissed the top of her head and whispered, 'My heart bursts with pride every single time I see you. I can't believe you are my family, and a few grass stains won't impact that in any way at all. Anyway, nobody will notice because I will walk into dinner with the most beautiful woman here on my arm, and you'll dazzle everyone so much that the dirt on the boys' suits won't even register.'

She smiled up at him and they locked eyes for a moment. There was no need for words.

Conor stopped Carlos on his way back from the kitchen. 'Any sign of that guy from earlier?' he murmured.

'No. Both Artur and the security manager have been keeping a very close watch, but nothing so far.'

'OK, good. I just got a bad feeling about him. Let me know if he shows up.'

'Of course. Also there seems to be an intermittent fault with the electricity to the smaller of the marquees. I have someone checking on it, but it really needs Artur...'

'Let's not disturb him if we can help it. He's having a well-deserved night off, so if it can be solved by the maintenance team, let's leave it at that. Don't worry. You take care of the dinner, and I'll make sure that the electricity gets sorted.'

'Fine.' Carlos was spare in his response, but both men understood each other perfectly.

'The place looks great and is running perfectly. Thanks, Carlos.' Conor was sincere.

'I'm glad you're happy. It's a beautiful place and deserves to be shown off to full effect,' Carlos said, a hint of warmth in his voice.

Dinner was announced and the gathered crowd filed into the marquee that had been set for 400.

It was a tight squeeze, even given the commodious space, but Carlos and the décor people managed it beautifully. The kids were out in a separate marquee where the music would be later but for now had a flat-screen TV showing cartoons. They were dining on fish fingers and chips, or as Chef called them on the menu, goujons of wild Atlantic cod in a brioche crust served with pommes frites. Joe and Artie were busy explaining to everyone that it really was just fish fingers and chips.

Conor watched everyone file in, telling Ana to go ahead as he wanted to oversee everything. He didn't intend to eat at all. He would take his seat at the table but excuse himself soon after the meal was served to check on the electricity situation. He'd explained it to Ana and she understood. They were to sit with her parents, Siobhan and Diarmuid, and Dylan and Laoise. Ana would be very happy in their company.

The chatter was louder inside than out, and everyone was blown away by the room. Though it was a tent, the interior designers had managed to make it all look like the inside of a castle. Flags of each town in the province, with their coats of arms, hung from the sconces on the realistic-looking stone walls. The long trestle tables were decorated with red and green, the colours of Castle Dysert, and the crystal and silver tableware shone.

Once starters were underway, Conor left. Everything was going fine. He popped into the smaller marquee to see how the kids were doing, and they were all having a great time, munching away and talking nineteen to the dozen. As he walked, Carlos rang to ask if he had sorted the electricity issue.

'Well, I was just in there and it seemed fine, but I'm on my way out to maintenance just to be sure,' he said, and hung up.

As he rounded the corner of the stable yard, he noticed one of the stable doors was ajar. There was a lot of expensive horticultural equipment kept there, and he made a mental note to speak to Nico's replacement about keeping it all secure. He was just about to lock it when he heard a noise from within, like someone whimpering.

He went inside. 'Hello, is anyone here?' he called.

The stable was dark despite the brightness outside, but he found the light switch and was horrified to find Laoise huddled on her knees by the wall, crying her eyes out.

Conor crossed the stable and gathered her into his arms as she sobbed. Her clothes were torn and she had scratches all over her face and neck.

'Laoise...Laoise, tell me what happened!' Conor was shocked. She had been fine just a while ago at the table.

'Some guy...' she sobbed, trying to get her breath. 'I w-w-went to go to the bathroom and then I r-r-remembered, I forgot the t-t-tuning fork for the harp.' She shuddered. 'I just ran out to the van...and he g-grabbed me...'

Conor imagined the worst. 'Who? Who grabbed you? Laoise, did he...did he hurt you?'

'N-n-no. I stopped him with that.' She pointed to a spade that was now lying on the ground. 'H-h-he heard you on the phone outside... H-he was g-g-going to rape me, Conor.'

The terror was so raw on her face that Conor couldn't leave her, but he didn't want whoever had done this to get away. He took out his phone and called Katherine. 'Come down to the stables now, on your own, please.'

The great thing about Katherine was she never asked stupid questions. She simply replied, 'I'm on my way.'

'W-Who did you call? I don't want Dylan or my dad. Can you get my mam?'

She looked so young and vulnerable that Conor felt the simultaneous emotions of both deep compassion and murderous rage. 'I will, pet, but for now, I'm going to bring Katherine O'Brien from reception down here. If I call your mam, the whole table will get suspicious. Katherine is really kind and she'll look after you. We have a doctor here, Doctor Kelly from the village, and she's lovely. We'll get her to check you over. You're OK now, pet. Don't worry.' He rubbed her back as the sobs subsided. 'Laoise, can you describe him?' Conor was gentle but he needed to know.

'N-not really. He came at me from behind and dragged me in here. He was strong and he...he had dark hair...I think. He smelled of booze.'

'Did he say anything?' Conor asked.

'He...he just mumbled, but I...I think he said Dylan... I...I don't know, Conor.' She started sobbing again and he just held her.

Katherine arrived and Conor explained briefly. Katherine immediately took over. Nobody who saw her day-to-day on the reception desk would have thought her capable of such gentle kindness. As they left, Katherine put her jacket around the younger woman's shoulders. 'I'll call the Guards. Don't worry. Sergeant Kenny will be discreet, but whoever did this will have to be found.'

Conor nodded and handed Laoise over. He'd have to get security as well and was just about to call them when he spotted someone behind the stables. Conor ran after the man as he tried to climb over the back wall to escape via the meadow.

Conor pulled the man back down by his feet and swung him around by his shoulder. Conor punched him straight in the face followed by a ferocious blow to the abdomen. The man doubled over with a grunt, and as he did, Conor caught him again on the chin. The guy came back with remarkable speed, punching Conor in the ribs and trying to get his hands around his throat. Conor managed to sidestep him and landed a blow to the side of the man's head. He fell backwards and slumped down. For a second, Conor thought he might have killed him. But he could see he was just knocked out; he was still breathing, albeit laboured. It was Larry Smith. Panting and clutching his aching ribs, which were almost definitely broken, he reached into his trouser pocket for his phone.

As he looked down, he saw his shirt was covered in blood, and he was sure it wasn't his own. He thought he may have broken a finger too, as his hand was throbbing. With his good hand, he called the security office at the main gate. He walked out of the stable yard in the direction of the castle in case anyone was about to help.

'Bill, it's Conor. Bring the guards and meet me at the –'

Conor felt a blow to his head but nothing more.

CHAPTER 32

Conor heard a voice, but it was coming from very far away. He tried to focus on it. What was the person trying to say to him?

He was lying on something cold and hard, and every part of his body ached. He just wanted to sleep.

'You must get up. Please, Conor, you must get up!'

Conor struggled to open his eyes.

'Wake up, Conor! You must save Joe and Artie! Wake up!'

At the mention of his sons' names, Conor tried very hard to focus on the voice. His eyes didn't want to open; he just wanted to rest. But something was dragging him back to painful reality. He felt something push at his shoulder, then heard the voice again.

'Conor, please. You must wake up. Please, wake up!'

He managed to open his eyes for a second. Pain seared through his head and his limbs seemed frozen. An image floated in front of his eyes – a child. Was it Joe? No.

'Artie?' he managed to croak.

'Conor, go and save Joe and Artie.' The voice was clearer now.

Conor opened his eyes for longer this time. Before him stood a small boy, no more than four or five years old, and at first, he thought it was a girl. The child had long curly hair and was wearing a very odd outfit, a sort of jacket with a sailor collar and short trousers.

'Where are Joe and Artie?' he croaked.

'In the playroom.'

The child stood motionless, and Conor realised who it was. He managed to sit up this time, but the pain in his head was so severe he thought he might faint. He smelled burning.

'What is that…' he asked.

'Go and get Joe and Artie, Conor. They came to play with me, but there is danger now. I wanted to play with them. They came with me. Please, Conor, you have to get them!'

Conor was confused but turned painfully in the direction of the castle. The heat and light were unmistakable. One side of the castle was in flames.

He pulled himself to his feet and gathered all his strength. He had to get to the top floor. In agony, he ran as fast as his battered body would allow around the side of the building that was not yet engulfed and went in the staff entrance. All the fire staff and security were focused on the other side, so nobody noticed him. The castle was deserted, presumably evacuated, and he managed to get up the stairs, even though the smoke was by now acrid and lodging in his throat and eyes, making him choke. He remembered that if you stayed low to the floor, the smoke wasn't so bad, so he dropped as low as he could while still making headway. His keys were still in his pocket, thankfully, but when he eventually reached the playroom door, it was closed but not locked.

He turned the handle and entered to find no trace of smoke in the room. Joe and Artie were sitting on the floor, playing with the train. They looked up and saw him, and Conor could have cried with relief.

'Dad, this place is so cool! Why didn't you take us here before? There's loads of toys, and the boy let us play with his train even though he said it was his favourite.'

Joe and Artie were delighted with themselves as the train circled around the track.

'OK, lads. We need to go now, though,' Conor said gently. Even though he was desperate to get the twins out, he didn't want to terrify them.

'Shouldn't we wait for the boy? He said he was a twin, the same as us. We asked him where his brother was, and he said he didn't know. We said he better look for him and for his mam and dad too because they'll be worried,' Joe began.

'And we said you and Mammy would go mental if I left Joe someplace or he left me and you didn't know where we were,' Artie finished.

'Dad, what happened to you?' Joe noticed the blood for the first time.

Artie then started to cry. 'Did someone hurt you, Dad?'

'No, lads, I'm grand. But we all need to get out of here. The castle is on fire, and we need to get out really quickly and back to Mammy.'

He could see the panic in their eyes. 'We'll be grand because we are the brave O'Shea men, right, and Mammy and *Didus* and *Babusya* are waiting for us outside.' Conor tore the curtains from the wall and took them to the ancient sink, specially installed by Samuel all those years ago for arts and crafts. He soaked them, then tore them into three pieces. He tied the soaking rags around each of their faces and held his sons' hands.

'Dad, will we leave the boy's train here for him, in case he comes back?' Joe asked.

'Do, Joe,' Conor said as calmly as he could.

He led them back along the corridor of the top floor and down the back stairs to the ground floor. The smoke was thick and sickening, but there were no flames yet. He opened the door to escape through the kitchen, but as he did, he was driven back by the flames. The gas barrels used for cooking were stored in the pantry, and he prayed they wouldn't explode before they got out. He closed the kitchen door again, half dragging, half lifting the boys as he tried another exit further along. But the heat of the fire made it impossible.

He had an idea. The breakfast room at the front of the castle was on the first floor but it was on the side yet unaffected by flames. He pulled Joe and Artie behind him up to the first floor. He opened the door, and sure enough, there were no flames, just smoke. The fire was all in the eastern wing for now, which was mostly bedrooms and storage rooms. He shepherded his boys, now choking from the smoke, to the window and tried to open it, but the original sliding sash windows, recently painted, had become stuck. Artie and Joe were coughing incessantly now, even though they were breathing through the rags. With aching arms and shoulders, he lifted a heavy chair and rammed the window, smashing the glass. He bashed out as much glass as he could and shouted out the window, though his voice was weak from the smoke.

Eventually, he heard someone shout that they'd seen him, and the gathered crowd gazed up at him. The firemen gathered below the window.

'I'm going to throw the boys – catch them!' he managed to shout.

A large net was stretched, and Conor lifted a terrified Artie into his arms.

'No, Daddy, don't throw me out the window! I'm scared! I'll di –' His words were lost in another bout of coughing.

'You'll be OK, Artie.'

Conor had no time to comfort him further. He removed his son's arms from his neck and threw him out.

He ran back for Joe, who was unconscious on the floor. Heaving his son's dead weight, Conor staggered back to the window. He saw that Artie was being attended to, having landed safely.

'He's unconscious,' Conor called as he threw his second son out.

Artie was in Ana's arms, and Artur and Danika lifted Joe to the waiting ambulance.

'Conor!' Ana screamed as the room behind him exploded in a ball of flame.

CHAPTER 33

'Daddy, *Didus* played soccer with us and he scored a goal on Joe, even though Joe says he was taking it easy because *Didus* is old…'

Conor looked up as Artie burst into the hospital room ahead of his brother and Ana.

Ana crossed over and bent to kiss him. 'How are you today? Little better?' She ran her hand through his silver hair.

'Better now you're here.' He grinned.

'Seriously, though, what did doctor say this morning? Can you come home? We miss you.'

'She was here earlier and says I'll be fine to go home. I'll need to come back and get the burns dressed every second day, but the stitches in my head are dissolvable and the hair will grow back eventually.' He grimaced as he tried to sit up. 'This sling has to stay on for a few weeks because of the broken fingers and ribs, but other than that, I'm grand. So if you still want Frankenstein's monster, I'm all yours.' He winked, even though the pain was worse than he let on.

The boys forgot their squabble and were ecstatic.

'Miss Carney said we don't have to do homework for a week in case we are too tired, and I got ten out of ten in my sums test, and me and Artie got the same marks in the poem that we learned.'

Joe was so proud of himself that Conor's heart nearly burst. In the two weeks he'd been in hospital, he'd had plenty of time to think about how much worse the outcome of the fire could have been.

'Actually, I got eighty-four percent and Joe got eighty-five, Dad,' Artie clarified, anxious that his brother get due credit.

'Well, aren't you the right pair of Einsteins?' He ruffled their hair as they sat on either side of him on the bed.

Ana sat on the chair beside him. 'Everyone is dying to see you. They've been calling every day, waiting for news. Corlene and Dylan tried to make the nurse let them in, but she say no, you not well enough, and also fear of infection, so they all the time asking me when you coming home. Dylan especially. He says every day he must speak to you, but I tell him no.' Ana looked tired; the stress of the past few weeks was taking its toll on her. The thoughts of what might have happened gave her nightmares; she'd confided in him on one of her daily visits.

She refused to discuss the future of the castle while he was in the hospital. In the first week afterwards, he was too sick to even talk, but in the past few days, he was desperate for some news. She told him that all she knew was that the man who attacked Laoise and then him was in fact Larry Costello, Dylan's father. Carlos had been interviewed and identified the man as Larry Smith, and he was in custody. The investigators were not finished with their official assessment yet of the possible cause of the fire, but Ana had been told on the QT by the local fire chief that they were fairly sure it was arson. Corlene was absolutely right; Larry Costello was not a man who took rejection well.

Last night, Ana had come alone to the hospital to tell him what Dylan had confided to her. He was racked with guilt because he'd lied to everyone. He blamed himself for the fire, as well as Conor being hurt and the attack on Laoise. Apparently, he hadn't told Costello to leave him alone by email as he'd informed everyone, but instead had brought him to Ireland, drove him someplace remote and beat him up. Costello must have been mad at Corlene for telling Dylan the truth, and then mad at his son for rejecting him, and he set about hurting them both. Conor and Laoise were caught in the crossfire. Ana said Dylan looked dreadful; he hadn't slept since the fire. He wanted to see Conor to say how sorry he was.

Conor didn't blame Dylan. He might have done the same in his shoes, and Dylan had no way of knowing what Costello was going to do. Conor told Ana to tell Dylan that he was fine and definitely didn't hold any grudge against him, but that he wanted him to go to the Guards and tell them the truth. Sure, he assaulted someone, but in the light of Costello's subsequent reaction, Conor doubted very much if charges would be pressed. And the Guards had to know all the facts to get a conviction. Costello needed to be behind bars for as long as possible, so the more evidence they could get, the better.

Conor really wanted to see Dylan to reassure him, and also to see Corlene and Laoise. He knew the building was insured, so they wouldn't lose everything, but he found thinking about the castle as a blackened charred mess so upsetting. So much effort had gone into it; so many people looked forward to it for their livelihood. He wanted to see Katherine and Carlos and make sure they were OK and provided for, but Ana told him to relax and take it easy. Corlene was on top of everything, and her strict instructions were for him not to worry. Easier said than done, though.

'So if we call the matron, she'll sign my release papers and I'm a free man!' he joked. He was feeling fairly rough but didn't want Ana or the kids to see that, and he certainly didn't want the doctors to change their minds. He'd assured the consultant that morning that he would be taken care of like a prize pig once he got home.

His head was pounding and no amount of painkillers seemed to touch it. He was assured it would settle down, but the blunt-force trauma to the skull in the form of a shovel wielded by a very strong, violent criminal had taken its toll. His fingers were fine although three were broken, but he'd broken bones before so he wasn't worried, and the ribs would heal themselves too. There was considerable scarring on his lungs from the smoke inhalation, and it hurt like hell to cough.

The burns were the worst part. Thankfully they were on the back of his body. The gas barrels for the cookers exploded in the kitchen below the breakfast room, and the force of the blast propelled him out the window only seconds after he managed to throw Artie and Joe out. Apparently, the strength of the blast had saved him. Thankfully, he had no recollection.

The surgeon had come in the day before. He'd examined the damage, which was to his back mostly, and gave him an assurance that he would probably heal fine. There would be scarring, undoubtedly, but if it wasn't tight or painful, then they could leave it alone, and if it was, then they could graft skin afterwards.

Last week, Ana had arrived with a parcel that Martin O'Donoghue had delivered to the house. It was a box wrapped in newspaper, and inside was a jar of some kind of vile-smelling ointment and a note in very scrawly writing.

Conor, rub this on the burns. Use it sparingly – it stings. The child is fine now. He's where he should be. Well done. Molly O'Donoghue

Ana had brought it to the hospital as Martin was insistent that Conor begin using the ointment right away. Ana wanted to check with the doctor if they should. Conor was fairly sure the surgical team would veto it, so he convinced her to say nothing and just to remove the bandages and rub the ointment on his burned skin. The sting was tear-inducing as Molly had warned, but he gritted his teeth while Ana used feather-light touches to spread it. Almost instantly, the sting changed to a soothing cool sensation. It was as if it were moisturising his skin back to life. When Ana saw the improvement after just a day or two, she was convinced as well.

The plastic surgeon was amazed at the speed of his healing. Conor said nothing about the ointment, but every day, Ana applied another little bit. He came to count down the hours until her visit, not just to see her but for the relief from the pain the ointment gave.

After Ana left that day, he took out the note again. *The child is fine now,* he read. He'd never said a word to Ana about the events of that night. He had no idea what had happened, but he knew if it weren't for the intervention of a little boy with curly hair in old-fashioned clothes, his darling sons would have died in the fire.

He would never in his life forget that evening, how he found Joe and Artie in the playroom. They'd spoken about Grenville King as if he were a kid like themselves. They'd told him to go home because his brother and his mammy and daddy would be cross and worried if they didn't know where he was – maybe that was what was needed, another child to tell him. Maybe it was because they were twins and he was a twin – who knew? They didn't seem remotely upset by it, though at the time, it was strange.

Ana had asked them why they were in the castle at all, and apparently some of the other kids wanted more ice cream and Joe and Artie said they'd go and get it, probably showing off to their friends that the hotel was their own private larder. They never said why they ended up in the playroom, and Conor never said it was where he found them. Everyone assumed they were in or around the kitchen. The boys never mentioned the playroom, or Grenville King, or anything else about that night. It was as if none of that part ever happened. Conor would tell Ana when everything calmed down, but for now she was traumatised enough.

The walk to the car was painful, but he tried not to let it show on his face as his boys skipped ahead and carried his bags. 'Strap them in first,' he whispered to Ana. He didn't want them to see the agony on his face as he tried to get into the car.

He hated being an invalid; he'd always been the strong one his whole life. Eventually, he managed to get into the car, the pain almost excruciating. He tried not to see the tears in his wife's eyes as she watched him.

* * *

'CORLENE IS HERE, but she say if you tired, she will go away?' Ana came into the sitting room where Conor was stretched on the couch with the boys watching the *Minions* film.

'No, I'm grand.' He dragged himself to a sitting position, wincing as he did so.

'OK, but not for too long?' She kissed his head. 'Go and wash your hands, boys. *Babusya* has made *varenyky* for dinner, and *pampushky* for dessert if you eat all your dinner.'

This news was greeted with delight. The Ukrainian filled dumplings were their favourite after fish fingers and chips, and the doughnuts turned in cinnamon sugar for dessert were only for very special occasions.

'She made them because you're home.' Joe grinned. 'We didn't get *pampushky* for weeks because Mammy says they aren't healthy – she only lets us eat fruit after dinner – but *Babusya* knows you love them.'

Joe was none the worse after his ordeal. He'd woken up in the ambulance, and both twins were really excited to tell their school friends they were in one, with the sirens going and everything.

Happily, they trooped off as Corlene entered.

'Thank God you're alive. When I think what could have happened...' She sat opposite him, afraid to touch him.

'I know. I spent many the long night in the hospital thinking about it all. Poor Ana, looking up and seeing us at the window. I didn't stop to think – I just had to get my children.'

'Is it very painful? It looks like it is.' Corlene was as upset as Ana.

Conor sighed. 'I'm putting a brave face on it for Ana and the kids, but yeah, it's fairly bad. That cream Molly O'Donoghue sent me – did Ana tell you?'

Corlene nodded.

'Well, that's working. I'm improving all the time, and it's the only thing to touch the pain. She sent a note with it.'

Conor told Corlene the story about the boys in the playroom and the train and everything. It felt good to get it off his chest. When he was finished, they both just sat there in silence, each immersed in their own thoughts.

'They know it was Costello who started the fire. The fire officer called me this morning. So it looks like he'll face charges of attempted rape, grievous bodily harm, attempted murder and arson. He's going away for a long time.'

'Good,' Conor said.

'I know. And it is of course good, but I just wish you and your family, and Laoise… Poor Laoise…'

Conor turned slowly to face her, wincing in pain as he did. 'None of this is your fault, or Dylan's for that matter. Larry Costello is an evil person, and he will pay now for the first time for what he did to you and God knows how many others. Laoise got an awful fright and she'll be fragile for a while, but she's tough, and in the end she'll be grand. My boys are fine, you saw for yourself, and I'll live too, so no real harm done.'

He asked Corlene to go to the shelf beside the TV and take down Molly O'Donoghue's note. She read it aloud. 'The child is fine now. He's where he should be. Well done.' She sat down again, just staring at the note.

'So since that issue seems to be resolved, what are we going to do now?' Conor asked.

Corlene studied the note. She was so different from the woman who had come on the tour with him all those years ago, and so different too from the brash, polished businesswoman who made him the offer of part ownership of a hotel. The Corlene who sat in his sitting room now was dressed in jeans and a sweatshirt, she wore no make-up, and her hair was tied back in a ponytail.

'Conor, I have no idea what happened there, but it was something way outside of my control and I've learned my lesson. The insurance will pay for the renovations, and while the damage is extensive, the castle is salvageable. The fire was started deliberately, and not by us – they are sure of that at least. Because the dinner was on, every one of the guests was in the marquee, and the staff had done two fire drills under Carlos, so they knew exactly what to do and all got out. We could have been looking at such a tragedy here.'

Conor gave a rueful smile. 'Well, it never occurred to you nor I to do a fire drill, so maybe hiring Carlos was the best thing we ever did, pain in the butt though he is. Are you sure you want to start again? After everything?'

'No. To be entirely honest, I'm not. But when I think about all the great staff we had, and how great it could have been, then I think why not? We might have to take Miss O'Donoghue on a day trip before we begin again, just to do a spook check.' Corlene chuckled, but both she and Conor knew what happened at Castle Dysert would remain with them forever.

'So how's Laoise?' Conor asked. 'I couldn't get her face out of my head when I was in the hospital.'

'She's doing OK. You're right – she is a trooper, that kid, though her father is very shaken by it. Diarmuid is such an easy-going kind of guy, but when he found out, I never saw rage like it. Siobhan calmed him down, assured him that Laoise was OK, but Costello better hope that he is sent back to the States or kept locked up for a very long time because if either Diarmuid or Dylan get their hands on him... When the cops arrested him, they both tried to take off for Ennis behind the squad car just to see him, and I've no doubt to rip his head off if they could. Siobhan stopped them.

'Poor Dylan feels so guilty for bringing him here. He hurt you and Laoise, and he could have killed Joe and Artie.' She shuddered. 'It's all been so hard on him, finding out how he came to be, the life I gave him, and now this...' Tears filled Corlene's eyes and Conor took her hand.

'Poor lad. Of course I don't blame him. Costello will hopefully get what's coming to him, but he's nothing to do with Dylan. Tell him I said that, and that if they want to call tomorrow, I'd love to see them.'

'I'm sure that will come as a relief. Laoise was telling him he was being stupid, but you know what he's like, too stubborn to listen to good advice. He gets that from me.' She smiled sadly.

Ana came in with tea and some of the delicious sugar-coated doughnuts Danika had made. 'What you think, Corlene – will he live?' She grinned while pouring. All animosity between the two women seemed to have dissipated.

'It's going to take more than that to kill our guy. And between your mother's cakes, your gentle touch and the potion from the old witch, I reckon he'll be back on his feet in no time.'

They talked on, and Corlene showed them pictures of the destruction and some reports from the assessors who were quantifying the damage. Conor was relieved that Corlene was willing to try again, just because so many people were relying on the castle for employment.

'The gardens are still fine and the wing that was gutted is going to take some renovating, but they assure me we can fix anything if we throw enough money at it. I reckon Nico taught those local guys we took on in landscaping and groundworks very well, and they'll be able to do some pretty fantastic things once they get going.'

Conor sat back and observed his friend. No matter what life threw at her, she got back up and still had the energy of a toddler. Such a setback as this would daunt almost anyone else, but Corlene was not like anyone else. Bert would be proud of her. She'd used his money to do good – not as in handouts, but by giving people opportunities to improve their lives on their own. And while the locals saw her as a great benefactor and provider of employment, Conor knew it was what made Corlene tick. She wanted to live up to Bert's expectations of her. If she stopped trying, she might as well stop living.

'He'd be very proud.' Conor smiled at her.

She nodded sadly. 'I miss him, Conor, I really do, but I'm glad you think so. So are you in? Can we start again?' she asked, the enthusiasm shining from her face.

'I think there's always a chance to start again. Let's do it.'

THE END.

I sincerely hope you enjoyed this, the third book in the Tour series, the next book is called

The Homecoming of Bubbles O'Leary

and is loosely based on a true story.

I was a tour guide of Ireland at one stage of my career, and this story really happened. I have embellished it of course, but the core of it is true.

You can get it here:Here's a sneak preview of the first chapter - I hope you enjoy it!

https://geni.us/TheHomecomingOfBubAL

The Homecoming of Bubbles O'Leary
Chapter 1

Chapter 1

'Very well, of course.' Katherine paused and gestured with her hand for Conor to stay beside her until she finished the call.

He tried to hide his impatience. Katherine was normally very efficient, keeping the day-to-day details of running the hotel under her control. He needed to get out of there.

'I'll tell you what, I'm sure we can accommodate you, but if I can call you back in just a moment, I'll confirm it all with the manager. Yes – Conor, that's right.' She laughed, a surprisingly girlish sound for someone so austere.

Conor looked at her quizzically. Katherine O'Brien managed the front desk at Castle Dysert effortlessly, allowing him to focus on other aspects of running the hotel. Initially, Corlene, the other owner, was worried that someone as forbidding as Ms O'Brien would put guests off. He had to agree that the dark suit, rail-thin body and severely coiffed hair pulled back off her pale face in a tight bun was not exactly the welcome look they were going for, but she was excellent at the job. She didn't suffer fools, and she struck fear into most of the staff, but underneath the hard exterior, she was unfailingly kind. She was invaluable and everyone knew it. He understood a lot of her nature came from finding some social interaction difficult. She didn't engage in idle gossip or chit-chat. If she had something to say, she said it, but silence didn't unsettle her. She was loyal to the last, and he would trust her with his life.

Since the fire last year that almost destroyed everything they had worked so hard to build, the business had gone from strength to strength, and there was rarely a night that they weren't fully booked.

Conor gave her a pleading look, tapping his watch with his finger, wishing she would just let him go. The way she held her palm up, ordering him to wait, brooked no argument, and he knew better than to defy her. If she was insisting he stay, it must be important.

It was Ana's birthday, and he wanted to get home early. The twins had made her a cake with the help of their beloved Babusya, Ana's mother, and Conor was taking her out to dinner. Things had been so busy lately, he felt like he hardly saw her or Joe and Artie.

Eventually, Katherine hung up. 'Can we go to your office?' she asked. Then, turning to Meghan, the junior receptionist, she said, 'Meghan, please attend the desk.' She pointed to a neatly arranged in tray. 'And ensure all those invoices are in correct date order.'

Meghan got straight to it; when Ms O'Brien gave an instruction, she expected it to be followed to the letter without question or delay.

'Be my guest.' Conor smiled, ushering Katherine ahead of him. He caught Meghan's eye behind the older woman's back and made a funny face. She giggled and blushed.

'I saw that,' Katherine said tartly as she closed the door, though she couldn't possibly have. 'Right. That was a man from America, and he wants to book in a large group. They're all patrons of an Irish bar or something apparently, and they want to come here to attend the Lisdoonvarna Matchmaking Festival.'

Conor was confused – normally she wouldn't involve him, she'd just take the booking if they had availability. He wished she would get to the point, but she was not a woman to be rushed.

'Fine, and can we do it?' he asked.

'Yes, we can.'

'And so…' He smiled encouragingly.

'They want you to take them around, be their guide and so on.' Katherine did not give anything away in her expression, but Conor was used to that.

'Ah, but sure I don't do that any more. But ring them back and tell them we'll find them someone else, someone great, and that'll be fine.' He grabbed his car keys.

'No. That won't be acceptable this time, I'm afraid – it has to be you. The booking would be very useful to us, and they would stay for six nights, so it's a significant saving on housekeeping and so on, not turning the rooms around. The person who rang, his name was Kevin Wilson, and he insisted that you should be the one to do it. Apparently, someone he knows remembers you from a previous tour. The reason I'm suggesting it, apart from the fact that they would be far too enthusiastic and chirpy for me to be dealing with every day – you know how I can't really do small talk, and Americans always seem to want to chat – Sheila Dillon's son is getting married that week and she wants the week off. If we had one large group in rather than lots of singles, the housekeeping team could hold the fort till she gets back. But if it's lots of one- and two-night guests, then we'll need a substitute for Sheila, and getting staff is proving impossible, as you know.'

Conor sighed heavily and sat down. Katherine was right – the Irish economy was booming again and getting staff was a huge issue. Sheila was invaluable as head of housekeeping, and she really needed her holidays.

'Is there no other way?'

'None,' she said with certainty.

'Sure maybe you could hit the matchmaking festival yourself, Katherine?' He winked at her.

Apart from a never-mentioned romance that went wrong years ago, to the best of his knowledge, Katherine had never had a relationship of any kind. She lived alone and was dedicated to her job. He knew she read a lot and studied online courses in history and philosophy all the time, but he would have liked her to have a bit of joy in her life. Though what kind of man would be suitable for her was anyone's guess. She wasn't everyone's cup of tea.

'Utter nonsense. The idea that a farmer with a big dirty book could arrange weddings, for goodness sake.' She rolled her eyes. 'No, Conor, I have no interest whatsoever in such foolishness. Now, can I telephone Mr Wilson back and tell him you are available?'

He sighed, knowing he would never wriggle out of it. 'Look, I'll ring him tomorrow and see what he wants to do. I might be able to swing it – I'll see. Now, I've got to go. I'm taking Ana out for her birthday.'

He had been for a swim in the hotel pool as he did every day, and got dressed and ready to go out afterwards. He was back in his casual clothes: dark jeans and a pale-pink shirt. He was tanned and muscular, and his silver hair was neatly cut. 'Do I look all right?' he asked with a grin.

Katherine raised a perfectly arched eyebrow. 'Yes, you look very presentable.'

He chuckled. Presentable was as far as she would go.

As he drove away from the castle, he planned the evening. Artur and Danika were looking after the boys, who at eight were full of energy. Luckily, their grandparents adored them. Conor thought having his parents-in-law living near them full time might be a bit of a strain, but he couldn't have been more wrong. They'd moved to Ireland two years ago from Kiev. Artur quickly made himself indispensable as head of maintenance, and Danika was a huge help to Ana with the boys.

He was taking his wife to a new fish restaurant out at Spanish Point, and he was really looking forward to spending a whole evening with her uninterrupted. She'd been so tired lately, what with the boys on summer holidays, and she really needed a break. They hadn't managed to take a vacation since the fire last year as there was so much to do.

He pulled into the driveway and was surprised that Joe and Artie weren't in the garden. They lived outside, playing football or hurling. He let himself in, glancing at the clock on the wall over the big stove. At ten past six, the place was usually a hive of activity with dinner and bath time, but the house was silent.

'Ana!' he called. 'Are you here?'

Something was wrong. If she wasn't going to be there when he got home, she would have texted him.

He looked out back; her car was there. He took the stairs two at a time and opened their bedroom door. There she was, in bed. Relieved but perplexed – she never took a nap during the day – he walked over to where she lay on her side. She was awake.

'Ana, what's wrong?' He bent down so he was level with her head. Her eyes were puffy and swollen; she'd been crying.

'Ana, please, are you all right? Where are the boys?' A growing sense of dread threatened to engulf him. She was not a drama queen – something was really wrong.

'They are with my mother. They went over to her house for dinner. My dad picked them up.' Her voice was not normal; it was as if every word was an effort. Her Ukrainian accent was more pronounced than usual.

'So what's the matter?' He felt his mouth go dry. This was so out of character for his wife.

She sat up and took a deep breath that seemed to come from her toes and threw back the covers. She was still dressed.

'Conor, I… Today I was going in the hospital. Last week, I find a lump here' – she pointed to the side of her breast – 'and so I go to see doctor. I know you will say why I don't tell you, but everything so busy in the hotel, and I think is nothing. But Doctor Moriarty make appointment for me, and tell me to go in hospital today just for to make check. They did a test, and they say there is something there. They take some out with a needle to test – I forget the name of that thing – and now I must wait.'

Conor could feel the blood thundering in his ears, his heart thumping in his chest. This can't be happening. His beautiful, lovely Ana couldn't have cancer. It's just not possible. He struggled to say the right thing.

'Oh, Ana, my love.' He drew her into his arms, and she rested her head on his chest. 'I'm in shock. I…I feel terrible, I should have gone with you. To get news like that on your own… You're so much more important to me than any hotel. I'm so, so sorry, pet.' He was struggling to keep his voice normal. His darling girl – she was so young, and so fit and healthy. 'How long before we get the results of the test – was it a biopsy?'

'Yes, this. A biopsy. They say to come back on Friday, but the other doctor, the special one for breast cancer, say she think it look suspicious. She said to call you, but my phone was dead, and anyway, I was not able to talk. I didn't want to tell you this on the phone, so I come home and wait.'

It was Tuesday. Friday seemed forever away.

'Oh, my darling, I should have noticed something. Can you see the lump or feel it?' He tried to keep the anguish he felt out of his voice; the last thing she needed was a hysterical husband.

'I just feel it in the shower. I was shaving under my arm, and I feel it. Look here.'

She took his hand and placed it along the side of her right breast. He pressed gently, and sure enough, there was a hard little lump. He swallowed.

Memories of his own mother, in bed and fading away from cancer when he was just sixteen, flashed before him. It was as if she had been erased before his eyes. It was horrible. He couldn't bear that to happen to his darling wife. He felt his chest constrict with panic and fear, but he tried to breathe through it. He needed to be strong for Ana.

'I will be right beside you, I promise. We'll do this together. We don't know what we're facing, but I love you so much, and the boys love you…' His voice cracked, and he couldn't go on.

She nodded sadly. 'I can't leave you all, Conor.' Her eyes filled with tears. 'I don't want to die.'

'You are not going anywhere, do you hear me? You're going to be fine. Things are so much more advanced now, technology and all of that, and they've caught it early.' He prayed he was right. He felt so guilty; if he'd been paying more attention to his wife and less to the hotel, maybe he'd have spotted it. 'How long has it been there, do you think? I should have noticed.'

'I think two weeks, not more.' She swallowed. 'Is okay, Conor, you don't have to be so strong. It's bad news.'

His eyes locked on hers. He felt the moisture on his face before he knew the tears had come, and they sat on their bed, clinging to each other, crying.

If you would like to keep on reading (I hope you do) just click this link,

https://geni.us/TheHomecomingOfBubAL

ACKNOWLEDGMENTS

The very first book I ever wrote was *The Tour,* and if someone had told me then I would write a series featuring those characters, I'd have said they were mad. But in the funny way life has of turning out, here we are.

I have many people to thank: my wonderful editor, Helen Falconer, as well as my proofreading and plot-hole-finding friends, Vivian, Joseph, Jim, and the amazing Collette, who is not only my *favourite* sister-in-law but also the most eagle-eyed woman I know when looking for a discrepancy.

This book is dedicated to the memory of a very dear friend and a character in his own right. The character of Martin in the story is based on a very real Martin O'Donoghue, who was so full of life and fun and mischief, it is hard to believe he is no longer with us. He did live in a train station, he did sometimes sleep in a caravan with his feet out the window, and you were as likely to be offered a glass of whiskey as a cup of coffee when you visited, no matter what the time of day. He was a singer, a musician, a storyteller, a master craftsman, a horticulturalist, a historian, and a great friend. We all miss him.

As always, my thanks goes to my husband, Diarmuid, himself a musician and singer, and also my biggest fan and my gentlest critic. Without him, there would be no books.

And finally to you, dear readers, who have supported me through this amazing journey. I do not take a single one of you for granted, and know that your purchase is keeping the lights on and the laptop charged in a stone cottage in County Cork. I love to hear from readers, so if you ever want to drop me a line, please do, to jean@jeangrainger.com.

Le grá,

Jean x

ABOUT THE AUTHOR

Jean Grainger is a USA Today bestselling Irish author. She writes historical and contemporary Irish fiction and her work has very flatteringly been compared to the late great Maeve Binchy of whom she is an enormous fan.

She lives in a stone cottage in Cork with her husband Diarmuid and the youngest two of her four children. The older two show up occasionally to main about the cost of living now that they are buying their own toothpaste. There are a variety of animals there too, all led by two cute but utterly clueless micro-dogs called Scrappy and Scoobi.

ALSO BY JEAN GRAINGER

To get a free novel and to join my readers club (100% free and always will be)

Go to www.jeangrainger.com

The Tour Series

The Tour

Safe at the Edge of the World

The Story of Grenville King

The Homecoming of Bubbles O'Leary

Finding Billie Romano

Kayla's Trick

The Carmel Sheehan Story

Letters of Freedom

The Future's Not Ours To See

What Will Be

The Robinswood Story

What Once Was True

Return To Robinswood

Trials and Tribulations

The Star and the Shamrock Series

The Star and the Shamrock

The Emerald Horizon

The Hard Way Home

The World Starts Anew

The Queenstown Series

Last Port of Call

The West's Awake

The Harp and the Rose

Roaring Liberty

Standalone Books

So Much Owed

Shadow of a Century

Under Heaven's Shining Stars

Catriona's War

Sisters of the Southern Cross

Made in United States
North Haven, CT
25 May 2024